The

House on

Salt Hay Road

The

House on

Salt Hay Road

CARIN CLEVIDENCE

Farrar, Straus and Giroux   New York

Farrar, Straus and Giroux
18 West 18th Street, New York 10011

Copyright © 2010 by Carin Clevidence
All rights reserved
Distributed in Canada by D&M Publishers, Inc.
Printed in the United States of America
First edition, 2010

Library of Congress Cataloging-in-Publication Data
Clevidence, Carin, 1967–
   The house on Salt Hay Road / Carin Clevidence. — 1st ed.
     p. cm.
   ISBN 978-0-374-17314-2 (alk. paper)
   1. Long Island (N.Y.)—History—20th century—Fiction.   2. Domestic fiction.
I. Title.
PS3603.L497H68 2010
813'.6—dc22

                                 2009043087

Designed by Abby Kagan

www.fsgbooks.com

10 9 8 7 6 5 4 3 2 1

For Jemma and Clement

Contents

PART ONE

A Floating House

The sound was the loudest Clayton Poole had ever heard, the noise he imagined a bomb would make if the Huns attacked Long Island. Twelve years old, a sturdy boy with freckles and a blunt boxer's jaw, he'd been sketching a line of sandpipers on the bottom margin of his Elson Reader. Pretty Miss Collier, in a brown-checked dress, stood with her back to the fifth- and sixth-grade children, writing a list of spelling words on the blackboard. The sound crashed around them like a breaking wave and the windows rattled in their casements. The chalk in Miss Collier's hand skipped across the slate like a stone on pond water.

Clayton was the first one to reach the window. To the west of Fire Neck, white smoke billowed against the sky. Maybe it *had* been a bomb. Where was his sister? What if she'd been hurt? At the front of the classroom, a girl in pigtails started to blubber. Clayton thought of the birds at Washington Lodge, where he worked every morning before school. The cockatoos were inside, he reminded himself, because of the man from Boston. "Sit down, children! Sit down!" cried Miss Collier. She slapped the desk with her ruler. But they stayed clustered at the window with their faces up against the glass like the turtles in the class terrarium.

Seeing his chance, Clayton edged toward the door.

Clayton's sister, Nancy, nineteen years old, was riding bareback down Old Purchase Road when the thunderous noise spooked her horse. She felt the animal contort beneath her, then surge forward like water through a broken dam. She hung on to the mane as they careered across the road, narrowly swerving around a child on a tricycle. Nancy saw a red cap and the round O of a mouth. Gripping with her knees, she hauled on the reins. The horse galloped into the woods that bordered the marsh. A flock of black ducks rose from Scheibel's Creek. Leaves and vines whipped against her, and Nancy crouched lower and tried to shield her face with her elbow. Then a branch loomed and she was scraped off the horse's back like mud from the heel of a boot. She landed on the damp ground among the skunk cabbage, rattled and indignant. It had been years since she'd fallen off a horse. In the distance she heard the sound of Buckshot crashing through the blueberry and the shadbushes.

In Fire Neck, just east of Southease, Clayton's grandfather woke with a start. In his dream a ship had run aground with all sails set and was breaking up on the sandbar. August Scudder had worked for most of his life in the United States Life Saving Service across the Great South Bay on Fire Island; his dreams were full of maritime disasters. Scudder jerked upright, surprised to find himself not in a lifeboat but in a chair on the front porch of his house. Out in the yard he saw his son, Roy, standing open-mouthed.

"What the hell?" Scudder demanded. Roy was staring over the trees at a ragged cloud smudging the blue sky. He wondered aloud if this might be war, if the town of Southease had been bombed by the Germans.

Scudder's thoughts leaped to his granddaughter, out riding her horse. The girl was his favorite, like her late mother before her, and he wanted her home. He distrusted horses at the best of times, skittish beasts, prone to shying. "Where was Nancy headed?"

Roy shrugged. Behind the house his hunting dogs barked and whined.

"And Mavis," said Scudder, thinking of his youngest child, "up at the lodge."

Washington Lodge, where Roy's sister Mavis worked, lay on a small rise between Southease and Fire Neck, much closer to the confusion. The two men exchanged a look. "Pigs," Roy said. "I'd better go and bring her home."

In the kitchen of Washington Lodge, Clayton's Aunt Mavis prepared to meet her maker. She'd scalded a goose and had just started to pluck it. There were two loaves of bread in the oven, and she'd opened the window above the sink to let out some of the heat. Then the room shuddered around her and a stack of dishes lurched to the floor. The goose slipped from her fingers. From the pantry came the tinkling sound of wineglasses breaking. Mavis, stout and ungainly, fell heavily to her knees and pressed her feather-covered hands together. Out the window an ugly gray cloud was rising above the trees. "Our Father who art in Heaven . . ." The cloud seemed to take on a shape. She could see it moving toward her. The fist of God, she thought, breathing in the smell of brimstone. She squeezed her eyes shut and prayed as fire whistles went off and dogs all over town began to howl. She prayed as flakes of ash as big as hands drifted in through the open window and brushed her face.

Rushing home, Clayton saw ashes dancing in the wind along the string of lanes that ran south toward the bay off Beaver Dam Road. They settled on the grass and on a half-empty laundry basket at the corner of Hawkins Lane, where a clothesline had been abandoned. The last shirt on the line fluttered a damp arm. Clayton rounded the corner onto Salt Hay Road, his shoes kicking up dust.

The Scudder house stood at the end of the lane, facing the uninterrupted marsh. Across the field, the Barto River flowed toward the Great South Bay. As Clayton turned into the yard, he could see the masts of the sailboats at Starke's Boatyard poking up over the far hedge. His grandfather stood at the door to the house, a sinewy man with a crest of white hair. His sharp nose protruded like a beak. "What happened?" Scudder asked.

Clayton struggled to catch his breath. "Where's Nancy?" Flakes of ash and charred paper drifted down around them. The stain in the sky had faded and spread toward them on an easterly wind that blew the sharp smell of gunpowder with it. Ash settled on the grass and on the yellow daffodils by the gate.

"Riding," Scudder told him. "Roy's gone to fetch your aunt. Why aren't you at school?"

"Riding where?" Clayton insisted. He had slipped out of school in the confusion, something he didn't care to explain, because his sister wouldn't like it. Now she wasn't home. What had started as a small uneasiness unfurled inside him, billowing like a sail in a gust of wind.

Scudder shrugged his bony shoulders. "Who knows where she goes on that animal. Run over to the Captain's house. See if he's all right."

Captain Kelley lived alone in a cottage across the field. He was an old man, almost as old as Scudder, and they had known each other since their days in the Life Saving Service. Clayton knocked on the door for form's sake before opening it. The small, dim house was overrun with cats. Two of them rubbed against his legs as he stepped inside. It took Clayton's eyes a moment to adjust to the darkness. In the front parlor, portraits of the Captain's mother and father hung on the wall, draped in dusty black lace. The shades were always drawn; Captain Kelley had once explained to Clayton that he hated looking out of dirty windows. From the sofa came the sound of snoring. Clayton tiptoed across the rug. The Captain was stretched out, with his head on a pillow and his mouth open. His white mustache rose and fell. The room smelled of fish and cats and standing water. Clayton closed the door softly behind him and stepped back into the sunlight.

Instead of going home, he skirted the field and headed into Southease. He knew his sister sometimes rode down to the Southease dock to watch the sailboats on the bay. Until he saw her, the jittery feeling in his gut would only get worse. At Hawkins Nursery, glass lay smashed at the base of the greenhouse like drifts of ice. A little girl stood barefoot on the porch next door and cried halfheartedly, rubbing her eyes with her fists. Across the street a man in a gray suit was stamping out a fire on an otherwise immaculate lawn. "What happened, mister?" Clayton called.

"The fireworks factory," the man said glumly. "Look at all this garbage!" Scraps of singed paper hung in the green privet.

Clayton asked if anyone had been hurt.

"I wouldn't be surprised," said the man in gray. "The blast nearly took my roof off!"

A policeman had blocked off Main Street with a sawhorse, forcing the traffic to turn back. On a lawn nearby, bits of orange and silver shone in the sunlight where a window had shattered and blown outward, along with an aquarium. Half a dozen goldfish lay strewn like bright fruit on the grass.

Clayton planted himself in front of the policeman. "Mister, have you seen a girl on a black horse?"

Intent and self-important, the policeman shook his head. He had a whistle between his teeth and blew it sharply, gesturing at a Buick convertible that had come to a stop and was now blocking traffic.

Clayton hurried on, past the fish market and the stationery store. A woman in curlers ran by, nearly knocking into him, a scarf clutched to her head. Clayton joined a cluster of people on the sidewalk. They stood watching as, across the street, firemen from the Southease Hook and Ladder hosed the smoldering debris that had once been the fireworks factory. Blackened and twisted shapes protruded randomly from the rubble. "I knew it the minute I heard it," a man in a houndstooth hat was saying. He had the stub of a cigarette in his mouth, unlit, and talked around it. "They were always testing something."

"Not like that," said another man, with a snort of derision or disbelief. "Not that loud. I thought it was gunshots."

A woman in the front of the group shook her head. "I knew it was fireworks. All that popping before the bang, and the colors. Red and yellow and green. Like a Christmas tree."

"Excuse me," Clayton said, pushing himself forward. "I'm looking for my sister. On a black horse?" An older woman with a shopping bag turned to look at him and tutted, sympathetic. No, no one had seen a horse.

The man with the cigarette stub spat it onto the ground. "Would have bolted," he muttered. "Miles from here by now."

Clayton felt their interest in his small problem ebb. The crowd turned back to the smoking wreckage across the street.

The fireworks at the Lights of Long Island were made by hand, packed one by one with a brief and particular glory, from penny snaps to aerial shells to set pieces that took weeks to construct. What had set them off was a rogue spark, a scrap of electricity. One squib shot up, then a few more. Then came the rolling explosion as the rest fired off together—the beehives and the Niagara Falls, the willow tree rockets and flying pigeons, the pinwheels, the crimson stars, the white-and-gold flitter, the revolving suns and the Saxon crosses—each carefully planned artifice of light reduced to smoke and noise.

Out on the Great South Bay, fishermen on their boats heard the loud report and saw smoke like a sudden thunderhead rise above the trees. In Southease windows shattered in houses and storefronts from Main Street to Oyster Lane. Burning debris hurtled through the air. A man on Ketchum Road later swore that the face of the Shah of Persia had appeared in lights above his vegetable garden. The stained-glass window in the Presbyterian church, the one showing Christ as a fisher of souls, fell in pieces. Greenhouses echoed with the sound of breaking glass. When the ground shook, people feared their homes were collapsing around them; a terrified mother tossed her baby out an open window. Wrapped in a blanket, he landed unharmed in the yellow branches of a forsythia.

While people panicked and dogs howled, the cloud of burned powder rose over the fireworks compound and the maple trees on the sidewalk. It broke up slowly, catching in the spokes of the windmills and the leafy tips of trees, curling south in wisps down Main Street. It drifted out over the tops of sailboats moored at the Southease dock, east over a stretch of oak and scrub pine, down Fire Neck Road, along the grasses and cattails of Scheibel's Creek. It spooled over the salt marsh, sifting powder and ash onto the spartina and high-tide bush. Beyond the marsh lay the Great South Bay, and beyond the bay stretched Fire Island, a long and narrow strip of sand clumped into dunes, where, days later, Clayton and his friend Perry would collect piles of blackened cotton and singed balsa wood that washed up along the beach.

Nancy stood and brushed herself off. The terrifying boom had come from Southease, nowhere near the elementary school where her brother was. The house on Salt Hay Road lay nearly a mile away; she had no doubt the horse Buckshot would be halfway there already. Much closer, just up the low hill toward Southease, stood Washington Lodge, where her aunt Mavis worked. Better to go there first, Nancy thought. Someone might know what was happening. Sirens sounded in the distance as she picked her way back through the woods to Old Purchase Road. The air had an acrid smell Nancy could taste in her mouth. With an uneasy feeling, she began to run, taking the shortcut that led to the back of the lodge.

Rounding the last of the trees, she saw the reassuring outline of Washington Lodge on the hill above her. A figure stood at the kitchen door, and Nancy put on a burst of speed. She was halfway up the hill when she realized the person in the doorway was a stranger. She slowed to a walk, surprised. He was a young man with a pale, freckled face and reddish-brown hair. The sleeves of his white shirt were rolled up. The way he stood facing her with his hand on the door it seemed, in the confusion of the moment, as if he were expecting her.

"I'm looking for my aunt," Nancy faltered, catching her breath. "She works here." There was a stitch in her side and her hip still smarted from her humiliating fall. The man opened the door wide, and she peered into the kitchen. The air smelled of burning bread, and also, faintly, of wet feathers. A stack of white china plates had fallen off the counter and lay broken in a gleaming line across the floor. Her aunt was kneeling under the open window with her back to them, head bowed over her clasped hands. Ashes sifted through the window. "Mavis," Nancy called gently. "Mavis, are you hurt?"

Her aunt did not turn. Nancy guessed the mumbling she heard was prayer.

She made a wry face at the stranger. "What happened?"

"I don't know." His voice was low and dry, and although he wasn't whispering, Nancy felt keenly that he was speaking to her alone. "It sounded like the Last Judgment."

Nancy's heart still pounded. She watched the stranger's face as he spoke. The noise had come out of nowhere, he said. "Like Armageddon. Without the trumpets." His name was Robert Landgraf, he told her, and he was visiting from Boston. Nancy thought his fair, freckled skin looked as if it would burn easily. She noticed ink stains on his fingers and the cuff of his white shirt. He'd heard glass shattering downstairs, he went on, and had searched the house in vain for other people. "I was starting to think the place had been evacuated without me. I found someone finally. Your aunt, I guess." He gestured toward the kitchen. "Then I opened the door and saw you." He smiled at her, and Nancy found herself smiling back.

The sound of a car on the pebble drive made them turn. Roy was behind the wheel. "She's in the kitchen," Nancy called as her uncle came toward them, looking concerned. She felt guilty for not venturing in before him. But Roy would do a better job of calming his sister, she told herself.

Roy paused at the door. "What the devil happened?"

"We think it's the Last Judgment," Nancy said with a nervous laugh, unable to restrain herself. Her uncle frowned. He glanced quickly from her to the man from Boston and back again before turning and stepping into the kitchen. Nancy knew she shouldn't make light of her aunt's religious fervor. She glanced down at her feet, abashed.

Nancy and Robert Landgraf stood in the doorway; like reprimanded children, she thought. Inside, Roy could be heard reasoning with Mavis. Glancing in, Nancy saw him helping her to her feet. He bent down to retrieve the half-plucked carcass of a goose and stood holding it for a moment, like a bachelor with a baby, before angling it into the gleaming white refrigerator.

"Let's all go home," Roy said firmly. He held his sister under the elbow and steered her toward the door. Mavis, pale with shock, blinked her wide eyes in the sunlight.

Nancy glanced at the stranger. It seemed unkind to abandon him. "Maybe Mr. Landgraf should come with us."

"Yes!" cried Mavis unexpectedly. "I'm supposed to cook his dinner. Mr. Washington won't be back till late." Roy nodded, shepherding them forward.

Robert Landgraf seemed grateful not to be left behind. Together they walked toward the car. A fresh wind brought another flurry of grit and the smell of burning. Mavis stopped to pull a handkerchief from her pocket and hold it over her nose. Roy handed her into the passenger seat of the Ford and opened the back door for the others.

Nancy hesitated. She couldn't bear the thought of riding back to Salt Hay Road with her aunt, who would pester Robert Landgraf with questions about his spiritual beliefs, embarrassing her. "I think we'll walk," she told her uncle. "Buckshot'll be back by now. But I lost my crop somewhere along the road."

Roy didn't protest. "Be careful!" Mavis called, waving her handkerchief from the window. The car sputtered down the white pebble driveway, leaving Nancy alone with the man from Boston.

She set off briskly. It seemed clear that while something had happened in Southease, maybe at the gas station, the ground would stay solid under their feet. Her brother was safely in school. Nancy's fear converted to nervous excitement, a sense of possibility. She felt acutely conscious of the man keeping pace beside her.

"Lively spot, Long Island," he said after they'd walked a few yards. "Ear-splitting booms, clouds of smoke. You locals must have nerves of steel."

Nancy laughed. "I grew up in Connecticut." She didn't want him to think she'd lived in the little town of Fire Neck all her life. "We're going to move back there in a few years. My brother and I. Once he finishes school."

"Still, I take it you're familiar with the local customs," Robert said. "You can translate the lingo, make sure I don't end up with my head on a stake." Nancy smiled again, trying to imagine what dinner on Salt Hay Road would be like with this stranger at their table. She could picture Clayton's pinched expression, sizing Robert Landgraf up, holding his white shirt and city shoes against him.

It had rained steadily for the past week and now the sun shone brilliantly. In the silence and the sunlight it was hard to credit the violence of the noise they'd heard before. The leaves on the trees were a bright acid green. Nancy left the road for a narrow trail that ran along Scheibel's Creek.

"You're in business with Mr. Washington?" she asked.

Robert explained that he was an assistant curator from the Museum of Comparative Zoology in Boston. "We heard a rumor there might be a rare bird here, a Carolina parakeet. Parrots are my specialty, so I'm the one they sent."

Nancy felt surprised that something as familiar as the birds at Washington Lodge should have caught the attention of a museum in Boston. "Did you find it?"

He shook his head, rueful. "No. They're similar, but it's not a *Conuropsis* at all. Something South American, in the genus *Aratinga*."

Nancy said, "You must be disappointed."

"Oh no. My hopes weren't high. And the collection is amazing." Robert whistled. "He's got African finches Peters would kill for. And a little psittacine I can't even identify. Maybe one of the New Guinea species . . ." His voice had become almost dreamy.

It still seemed incredible that the birds her brother fed and watered every morning were that remarkable. She asked, "But where does he get them?"

"He knows every ship's captain in New York Harbor, and he pays well. They bring him specimens from all over the world." Walking in front, unable to see him, Nancy listened to his disembodied voice listing the exotic names of the birds, *honeycreepers, jacamars, bee-eaters*; it was a strangely intimate arrangement, like talking in the dark. They were nearing the creek, and the air smelled damp and earthy. The brown spikes of cinnamon fern poked up from the undergrowth. She lifted a thorny strand of catbrier aside and held it. Robert took it from her, ducking his head.

"Where are you leading me, Miss Poole? Not into more danger, I hope."

Nancy had an image of him materializing out of the explosion, as if from an alchemical reaction. He had stood at the door of the lodge, she thought, waiting for her. A shiver rippled down her back. She said, "Call me Nancy."

It was late when Clayton got home from Southease. From the door on the front porch he could hear the clink of forks and knives on china, snatches of conversation: *train from Boston*; *brushfires*; *can't rebuild there, that's for sure.* Stepping in quietly, he saw that the family was sitting at the long table in the rarely used dining room, instead of in the kitchen: His grandfather Scudder sat at the head, with Roy to his left, then Mavis. Beside Mavis sat his sister, unharmed, holding out a bowl. At the sight of her he felt the worry that had drummed through him all afternoon subside, like the vibrations of a cymbal quieted by the pressure of a finger. And then he noticed the stranger beside her. A man with reddish hair and a foxlike face. As he watched, the man leaned toward Nancy and whispered something. A quick pink stain spread across her cheeks and throat.

"*Here* he is," cried his aunt, catching sight of Clayton. She gestured him toward the remaining chair and began to ladle stew into a bowl. "Now we're all together." She passed the bowl to Clayton and solemnly lowered her chin. "Let's say a prayer of thanks for keeping our family safe." Nancy made a face at him from across the stew pot.

Clayton sat and surreptitiously looked around him. The presence of the stranger at their table made him study the familiar faces as if he were seeing them for the first time. His plump aunt's mouth was moving faintly in her wide, soft face as she murmured grace. Beside her, his uncle Roy sighed with impatience, his dark hair falling onto his forehead. Tall and rangy, he shared only his coloring with his sister. His eyes closed, Roy seemed more solidly there among them. Often, Clayton felt, his uncle's gaze was held by something just out of view. Nancy, eyes shut but still irreverent, seemed to be smiling at some private joke. At the head of the table, his grandfather Scudder hadn't closed his eyes at all. White-haired, gaunt, his beaky nose protruding from his weathered face, he studied the stranger sitting next to Nancy with a severe expression.

Clayton and Nancy had moved to the house on Salt Hay Road five years before the fireworks factory turned itself inside out. He'd been seven then, Nancy fourteen. Before their mother's death they'd lived in a big house in Stonington, Connecticut, overlooking Long Island Sound. Confined to a daybed downstairs as the cancer whittled her away, their mother had liked to watch the sailboat races on fine days with a pair of opera glasses. Clayton didn't remember his father at all. He'd died of a heart attack the year Nancy was ten, Clayton barely three. "He used to swing you onto his shoulders when he came home from work," Nancy had told him. "You'd grab at his mustache to keep from falling. Don't you remember?"

What Clayton did remember was their arrival on Salt Hay Road. This would have been after their mother's funeral, though he recalled the two events separately, as though they'd occurred on different continents. First there'd been a church thronged

with well-dressed strangers, where the collar of his shirt scratched
him and his neck grew stiff from keeping still while perfumed
women murmured into the air above him and stroked his hair.
He'd realized with relief that he could hold his sister's hand
without censure; he kept close to Nancy and stared down at the
floor. In his mind he could still see the tops of her slightly too-
large shoes, the little gap between the stockings and the black
patent leather.

Later they were on the ferry. It was night. His grandfather
and aunt and uncle must have been there, but he did not remember them, only his sister standing at the rail. Clayton
clutched her hand. The wind tangled her hair, long then, and
whipped it across her face as she cried. He shivered in the cold
and wished she would notice him and go back inside the cabin.
But the minutes passed and she stayed at the rail, and he could
not imagine going anywhere without her. The wind came at
them off the water and his eyes teared. He wiped his nose on
his sleeve. In front of them the lights of distant houses trembled
on the black horizon.

Then they were riding in a car, and the warm, close air
smelled of leather and dogs and his aunt's flowery perfume. He
fell asleep leaning on his sister's shoulder. After what felt like
hours, he half woke as the car slowed and began a series of
turns. Clayton found his muscles anticipating the route, waiting
for the turn off Beaver Dam, the long bumpy stretch of Salt
Hay Road, as though it had been mapped into his growing
bones from the time he was a baby in his mother's arms. He felt
the car turn and slow down, the tires laboring over the potholes
where he'd watched flocks of sparrows bathing in the puddles
after a rain. The ruts on the east side were deeper than those on
the west; his grandfather Scudder said the car listed to starboard

on the outbound tack and port on the homeward. Clayton was jostled against his aunt as the car pulled into the pebble driveway with a crunching sound.

The doors opened, letting in the chirping of crickets and the brackish, peaty scent of the marsh. The night was very still. Clayton, fully awake, kept his eyes half closed as his uncle picked him up off the backseat of the car and carried him into the house, ducking through the door and into the kitchen, where his aunt was already lighting the burner on the white enamel stove. Everything was just as he remembered it from summer visits: the smell of bread dough and potato peelings; the red-and-white-checked curtains at the window above the sink; the poster with the curled edges on the pantry door, showing different breeds of horses; the lampshade stippled with the outline of a square-rigged sailing ship. Clayton felt as if he were waking finally from a long nightmare. A knot loosened in his throat. His face tingled painfully, and he clenched his eyes to keep back the tears. Roy was still holding him, slung with careless affection over one shoulder. "Take him upstairs," he heard his aunt say. "The sewing room's his now, poor thing."

On that first night in his grandfather's house, after his mother's funeral, seven-year-old Clayton woke in the dark, confused by the smell of apple pie. In the morning, coming downstairs, he saw his uncle eating fresh pie for breakfast with a cup of black coffee and knew he hadn't dreamed it. Over the next few days he discovered that his aunt often baked at night, after the rest of the household had gone to bed. The old sewing room was just above the kitchen, and on nights when his aunt baked, he would lie in bed and breathe in the scent of ginger cake, cinnamon rolls, corn muffins, black walnut pie. Sometimes he heard her singing to herself while she rolled out the dough. Then he would slip out of bed and sit on the dark stairs, out of sight, but close enough to hear her. The songs she sang were the ones she'd learned at the piano with his mother when they were girls: "Annie Laurie," "My Darling Clementine," "My Sweetheart's the Man in the Moon." With his eyes closed, he could almost believe it was his mother singing.

His sister also noticed that their aunt had trouble sleeping, especially on moonlit nights. "Probably because she's so fat," Nancy remarked, unfeelingly. Clayton imagined the full moon tugging at his aunt's large body like a boat on the tide, dragging her awake and down the stairs. Over time, moonlight and the smell of baking linked themselves in his mind, and the full moon stirred in him a craving for fresh bread and cream.

The explosion of the Lights of Long Island fireworks factory killed four workers who were in the building at the time, and set over fifty homes alight in Southease and Fire Neck. What people talked about more than anything was the suddenness of the devastation, its unexpected force. "No warning at all," friends and neighbors repeated to one another, shaken. "Out of a clear blue sky."

In the house on Salt Hay Road, one of the matched pair of upstairs windows had been cracked by the blast. The windows were shaped like fans and set on either side of the chimney. According to Scudder, it had been the charm of those same windows, like winking eyes, that had tempted his father to bid on the house in an auction he attended in East Moriches by chance nearly seventy years earlier. After the auction he learned that the house was all he had bought; not a foot of land around it was included in the price. The house sat on the bank of the

Terrell River and the owner wanted the price of the house again for the waterfront lot.

Scudder's father said he'd be damned if he gave the land shark another penny. He took careful measurements and waited for the next high tide. Then he and a group of relatives and friends jacked the house up off the ground and rolled it on logs to a flat-topped barge they borrowed from Starke's Boatyard. They floated the house down the Terrell River to Moriches Bay and then southwest along the shore, past Forge River and Pattersquash Creek to the Barto River.

Scudder had not been allowed on the barge with the house, being only ten at the time. He'd waited on shore with the others as it came up the river from Taffy Point. Scudder remembered watching the house appear in the distance and how strange the silhouette of it seemed, like a boat built by someone with no understanding of water or wind. "She had an awkward look," he told Clayton nearly a lifetime later. He struggled to describe the odd sensation that had come over him as he watched the house float toward them, the water splashing up the white walls and around the door, a yellow curtain swaying in one of the windows. It had seemed almost spooky, he told his grandson; not the house itself, but its limping, stubborn progress across the waves.

This was where Scudder had lived ever since, in this solid, narrow house of two and a half white clapboard stories. Later, after his parents died and his brothers married and moved out, Scudder stayed on alone. For years he worked at the Smith Point Station across the bay on Fire Island. Then the house would stand empty for most of the year, while he bunked at the station with the rest of the Life Savers. The worst storms struck in the fall and winter, but the crew remained on duty through the spring. Patrolling the beach, Scudder collected flotsam: the name board from a ship called the *Heron*; a blue-and-orange pennant; planks of yellow pine; a music box, its gears clogged with sand. Every summer the crew disbanded for the season and Scudder returned to the house on Salt Hay Road.

Scudder used the salvaged lumber to build a storage room off the side of the house. When a branch came down on the kitchen roof, he sawed it into usable pieces and patched the hole with it. The house absorbed the smells of salt marsh and mud and waterlogged pine. Scudder hung the name board from the *Heron* on the porch and flew the pennant from the weather vane. When the *Water Lily* wrecked on a sandbar in a bitter sou'wester, his future wife fell out of the breeches buoy into his arms. Scudder told his grandson that everything he had came out of the sea.

Genevieve Chaffey had grown up on a cattle ranch in Arizona. She and her mother and two cousins had been returning on the *Water Lily* from a tour of Europe. Though she accepted her relative poverty as a fair price for marrying for love, there were times, hanging diapers out to dry in air heavy with the dampness of the marsh, or lying in bed at night listening to the whine of mosquitoes, that she missed her childhood home in Arizona, the bone-dry air, the soft-spoken servants. During the first years of her marriage, she tried to coax a line of weeping willows to grow along the southern edge of the property. The salt water proved too much for them. She had more success with the wisteria and the climbing pink roses she planted on either side of the kitchen door, and with the blue hydrangeas along the front walk.

Later, when she inherited some money, she suggested they look for a house in tonier Southease. Scudder refused to consider it. So Genevieve improved Salt Cottage, as she called it. She hired a good architect to enlarge the kitchen, add a porch to the east and a large, sunny room to the south, which she filled with potted plants. From the outside, the two parts of the house looked entirely harmonious. Inside, despite fresh plaster and coats of paint, the original rooms still exuded the faint but unmistakable odor of the sea. At night the posts and beams of the old house would creak, like the timbers of a ship under sail.

The morning after the explosion, Clayton peered into Nancy's room and saw an empty bed. He was often out of the house before she even got up; now, in his confusion, he feared she'd been kidnapped like the Lindbergh baby. He glanced wildly about, looking for clues. Beside the disordered bed, on the bureau, stood a photograph of himself on his mother's lap, a boy of two or three. His mother smiled calmly, her hair in neat waves, her eyes tired but still beautiful as a movie star's. The boy, in a neat-fitting sailor suit, stared back at him, chin thrust forward. Clayton felt angered by the photograph, as though it were a fake. He could not remember ever sitting on his mother's lap or wearing such ridiculous clothes. Since her death, he'd tried without success to imagine his mother watching over him. But it was Nancy who did that, Nancy who mattered most. He turned and clattered down the stairs.

Clayton had known his sister to be seriously ill only once. Not long after they'd moved to Salt Hay Road, when she was only fourteen, she'd had a fever for three days. He had watched her anxiously as she slept, her cheeks flushed, her hair dark with sweat. Mavis told him to go play outside, but as soon as she wasn't looking, he crept back in. When Nancy woke for brief stretches, her eyes glittered. Finally the fever broke. She slept for a day and a half, and Clayton realized she wasn't going to die.

That was when he'd formed the habit of checking on her first thing in the morning, before he went downstairs. He would have been embarrassed if anyone had seen him, but he found himself doing it nonetheless. If he could verify from the doorway that she was breathing, if she stirred a little in her sleep or if he caught the movement of the blanket as her chest rose and fell, he could almost pretend he hadn't needed to check on her but merely wanted to see if she was awake. If she lay with her face to the wall, or obscured by one of her many pillows, he felt compelled to tiptoe into the room until he could satisfy himself that she had emerged safely on the other side of the night, that dark tunnel. Once, she'd startled him by opening her eyes just as he leaned over her. She sat up, annoyed, and demanded to know why he'd woken her. Clayton had stammered an excuse and retreated as fast as he could, his heart pounding.

Now he found her downstairs at the kitchen table, leafing idly through the morning paper with a cup in one hand. Clayton hid his relief by humming "At the Codfish Ball." She glanced up, and he caught the feverish sheen in her eyes. It looked as if a reflection of the fireworks had somehow lodged there.

Nancy put her cup in the sink and stepped over to the little mirror in the hallway. "Do you think I'm beautiful?" she asked. She brushed the glass with her hand. It was an old mirror, the surface more gray than silver.

"I don't know," Clayton muttered. She wore a green puckered blouse and the brown riding pants that Mavis didn't like. Her short, dark hair had been brushed back away from her face and tucked carefully behind her ears. As he watched, she bit her bottom lip and rubbed her cheeks. Her skin reddened under the tips of her fingers. She seemed to expect him to say more.

"Perry's brothers think so," he admitted finally. He'd heard Charlie Gilpin whistle from the yard as Nancy rode by on Buckshot, and then say something about horses and luck. When he asked what that meant, Fred told him, "Your sister's a looker." Clayton felt annoyed by this, though he understood Fred meant it as a compliment.

"Oh, the Gilpin boys." Nancy dismissed them with a toss of her head. "What do they know?" She straightened her shoulders and gave the mirror a bright, intense look, as if she meant to stare it down.

Clayton loved all the Gilpins, and Perry's older brothers particularly. They worked on the bay every summer, and Clayton longed more than anything to have a job like theirs someday. "They know everything about clamming," he told Nancy loyally.

His sister laughed and turned away from the mirror. "Exactly," she said. Clayton was relieved to see her look more like herself.

In the aviary at Washington Lodge, Clayton was halfway through his morning work. He'd opened the heavy drapes and the sun streamed in through the many windows, thick as honey, and lighted the bits of down that floated in the air like the fluff from sea myrtle in the fall. He had changed the lining on the cages that hung against the wall and distributed fruit to the parrots, the cockatoos, and the trogons, neatly avoiding the quick beak of the African gray. He marked his progress through the maze of cages by species: he was in the smaller bird section now, moving slowly to avoid startling a pair of green lorikeets. Clayton refilled the lorikeets' water and placed a spray of millet on the tray. Over the screeches and the rustling of the birds he heard the rattle of the door.

A steaming cup in his hand, George B. Washington skirted the cages in a red brocade dressing gown and leather slippers. Washington had made his fortune during the Great War with his invention of instant coffee. When the U.S. Patent Office refused to let him sell George Washington Powdered Products, he'd simply added the initial *B*. His real name was unknown, though he was clearly a foreigner. Some believed he came from Eastern Europe, others South America. His manners were faultless and his English excellent, but he betrayed himself in small eccentricities: a fondness for yellow silk scarves, a disinterest in sailing, his huge collection of rare and exotic birds.

Mr. Washington stood near the open window and tipped his head, sniffing the air. Over the smells of the aviary, Clayton caught the harsh, lingering scent of gunpowder. "I sold firecrackers once," Mr. Washington murmured, almost to himself. He was staring out the window, and the steam from his coffee fogged the pane. "With my brother on the street corner. Many years ago." Mr. Washington was not given to conversation and usually spoke to Clayton only with instructions about the birds. "My first job," he added, surprising Clayton further by turning and addressing him directly. "I wanted the money for a pair of shoes. My mother took it to buy a pig." Clayton, standing with the tray of fruit and millet in his hands, glanced down at his employer's immaculate leather slippers. Then he caught Mr. Washington's wry smile. "Yes." The older man nodded. "But the boy I was then"—he pressed the fingers of one hand together and then opened his palm with a little snapping motion—"still shoeless." Clayton tried to imagine Mr. Washington, with his elegant black mustache, his dressing gown with the tasseled belt, as a barefoot boy with firecrackers spread out on a cloth. He opened his mouth to ask where that had been, then thought better of it, suddenly shy. Mr. Washington had turned back to the window and was studying the temperature gauge. "Warm enough for the cockatoos today," he said. The moment had passed.

On sunny mornings in the spring and summer, the sulphur-crested cockatoos were allowed into the branches of one of the copper beeches that lined the white pebble drive. A short chain tethered each bird by one foot to its own metal hoop. Clayton carried the birds out one by one, riding like pashas on his shoulder, the hoop clutched in his fist. The cockatoos' sharp claws dug into his skin, but even so, it was his favorite part of the job; they understood exactly where they were going and shrieked and whistled with excitement, making his ears ring.

Carrying the birds, Clayton considered how Mr. Washington had come from somewhere else and made his home here too. It seemed funny that Clayton had never looked at it that way before. He would save his own wages, like Mr. Washington had. Not for something dull, like a pair of shoes or a pig. Not even for an aviary full of birds. He would save up for a boat. He pictured it in his mind, a cockpit runabout with a six-cylinder engine.

He used a long wooden pole with a hook at the end to hoist the birds into the air. One by one, he fitted the hoops onto hooks in the branches of the tree. Secured among the leaves, the cockatoos stretched their wings and cocked their heads, gazing down at Clayton with smug benevolence. The sun glinted on their white feathers. They blinked their gray, hooded eyes. When the last bird was aloft, it looked like the copper beech had blossomed with enormous gardenias.

Mavis had walked to the lodge with Clayton to prepare Mr. Washington's breakfast and then his large lunch. Because he ate his main meal at two in the afternoon, she was usually able to go straight from Washington Lodge to Salt Hay Road in the late afternoon, leaving something light for Mr. Washington's dinner. All this changed when he had guests. The afternoon after the explosion, Mavis was preparing partridge in the kitchen. The partridge was in honor of the visitor from Boston, and it meant that she would not get home until after eight.

Mavis cut the fat salt pork into strips. Now and then she glanced out the window, remembering the cloud of smoke in the shape of a fist. The housekeeper had removed all evidence of ash and broken plates, and scrubbed the kitchen floor, but Mavis still felt nervous here and wished she were home on Salt Hay Road. If only she were certain what the explosion presaged. Danger, she thought, but from where, from whom?

A knock on the kitchen door startled Mavis badly. She jumped, nearly slicing her thumb, as her niece stepped in. Nancy's cheeks were pink from riding. "Hello," she said brightly, pulling off a pair of brown kid gloves. "I was out on Buckshot and thought I'd drop by."

The girl wore her riding breeches, something Mavis did not approve of, and a cropped, boyish jacket. Mavis was sorry Roy had allowed her to take up riding after Helen died, giving her free use of the two horses. Mavis loved her late sister's daughter, of course she loved her; she had welcomed her into her home. But the girl never reciprocated her affection, pulling away stiffly, even after her mother died, if Mavis tried to hug her. She was indifferent even to Mavis's cooking. Mavis had made an orange sponge cake for her eighteenth birthday, as a special treat, and her niece had poked at it with the tines of her fork, unimpressed, as if oranges were as common as apples.

There was a small mirror on the wall by the door. Mavis watched Nancy peer into it with a quick, critical look and tuck a loose strand of hair behind her ear. The girl knew she was pretty, Mavis thought with a flash of old bitterness, though she would never match Helen's cool and perfect beauty.

"Clay around?" Nancy asked.

"No," said Mavis. She resented being interrupted in her work. "I haven't seen him since this morning. He's probably just getting out of school." She rummaged in a drawer for the larding needle, found it, and threaded a strip of salt pork through the wide eye. "If you hurry, you'll be able to catch him."

Instead of leaving, her niece leaned indolently against the counter. "What is that?"

"Partridge," said Mavis, in the tone of someone stating the obvious. She took a long, shallow stitch with the needle, drawing the salt pork at a right angle to the narrow breastbone.

"Why are you poking it like that?"

Mavis sighed. Larding a partridge was a tricky job, requiring all her concentration. She picked up a second strip of salt pork and fitted it through the eye of the needle. "I'm larding it, of course. To keep the meat from drying out."

Nancy sat down at the table and toyed with a paring knife. Her thick, bobbed hair fell around her face, hair as glossy and dark as her mother's. *She'd* never had to work for a living, Mavis thought as she leaned over the puckered flesh of the partridge, her hands slippery with grease. No one had ever called *Helen* a dumb broad, or taken all her money, or walked out on her. Helen had been treated to a Grand Tour of Europe by Granny Chaffey when she turned seventeen, and a Venetian count had kissed her hand and called her a flower of America. Mavis, six years younger, had not been taken anywhere. Europe had gone to war, and Granny Chaffey broke her hip in a fall and never fully recovered.

The clock in the dining room chimed and Mavis realized she'd forgotten to take in the tea. She glanced at her niece, who did not look especially presentable in her breeches and cropped jacket. Mavis felt glad Mr. Washington wasn't home; the fellow from Boston wouldn't notice the irregularity. "Run the tea in, would you? You made me forget all about it. To the aviary. The farthest door on the right."

Nancy surprised her by jumping up and grabbing the tray before she'd even finished talking. Flighty, Mavis thought with irritation. She called down the hall, "Careful with the china."

"Guess who?" Nancy said lightly, brandishing the tea tray so that the cup and saucer rattled. Robert Landgraf was standing at the window beside a cage of bright green birds, a camera in one hand. She'd intended to say something funny about moon-lighting as a parlor maid, but the look of pleasure on his face as he turned drew her up short. She felt her cheeks flush. Behind her the swinging door creaked to a close.

"I'm just helping my aunt," she told him. "I'll set this down here." She moved toward a table strewn with papers, rulers, and calipers of different sizes in the middle of the room.

Robert bumped against two birdcages, causing a screech and a panic of flapping wings in his attempt to reach the table before Nancy did. He flipped the sketchpad closed and pushed the charcoal pencils aside, too late to keep her from glimpsing the drawings of a girl in a riding jacket. She recognized her own short, dark hair, the set of her mouth.

"I didn't expect to see you," Robert said.

"I stopped by to check on my brother." Together they looked down at the tea tray. This was where he'd been when the fireworks factory exploded, Nancy thought. She remembered the way the sound had lurched through her, flattening her heart against her rib cage. Robert Landgraf would have felt that too. Nancy glanced back toward the sketches he'd covered up and a wave of giddiness surged inside her. "My aunt asked me to bring the tea in. She's busy darning your partridge."

"Darning my partridge?"

"With a needle. There must have been a hole in its heel."

"A specialty of the region?" Robert asked. "I can't wait to try it. In the meantime, can I offer you some tea?"

Nancy smiled. "There's only one cup."

"You drink from the cup? That's handy. In Boston, we prefer the saucer."

When Clayton arrived at Washington Lodge, he was surprised to see Nancy's horse cropping the grass at the base of the bird feeder by the kitchen door. He gave Buckshot's neck a tentative pat. Inside, the kitchen was empty. "Hello?" Clayton called, throwing down his schoolbag. When no one answered, he climbed quickly onto a stool and reached into the shelf of baking supplies. He didn't think his aunt would begrudge him a handful of raisins, but he'd never risked asking.

The raisins were a way to befriend the peacock, or at least conquer his fear of it. The bird menaced Clayton when he tried to collect the peahen's eggs. Once, it had attacked him from behind, pecking hard with its sharp beak and leaving a bruise on his calf that Clayton watched with interest over the following days as it turned from deep to lighter purple, blue, green, and finally yellow, not unlike the colors of the peacock itself. After that, Clayton entered the pen with a stick and held the peacock's gaze until he'd backed out again. Now he tossed the raisins into the cage and watched, fascinated, as it gobbled them up, its neck snaking out as if the raisin were prey that might escape.

Engrossed, Clayton didn't notice his aunt coming around the corner. Her voice made him jump. "Have you found your sister? She's looking for you." Clayton shook his head, turning toward the beech trees as if to check on the cockatoos. "What are you feeding that bird?" his aunt demanded. Clayton glanced down. The peacock, moving with ferocity, had swallowed the last raisin.

"Crickets," he lied. As soon as he'd said it, he felt ashamed of his mistake: it was spring, and the crickets wouldn't be out till summer.

Nancy rode back down Old Purchase Road from Washington Lodge. The sun shone through the green maple leaves. Here and there along the road lay bits of ash and charcoal-edged debris among the daffodils. Now that it was in the past, the fireworks factory explosion struck her as proof that anything might happen, even here in Fire Neck. Nancy nudged Buckshot into a trot and then, almost immediately, a gallop. They hurtled along the side of the road, the green trees blurring. Happiness bobbed inside her like a silver bubble.

At the intersection of Old Purchase and Beaver Dam, Nancy reined in, slowing to a trot. They turned onto Beaver Dam, and the horse tossed his head and snorted. Nancy was conscious of the figure she cut, up on Buckshot's dark back, and she thought of the charcoal sketches she'd glimpsed in the bird-filled room at Washington Lodge. The bubble expanded inside her. Laughing, she leaned forward and dug her heels into the horse's sides. They charged off again down Beaver Dam Road. From behind them she could hear the squawking of the Scheibels' chickens.

As they turned onto Salt Hay Road, Nancy's exhilaration faded. The familiar ground with its potholes and dandelions seemed disappointing, as if, riding so breathlessly, she'd almost expected to arrive somewhere else, somewhere new and different. At the barn, Buckshot breathed gustily as she dismounted. Standing on her two legs again, she felt puny, diminished. Already the conversation with Robert Landgraf in the aviary at Washington Lodge seemed like it had happened to someone else. Steam rose from the horse's back as she lifted the saddle and then began to brush him with the curry comb. She measured out extra oats and pulled off a clump of hay, scattering the fragrant dust.

Nancy was nearly twenty; her best friend from high school, Enid Snow, had already married the year before and moved to Brooklyn. Nancy didn't think much of Enid's husband, an X-ray technician with a nasal voice and strong views on politics and the economy. Enid sensed this, and a coolness rose between them. In high school Enid had daydreamed about studying architecture like her father. Nancy admired her for this, picturing Enid one day at work over a desk strewn with blueprints. She tried to imagine herself with a job as well, supporting her brother, and remembered the self-assured secretaries in her father's gleaming office and the way they could look her in the eye and type at the same time, their fingers rattling the black keys while they chatted. Instead, Enid had fallen in love, and soon afterward she left Fire Neck for Brooklyn. Nancy wondered what Enid's new, married life was like and whether she still made sketches on graph paper of mansions with glass domes and balconied windows.

Inside, the house was dark and cool, the rooms hushed. Nothing seemed to change here. The upholstery on the chairs in the sunroom had faded, the yellow flowers bleached nearly white, and the sewing room where her grandmother had made dresses for Nancy's dolls had been turned into Clayton's bedroom. But the rugs with the sand worked deep into the nap of the wool were the same, frayed a bit more around the edges. To Nancy, the house felt suddenly like something that had been given up on. While her grandmother was alive, it had been well kept, with fresh flowers on the dining-room table all spring and summer. Now the table was cluttered with her uncle's tools, with bits of string and scraps of cloth, and her aunt's books and pamphlets with titles like *Startling Facts in Modern Spiritualism, Psychic Science and Philosophy*. Everything felt worn thin, from the sheets on the beds to the chipped green-and-brown plates in the cupboards. The kitchen was the worst. It was a dark room with an ancient and temperamental cookstove and a low ceiling, made darker by the overhang of the porch outside. The pockmarked counter, though always clean of crumbs, had a stickiness to its wooden surface that seemed to resist soap and water. When Nancy asked once about replacing it, Mavis acted scandalized; she told Nancy there wasn't money for fripperies.

Nancy thought of her aunt, bent over the partridge in the kitchen at Washington Lodge. When she and Clayton first came to live on Salt Hay Road, Mavis had made a clumsy little speech. "Welcome to this house," she'd told them, as if they hadn't come to visit every summer since Nancy was a baby. "This is your home now. We're your family." Mavis tripped a little over the words, twisting a napkin in her hands. "You'll always have us." She sat down and patted her eyes with the napkin. Fourteen-year-old Nancy felt a spasm of rage, like a charley horse in her chest. She and Clayton had each other; that was enough family for them. No one could replace their mother. She glanced angrily at her little brother, who stared at their aunt and uncle with a devoted look that reminded her uncomfortably of one of the dogs. She cleared her throat loudly, so that he turned toward her instead, and the torturous moment was over.

Nancy watched Mavis closely after that, waiting for her to try to insinuate herself, to play at being a stand-in for their mother. She made it clear that her brother was her responsibility. When he wet the bed, she was the one who washed the sheets the next morning. When he broke his leg, she was the one who sat by his bed and read Sherlock Holmes stories, who bought him fat books of Buck Rogers and Tailspin Tommy comics with her carefully managed allowance. She rebuffed her aunt's offers of help and advice, until Mavis learned to stop making them. Working at Washington Lodge most of the day, she was easy for Nancy to avoid. Roy showed no interest in interfering, though he was kind to both her and Clayton in his distracted way. Her grandfather was the strongest presence in the house, and Nancy had always known she could wrap him around her finger. Within the walls of the house on Salt Hay Road, Nancy made a separate space for herself and Clayton. "She's very *independent*," she heard Mavis remark to Roy in an aggrieved tone, soon after they'd arrived. She'd carried the word like a talisman ever since.

Nancy went upstairs, to the small room that had once been her mother's. On the desk by the window stood her father's old black Remington portable, with her typing booklets beside it. Nancy picked up *Tips for Typists*. Squaring her shoulders, back straight, she started with a sample business letter: *Dear Sirs, We are pleased to inform you that in the matter of . . .* The *e* key, sticky with age or humidity, needed to be struck especially hard. Nancy had been practicing for three weeks now, after hearing that Enid Snow's older sister had found a typing job at an office in Patchogue. In spite of her improving speed, Nancy still made six or more mistakes per page. The problem, she thought, was the tediousness of it. She looked through the pamphlet of suggestions by Albert Tangora, the World Typing Champion, but it was evidently not a subject he felt the need to address.

In a fit of dissatisfaction, she stripped her bed and remade it with fresh sheets from the linen closet. Spring cleaning, she told herself. The typewriter could wait. She hauled up the green braided rug off the floor and dragged it down the stairs. Out in the yard, she draped it over the clothesline and beat it with a broom. Dust rose in satisfying clouds, and she had to move upwind. The rug had belonged to her mother. As she worked to beat it clean, she thought of the furniture from the house in Connecticut, nearly all of which had been sold at auction after her mother died. It had not occurred to anyone that she and Clayton might one day have a use for it in a place of their own, and this was something Nancy resented. Mavis or Roy, someone should have thought of that. But her aunt and uncle were entrenched in the day-to-day, as worn and unchanging as the house itself. There was nothing they were moving toward, no beckoning future. She felt an unfamiliar pity for her aunt, abandoned by her unfaithful, gambler husband, living in her childhood home and working as a domestic. Her own life would be different, the way her mother's had been.

As a typist, Nancy thought, she could find work anywhere big enough to have office buildings. She pictured herself in a busy office, like her mother's friend Georgia Spencer, a buyer for a furniture company in New Haven. Mrs. Spencer wore beautifully tailored clothes and exuded a confidence that Nancy attributed to working all day with clever men in suits.

The rug was still releasing dust, but Nancy's arm was tired. She dragged it back upstairs and rolled it out on the floor of her room. If they lived in Connecticut, they could still visit Fire Neck in the summers, she thought, as they'd done with their mother. Some of her earliest memories were of walking on the boardwalk that led to the beach at Old Inlet, her bare feet on the warm gray planks, the men around her carrying picnic baskets and a ukulele, and her mother scandalizing the local women with a swimsuit they would copy as best they could the following season. The rest of the year, Nancy decided, she and her brother would live in an apartment on the top floor of a tall building. She wanted Clayton to have a wider view of the world, a sense of greater possibilities than the ones that existed here. He'd have a job himself, she supposed, though this was something she could never actually picture. When she thought of the future, Clayton was the same little brother she'd been watching over from the time she was seven years old.

When the letter from the lawyer arrived, less than a week later, it confirmed Mavis's fear that the fireworks factory explosion had been a warning. She picked up the mail, as usual, at the post office by the Fire Neck station on the way home from Washington Lodge in Roy's Ford. It was raining lightly, a thin spring drizzle that made the air smell like grass and leaves, and Roy waited in the car while Mavis went into the post office. Leafing through the bills and circulars, she was surprised to see her name on a heavy cream envelope. The return address was a law firm in Fresno, California.

Mavis had put her failed marriage from her mind as much as she could. When she thought of her husband during the day, she threw a pinch of salt over her shoulder to ward off bad luck. She had come back to Fire Neck a few years before her niece and nephew, when only Roy and Scudder were living in the house on Salt Hay Road. Mavis had written to them from Ohio, saying simply that she was coming home alone, and for good.

On the afternoon of her return, it occurred to Roy at the last minute that the kitchen was not entirely clean. He spent twenty minutes swiping halfheartedly with a damp sponge, and then, on his way to the station, the Ford ran out of gasoline. Roy had to walk all the way to Southease with the gas can.

So Mavis stepped off the train at Fire Neck to a deserted platform. The ticket collector helped her with her luggage. Then the train pulled away in a flurry of dust. There were six barrels lined up along the track waiting for a westbound train, and as Mavis sat down on one of them, she felt the purpose and activity that had sustained her across three states drain out of her like blood. Her husband, Ramsay White, had abandoned her in Cleveland, taking with him the last of the money she'd inherited from her mother. Mavis knew he would not be back. She had felt relieved, even as failure settled on her heart like a hen on an egg.

She sat on the barrel and twisted the ring on her left hand. When her brother arrived, more than half an hour late, she almost resented being interrupted in her vacancy. She came back to Salt Hay Road in a listless daze. And it was only the extreme and unexpected squalor of the kitchen, with its smell of dogs and its strangely streaked windows, that roused her.

It took two weeks, cleaning from morning till night, to restore the kitchen to order. After their mother died, Roy had taken to feeding his dogs there. The pantry had been abandoned to the squirrels. In the bird's-eye corner cabinet that had been part of her mother's dowry, she found a desiccated sparrow in a soup tureen, its clawed feet gripping at nothing.

Mavis had always been a fitful sleeper. When she woke at night, she felt grateful each time to find herself in her own narrow bed in the house where she'd grown up. She kept the top curtains open so that she could look out her window and be sure of where she was. The moonlight often woke her. After she'd lain awake for an hour, she'd pull a flannel robe over her nightgown and go downstairs. She moved as quietly as she could in her stocking feet, her thin hair loosening from its braid. Some nights she could go back to sleep after cooking a pan of cornbread. Other nights she baked till dawn. Once, Roy found her asleep at the table when he came downstairs at six, with two loaves of bread, a nut cake, and a blueberry pie cooling beside her.

It was baking that drove Mavis to employment. Her father wasn't mean, but he was thrifty, and Mavis felt guilty spending his money on butter and sugar, let alone the poppy seed and candied ginger she craved. One day after she had surreptitiously given away an apple pie and a loaf of soda bread, she overheard the fish man tell her brother that George B. Washington had advertised for a cook. "I wonder what he eats, anyway, with all his money," the fish man grumbled. "Not what I'd call overfond of fish, I can tell you."

She knew her mother would have been ashamed to see her working. Part of Mavis was grateful that her mother had died while she was still in Ohio, before her marriage had come apart at the seams. Genevieve Scudder had been old-fashioned in her views and thought a wife's role was to ornament the home. Her father and brother accepted Mavis's job at Washington Lodge without complaint. She saved half of her earnings and put the rest into housekeeping. With Mavis away most of the day, Roy could enter the house without removing his boots, and if his dogs slipped into the kitchen, no one raised a fuss.

Now Mavis got back into the car mechanically, the mail clutched damply on her lap. She had no reason to correspond with lawyers. Unless it had to do with a will. Her mind sprang like a trap: maybe Ramsay was dead. The idea brought a rush of feeling so strong it shook her. She had never wished him harm, she reminded herself quickly. Even when he was at his worst, when she realized he was penniless and had courted her on the slim hope of her Chaffey inheritance, the most she'd ever hoped for was only that he would leave her alone. But now for the first time she saw how cramped the world felt with him at large in it. All these years she'd felt him lurking in the shadows. If he were dead . . . She would finally be safe from him, from the menace he represented and that she was certain he would exert over her until he died. She'd be a widow instead of a discarded wife. Dead, he could never reappear, never make any further claims or threats. She hoped, virtuously, that his end had been painless. Knowing him, it seemed unlikely.

"All right there?" Roy asked. Mavis didn't trust herself to speak. She nodded, keeping her eyes on the road.

Back at the house, Mavis took the envelope upstairs and opened it in the privacy of her room. Unused to the stiff, official language, she read for a full minute before she realized that her husband was not dead after all. He was missing. The lawyer was attempting to contact him on behalf of a client.

Stricken, Mavis leaned against the door. The bitterness of her disappointment brought tears to her eyes. She told herself she was an evil woman for jumping to such a conclusion, for entertaining such a hope. Taking the letter downstairs, she felt that she deserved whatever trouble it foretold. Roy was mixing up a salve for his dogs, and the kitchen smelled of turpentine, something Mavis would usually have complained about. Instead, she handed him the envelope. "I don't know what to do," she said, dropping heavily onto one of the kitchen chairs.

Roy scanned the cream-colored page with its perfect knife's-edge creases. "Do you know where he is?"

She shook her head.

Roy shrugged. "Why don't you write back to tell them that?" He tossed the letter on the table, and Mavis saw a smudged thumbprint where he'd held it. The smudge seemed to strip the letter of some of its power. It was only a piece of paper, she reminded herself. "He probably owes someone money," Roy went on. "Write back and explain that you haven't seen him in however many years. I imagine that'll be the end of it."

"Do you think so?"

"Sure," Roy said easily, stirring the salve with a wooden spoon. The smell of turpentine was very strong. "I wouldn't worry."

Mavis watched her brother lift the pot and pour the mixture into an empty jelly jar. Part of her longed to confess her deepest fear: that her husband was trailing her, like a fox tracking a rabbit. That any day he might show up here on Salt Hay Road. She avoided saying his name, afraid of conjuring him inadvertently. Since the day of the explosion, she had not slept well. In her dreams she saw the ugly gray cloud moving toward her, and then she knew that her husband was here in Fire Neck, on Salt Hay Road, he had opened the kitchen door, he was mounting the stairs. She would wake up with her heart hammering like a sparrow's. As close as she was to her brother, as dearly as she loved him, she had never told him much about her marriage.

She felt instinctively that her fears were better left unstated, as if putting them into words could somehow bring them about.

Roy had finished wiping the jelly jar with one of her dish towels. Whistling for his dogs, he made his way out of the kitchen. Mavis stood for a moment by the counter and silently prayed: *Please, Lord, keep my husband away from here.* Then she remembered her evil hope of a few moments before and despaired. She didn't deserve God's protection. And yet, she thought miserably, she needed it so badly. She took the letter and carried it back upstairs, grateful for the smear Roy's thumb had made. If her husband did track her, her brother would be here. She would not have to face him alone. That thought, more than any other, calmed her.

It was impossible for Nancy to pretend she'd arrived at the train station by chance. She sat waiting by the platform on Buckshot as Washington's car pulled in. Robert Landgraf, emerging from the backseat, spotted her immediately. He started toward her, smiling. Nancy slid off Buckshot's back and gripped the reins.

"Hold on," the driver called. Nancy heard him explain that Robert would have to buy his ticket on the train. "In Boston you probably have a big station. Here we just have this." The driver gestured at the little wooden platform.

"Thank you," Robert said, picking up the bag. "I'll wait by the tracks."

"Not too close," the driver admonished. From down the track they heard the whistle of the train. "Be careful in New York," the driver added, getting into the car. Robert turned at last toward Nancy with a mocking, secret wink. The train, throbbing down the tracks, stirred up clouds of dust. Robert stood holding the handle of his suitcase, tipped slightly to the side by the weight, as if some force inside the tracks were drawing him toward them. He was heading into New York City to see colleagues at the Museum of Natural History before continuing back to Boston.

Nancy wished suddenly that he would ask her to go with him to the city, just for the day. She wouldn't, of course, it was out of the question. But she wanted to be asked.

"Would it be all right," Robert said over the noise of the approaching train, and for a moment she thought he was thinking the same thing, "if I wrote to you?"

"Oh, of course," Nancy told him. "Sure. Box 17." She tried to act breezy, as if men wrote to her all the time and one more or less was not of much consequence. But she had to raise her voice as the train pulled in, and it sounded thin and childish to her ears. She felt angry at herself for not staying away. Buckshot whinnied, pulling against the reins as the train squealed to a stop. The conductor was opening the door at the top of the steps. "Goodbye," said Nancy, trying to smile. "It was nice to meet you."

"Westbound!" shouted the conductor. Robert was gazing at her with a fixed expression, as if he had just asked a momentous question and was waiting for her answer. Buckshot shuffled and snorted behind her. She gave the reins a yank, exasperated and close to tears.

The conductor shouted again. Robert turned. With a little wave in Nancy's direction, he stepped onto the train. He hadn't kissed her, Nancy thought bitterly, he hadn't even held her hand. Now it was too late. She would probably never see him again. Above her on the train, she saw Robert struggling to lower the window. It was stuck in place. He reappeared in the next row. The train pulled away, gathering speed. The window flew down and Nancy saw Robert's face protrude, his expression earnest. He called something down to her, but the noise of the engine drowned him out. Nancy stood and watched the train grow smaller before it rounded the corner and hurtled out of sight. The unheard words seemed to hang suspended in the smoke and dust.

Scudder was of two minds about the haircut. He sensed, in his granddaughter's offer, an urge to make him more presentable, something he naturally resented. On the other hand, and although he claimed to feel like a prize pig at a county fair, he secretly enjoyed being fussed over by Nancy. It was rare that he had her full attention lately. At first he'd been relieved when her typewriter went quiet and she stopped talking about secretarial jobs in Patchogue. He hadn't liked the idea of her in an office full of men, most of them undoubtedly married, though of course he hadn't been able to tell her so. But she seemed distracted, even sulky. She'd turned down his offer of going sailing twice in the last two days. He suspected the haircut was her way of making amends.

With a show of reluctance, he allowed her to set a kitchen chair in a patch of sunny lawn and submitted to a towel thrown around his shoulders and fastened with a clothespin. It was a still morning, the spring air warm and heavy with the promise of summer. A kingfisher flashed above the pond, making its cheerful racket.

Scudder leaned back in his chair. White hair drifted onto his lap and onto the green grass. "Mattress stuffing," he said, poking a tuft with his boot. What it reminded him of more than anything was the ash that had fallen from the sky after the fireworks factory explosion. Scudder wondered if it was the explosion that had affected Nancy's moods, or the weedy-looking guest from Washington Lodge who'd come to dinner that night; first she'd been so agitated, now she seemed inclined to mope. He closed his eyes, feeling the sun on his face and the movement of Nancy's hands as they tugged and snipped. Well, the man had gone, he knew because he'd asked Mavis, and it seemed unlikely that the explosion would have shaken someone with nerves like Nancy's. The girl thought nothing of danger, you could tell by the way she rode. Scudder had tolerated horses on the property ever since his marriage; his late wife had grown up around the animals on her family's ranch, and she'd insisted the children learn to ride. But the sheer bulk of the beasts had always bothered him. His granddaughter seemed so slight, so precariously perched.

He remembered how once when Nancy was still in diapers they'd found her at the top of a ladder set against one of Roy's greenhouses. She was bobbing happily above their heads, directly over the bright expanse of glass. Scudder had felt his heart seize like a clogged bilge pump. His daughter Helen stifled a scream.

"Boat-th!" shouted tiny Nancy, pointing out over the greenhouse roof. "I thee boat-th!"

"Ahoy," Scudder called, forcing himself to speak. "Can I have a look?" He'd moved up the ladder slowly. In the Life Saving Service he had climbed masts after sailors who'd taken refuge there on listing ships and then grown too cold or too terrified to get down. Once a man toppled just before Scudder reached him; Scudder grabbed for him as he fell and caught him by the jacket, the dead weight nearly dislocating his arm. The ladder shifted as Nancy bounced on her small bare feet. Below, Scudder could see roses through the clear roof of the greenhouse, a mass of yellow, a mass of pink, a mass of red. "Easy, missy," he said when he reached her, wrapping his arm around her waist. His hands were shaking. "Why don't I whittle you a boat out of wood?" She let him carry her down the ladder. Her skin smelled pleasantly of soured milk. Helen had wanted to beat her with a hairbrush, but he wouldn't allow it.

Sitting in the warm sun, he felt a chill as he remembered her at the top of that ladder, oblivious to the danger beneath her rosy feet. "You ought to be more careful on that horse," he said. He felt her fingers pause for a moment. Then the scissors resumed their snipping.

"Of course I'm careful."

"I knew a man, one of the Life Savers. His wife was thrown by a horse and died."

"Maybe she wasn't a very good rider," said Nancy bluntly.

"And don't forget Kelley's brother," Scudder added. The Captain's brother, dead now, used to visit him from Pennsylvania every summer. He'd been kicked in the throat and spoke in a rough whisper, fascinating the children so much that they kept up a long string of questions simply for the thrill of hearing his raspy voice, which made anything he said seem fraught with peril and romance, even if it was only "Get out of here, you wretched whelps! Can't a man rest his head a moment?"

"It was a mule that kicked the Captain's brother." Nancy moved his head to the side, and he felt her begin to cut around his left ear. "Mules are different from horses."

"They're unpredictable," Scudder said. "Either one."

"Oh, I could live on horseback." Nancy's tone was cheerfully emphatic. "Like they do in Mongolia."

Scudder sighed. How ridiculous, he thought, that one of the things he loved most about his granddaughter was her disdain for his advice. Why should that be? He demanded obedience from his own children, but Nancy had a spark of mischief he couldn't help but admire. He felt the comb rake through the hair on the top of his head, and then a tug as the girl snipped without hesitation. He had watched her throw herself into the saddle of that monstrous horse and handle the reins with the same assurance with which she now wielded the scissors. Mavis, poor thing, was nothing like that. Not her fault, of course, Scudder admonished himself, just a woman built along different lines. Mavis put her faith in God and good-luck charms, and a lot of spiritualist hooey that had started when her mother died and worsened since her husband left her.

From the direction of the driveway he heard the engine of the car start and then sputter. Roy was tinkering with it again. He remembered his late wife worrying before she died that Roy would never marry. He'd been surprised by how agitated the thought made her; their own marriage had been happy, in the main, but they'd had their share of difficulties, especially early on, and his own advice, had he and Roy ever spoken of such things, would have been against making a hasty decision.

"Almost done," Nancy said. "I'm just trying to even this out."

Scudder closed his eyes, happy to feel her fingers in his hair. He would look like a shorn ram, he thought; it didn't matter.

Since she and Enid Snow had fallen out of touch, Nancy rarely took an interest in the mail. Her aunt usually stopped for it on the way home from working at the lodge. But after Robert Landgraf returned to Boston, Nancy found herself riding past the post office every afternoon. It was around the corner from the train platform in a small shop that sold candy, pens, boxes of envelopes, powdered milk. Inside, Nancy studied the dusty pencils, the postcards showing sailboats at the mouth of the Barto River. She could feel Miss Reese, the postmistress, watching her from behind the counter. Miss Reese was past seventy and devoted to her job: she read every postcard and held each envelope up to the light to glean what she could of the contents. She was a small woman with a large head, and her gray hair sat on top of it in a tight bun, like a rock cairn on a mountain.

Now her small, sharp eyes glittered at Nancy. Robert had been gone less than a week, and Nancy told herself again that he probably hadn't written, probably never would. But she refused to let herself be intimidated by a gargoyle like Miss Reese. She sauntered to the counter and asked if there was anything for Box 17, then waited, forcing herself not to fidget, while the postmistress checked the cubbyholes of mail. For five days she had tried without success to put the possibility of a letter from her mind.

Miss Reese turned back with an envelope in her hand, and Nancy saw her own name in an unfamiliar, masculine hand. Her heart stuttered. "Thank you," she said, smiling in spite of herself. Miss Reese pursed her ancient lips.

Outside in the sunlight, Nancy sat for a moment holding the envelope. She felt almost frightened to have an actual letter from him in her hands. She opened it carefully and smoothed the folded paper. *Dear Miss Poole*, she read. *Do you, by some miracle, actually exist? Here in my familiar rooms, surrounded by the objects of my prosaic days, I find myself thinking about you and the strange circumstances of our meeting. I remember standing at the back door of Mr. Washington's house, and the way you ran toward me across the lawn. I have a hard time concentrating on the lifeless specimens here in the museum. Will you take pity on me and write? I would be grateful for some proof that I did not imagine you.*

Nancy got up from the bench outside the post office and walked quickly around the building, and then sat down and read the letter nine more times. She'd had admirers, shy local boys who worked on the bay and boys from Southease eager to show off their fathers' cars. But they seemed now to belong to a different category altogether. With her finger she traced the letters that formed her name in Robert's large, orderly script, and the silver bubble bobbed wildly inside her.

Summer 1937

Roy Scudder was a gentleman farmer, which meant he dabbled in agriculture. He liked horses and would have been a rancher, he used to say, if only he had a hundred more acres. For a few years, after he'd come back from college, he threw himself into growing flowers. With money from the Chaffey side, he built two long glass greenhouses and filled one with roses and the other with carnations. Later he added sweet peas and violets, but never turned much of a profit. Then he became interested in duck farming and had blueprints drawn up for a duck barn that would empty into the pond. By then the money had dwindled, and when he learned he'd have to pay pluckers up to five dollars a day, he got discouraged and abandoned the plans. For a while he raised quail in large wire pens set off the ground and sold their tiny, speckled eggs to restaurants in Southease and Moriches. There was a pigeon loft, for squab. He'd kept pigs, both Durocs and Chester Whites. For several years he'd raised hunting dogs to sell, adding a series of pens along the edge of the horse barn and building a long, narrow barn for goats, which he kept to produce extra milk for the puppies. Roy cooked the dog food, a mixture of meat scraps and cornmeal, in kettles on the big stove just inside the kitchen, waiting till after Mavis had left for work at the lodge.

Though they never spoke of it, Roy suspected his father looked askance at his efforts to make a living; Scudder seemed to think the Chaffey money had softened him. By the mid-1930s, when Clayton and Nancy came there to live, the out-buildings behind the house on Salt Hay Road were already falling into disrepair. Roy had gradually lost interest in every-thing but the hunting dogs he kept for his own use and his horses, Buckshot and Hardscrabble. He spent his days on the marsh and his weekends with friends from the boatyard and the Pattersquash Hunting Club.

Roy was fond of his niece and nephew, and glad to have them join the household after Helen died. And yet they left him somewhat at a loss. They cleaved together, naturally. He worried that he should be doing more for them, especially Clayton, without knowing exactly what. He wished he could somehow make up for the loss not only of their parents but of their once-considerable inheritance. Roy knew the details of this, because he had traveled to Connecticut after his brother-in-law died of a heart attack, with the idea that he might be of some use to his older sister.

He had found Helen pale but perfectly composed. Black suited her; in her simple dress she looked like a model in a magazine, and Roy felt slightly chilled by this, as if she should be unkempt, somehow; unmoored. Helen had never been demonstrative. Mavis, nervous and uncertain, relied on him, and so he tended to know what she was thinking. Helen kept her feelings to herself. Bertrand Poole had fallen in love with her at a beach party on Fire Island, after she'd won the Women's Sailboat Regatta for the third year in a row. Roy remembered her raising the gleaming cup in triumph, laughing, her teeth white in her tanned face, her hair tousled with wind and salt. The next day Bertrand had three hundred roses delivered to the house on Salt Hay Road. Their mother ran out of vases, and there'd been roses in canning jars, red, pink, and white, in buckets and tin cans. The house smelled like a perfumery. Helen accepted them without surprise, as if roses were her due, and Roy found himself wondering if her beauty had spoiled her, the way she'd been spoiled by Granny Chaffey and her trip to Europe. Later, after her marriage, it was Roy's private theory that she hadn't taken her adoring husband seriously because, for all his success in the world of business, he didn't know how to handle a boat. "He's so clever," Roy overheard Mavis tell her at the wedding, with a touch of awe.

"In his way," Helen said carelessly. "But he's *helpless* on the water."

In Stonington, after the funeral, Roy worked to shake the feeling that Helen should be more distraught. Together they met with her late husband's business partner. Bertrand Poole had left a generous legacy. His partner, Mr. Connell, went over the details. There was a certain amount in a savings account, he explained, addressing himself to Roy, man to man. The rest was in a carefully chosen portfolio of stocks and bonds.

"Why do I need those?" Helen asked. She pulled a white handkerchief from her purse and patted her nose. "I'd rather have it all in one place."

Mr. Connell explained that stocks were shares in a company, almost like loans to that company, and that bonds were like loans too. Having them in different places helped to balance the risk. Hers were doing very well, he assured Roy. Returns on some were over 10 percent.

"*Loans?*" Helen looked at Mr. Connell sharply. "I don't

think we want *that*." Turning, she addressed Roy, "Remember how Grandfather kept all his savings in a canning jar in the cellar? And Grandpa Chaffey only invested in land. Good and solid."

"Ha-ha," said Mr. Connell, and then, as Helen regarded him stonily, "Should we discuss this another time?"

Helen shook her head. She was taking the children down to Long Island the next day for a visit, she explained, and she'd like all the money now, in a nice lump sum.

"My dear Mrs. Poole, I don't think you understand. We're talking about hundreds of thousands of dollars."

It was the wrong approach to take with Helen. Roy could see her elegant shoulders squaring ever so slightly in the black silk dress. "If I don't understand," she told Mr. Connell briskly, "it's because the money seems to be spread all over the place. Naturally I want it all together, where I can see it."

"I'll arrange for you to have as much as you need, my dear. The rest is doing very well in the stock market." Here he suggested a number, holding up a slip of paper. It sounded like a great deal of money to Roy. Helen shook her head firmly, giving Mr. Connell a withering look.

Mr. Connell doubled the number, holding up another piece of paper with a sigh that indicated he was being more than reasonable. Now Helen hesitated, turning to Roy. He couldn't remember another time that she had asked for his advice. But what did he know about stocks and bonds? Mr. Connell appealed to her wifely feeling. "Your late husband was a man of business. I'm sure he'd want you to leave everything just the way it is."

Helen clutched her purse, and Roy knew she was tightening her grip on an imaginary tiller. "Bertie couldn't even sail a catboat," she began.

Roy felt compelled to step in. "Helen, please. Leave it alone for now. You can get the rest when you need it." She sighed and closed her eyes, and Roy saw the grief in the lines of her face. The handkerchief in her hand drooped like a small white flag. Roy and Mr. Connell shared a brief but relieved glance over the top of her head.

A year later, when the stock market crashed, Bertrand Poole's legacy vanished overnight. Roy had wished many times since then that he'd backed his sister up that day in Mr. Connell's office. But how could he have known that she was right and Connell wrong? At least the money she had insisted on taking with her had made her last years comfortable. What was left for the children came from the sale of the big house in Stonington after she died.

Clayton loved the outbuildings just as they were—the barn with its hayloft and smell of horses, the empty pigsty, where the rich, dense odor of pig manure still lingered, especially after a heavy summer rain. He and Perry liked to scramble up the side of the A-frame pig house, their fingers gouging the moss-slicked shingles, and sit on the ridge of the low roof beneath the chokecherry branches. The small red cherries were tart on Clayton's tongue. He and Perry spat the pits high into the air and watched them skitter down the slanted roof.

Closer to the road, a lush abundance of oversized weeds and saplings thrived in the abandoned greenhouses. Inside, it was always several degrees warmer, the air moist with the smell of damp soil and rot. Clayton and Perry played long games of Jungle Hunter, taking turns as the Wily Beast, games fraught with real danger due to the broken glass on the dirt floor and the weakness of the remaining frames. In the tangle of vegetation they sometimes came across a splash of white carnations or yellow roses. Every so often Roy would decide to fix the greenhouses up, this time to grow tomatoes or lettuces to ship to New York City. He might spend a whole day reviewing the necessary repairs and scribbling with a thick pencil on the back of a brown paper bag. Once, he had a glazier come by, and the two of them walked in and out of the greenhouses, pointing and discussing prices and materials. In a box in his room Clayton kept the red and yellow stubs of Roy's discarded builder's pencils. It took some time for him to realize that nothing came of Roy's bursts of initiative, that the greenhouses, like the pigsty and the pigeon loft, were safe from improvement.

As soon as school let out in June, Clayton spent much of his free time at the boatyard. *Playing*, Nancy called it, as if he were six years old and he and Perry were shooting marbles. She had taken a morning off from typing practice to get a list of recommended titles from his teacher, Miss Collier—*All Set Sail*, *The Good Master*, *Young Fu of the Upper Yangtze*—and now she plagued him to start one, ignoring the fact that September was two and a half months away. "Don't play too long at the boatyard," she said. "There are books you should be reading."

Clayton and Perry knew every boat docked at Starke's, from the smallest leaky rowboat to the 42-foot cabin cruiser with the plum stem grandly called the *Coronet*. Perry's favorite was a long, sleek motorboat with an open cockpit that belonged to a lawyer from the city who used it only once or twice a month. Clayton liked the sturdy clamming boats with the wide, flat decks and rounded bows. He would have at least three boats when he grew up, he told Perry: a work boat, a sailboat, and a cruiser.

Today Clayton sat in the shade of the boat shed alone. Perry had been made to stay home with his little sister, Pearl, who had a toothache, while their mother went into town. Sam Burnett and George Rowley were mending eel pots and discussing a racing schooner being built in Patchogue. Clayton listened to the men, hoping to pick up a new phrase or technical term to impress his friend.

Theron Greaves came around the corner of the boat shed with a bucket in one hand, a flat blue cap low on his forehead. He was an older bayman with a face like leather. Clayton knew his boat, a 21-foot cat skiff called *Leda*. In the winter Theron coated his cotton jacket with fish oil to keep out the cold, and all year his clothes smelled of rancid fish and tobacco. A little black dog with a spotted face followed behind him and sat with an air of resignation as Theron joined Sam Burnett and George Rowley at the eel pots. Clayton, listening intently, heard him say he needed a scapper for the season.

Clayton was on his feet almost before he knew what he was doing. "I'll do it!" The three men turned, surprised, and he realized he had shouted. "I can scap," he said, forcing himself to lower his voice. "I'm good with a net. I can do it. I'll show you."

Theron Greaves gave him a long, appraising stare. Clayton felt like an eel on a slab of ice. He stood up straighter, trying to appear taller, and wished with all his heart that he looked more like one of Perry's muscular brothers.

Theron did not seem particularly impressed. He turned toward the other men and jerked his head in Clayton's direction. "Sober fellow?"

Sam Burnett grinned. "Sure. That's Scudder's grandson. Roy's nephew."

"Got all his fingers?"

"I suppose he does," said Sam. The three men looked back at Clayton. Confused, he held up his hands to show them his digits.

"Scap good?" asked Theron. He glanced around the boat-yard, as if hoping for other, more likely, candidates.

"Could do," said Sam. "You give him a try with the net."

"Two o'clock tomorrow, then," Theron said, addressing Clayton for the first time. "*Leda.*" He nodded to the other two and walked off in the direction of the canals with his bucket, the black dog trotting after him.

Clayton punched the shingled wall of the boat shed in his excitement. A job on the bay! A job with Theron Greaves! If only he didn't mess up. He'd crabbed off the docks plenty of times with Perry: they'd put a fish head or a piece of chicken neck on a string and lower it into the water. When a crab went for the bait, the string tightened and began to move. Then one of them pulled the string in slowly while the other stood by with the net. When the crab came into view, clutching the bait, the scapper scooped it out of the water. The trick was in the timing. If he scooped too soon, the crab would scuttle away before the net reached it. If he waited too long, the crab grew nervous and abandoned the bait. Clayton went over the proce-dure in his mind step-by-step, more anxious than he'd ever felt before a test at school.

Nancy sat on the porch, working on a letter to Robert Land-graf on her portable typewriter. His were playful, asking what had spontaneously combusted lately while lamenting the drea-riness of his days spent roughing out specimens in the museum basement, "in grave danger of forgetting what a live bird looks like, always excepting the pigeons." Nancy, trying to respond with something clever, gave up in despair after half a stilted page. Far in the distance she could hear the drone of an airplane. The smell of the lilacs outside the door hung sweet and heavy in the air. She tried to imagine Robert in Boston, but she couldn't picture where he lived, or the museum where he worked, or where he ate his dinner, or with whom. "I have never been to Boston," she wrote finally, stopping to unjam the keys. "Can you tell me more about it? My uncle swears someone once drowned there in a flood of molasses."

What Robert liked about Boston, he'd written, was the press of people, the sense that he was in the thick of something. He lived in an apartment "smaller than a bread box, but with much the same charm." He'd grown up in Winslow, Maine, where his father and older brothers ran the family dairy farm. Sometimes he still missed the bobolinks, he told her, the way they flung themselves from the branches in the spring when the air was full of cottonwood fluff. Reading this, Nancy thought of Clayton and the fascination with birds' nests and turtle shells he'd developed since they'd come to Fire Neck. It pleased her to draw that little parallel between them.

In his latest letter, Robert asked what she liked most about Long Island, "besides the clouds of smoke, of course." Nancy tapped at the shift key. Since Robert left, she'd felt more dissatisfied with Fire Neck than ever.

She thought of her mother growing up in this same house, and wondered if she had felt a similar impatience with the unchanging rooms, with her family. Nancy's father had fallen in love with her in the course of a single evening on the beach. Nancy had heard the story so often she could see it in her mind: her mother with her sailing trophy on her lap, her face lit by the flames of the campfire. Six months later, they were married and living in Stonington, another sailing town. Nancy allowed herself to wonder for a moment how it would feel, not the move from the house on Salt Hay Road so much as the leap of faith, the trading of one life for a different one. Of course, her mother would have taken it in stride fairly easily, Nancy thought. She was a woman unsurprised by her own successes.

Glancing up from the Remington, Nancy caught sight of Clayton coming across the field. He'd been hanging around at the boatyard, she guessed. At the fence he stopped and she saw him make a series of odd, scooping motions in the air with his arms. His face, pinched in concentration, made Nancy remember the way he used to frown, biting his tongue, back when he was learning to read. "What are you catching out there?" she called merrily, and Clayton jumped. Nancy thought again how much he'd changed in the last year. He had grown gangly and secretive. Sometimes she found herself missing him, though of course he was right there. "Come sit with me a minute," she called. Her brother paused and then walked over, hands in his pockets, his shirt in need of a wash.

"Do you ever think about what kind of job you might want?" Nancy asked. She worried that he didn't apply himself at school. His teacher had told her that Clayton often scribbled pictures in his workbooks and that he needed to pay closer attention. He'd been caught playing hooky. "Later, after you're through with school?"

Clayton looked startled. He moved his head in a noncommittal gesture.

"It's just that you know so much about birds and insects. You might be able to work in a museum someday."

He shot her a suspicious look. "I like being outside."

"Of course," Nancy said. "Of course you do now. I meant later, when you're older."

"I won't want to be inside then, either."

"It was just a thought." Nancy didn't want to argue about it. She knew how stubborn he could get. But now Clayton was looking at her with a shy smile.

"I might get a job tomorrow," he confided. "Maybe. A job on the *bay*!" He sat back, pleased with himself. Nancy realized that the fierce concentration she'd seen on his face earlier had been connected to this, and she felt a twinge of disappointment; clamming or crabbing would never translate into a job at a museum, a career. "I'm not sure, though," Clayton added, suddenly sounding anxious. "I don't know if I'll be good enough."

Nancy reached over and squeezed his hand. "Sure you will." He smiled at her again, grateful, and she seized her chance. "Now promise me you won't skip school anymore."

Clayton glanced at his lap. He shrugged elaborately. "It's the *summer*," he pointed out.

Nancy held his hand tight as he tried to withdraw it. "Promise me, Clay. It's important."

He rolled his eyes. "Fine, I promise!" He pulled his hand away, but not unkindly, and trotted off in the direction of the barn. He was just a kid, Nancy thought, half sorry she'd been so stern.

Clayton arrived at the *Leda* ten minutes early. Across the canal, red-winged blackbirds burbled in the reeds. He waited nervously, worried the job had been a joke on him, until Theron Greaves appeared, carrying his bucket. The old bayman nodded to Clayton. The bucket was half full of pieces of pungent salted eel. From underneath the bow of the *Leda*, Theron passed Clayton a huge spool of line, tied with lumps of old eel skin that looked like black gristle. They sat down on the dock with the spool and the bucket beside them. Wordlessly, Theron showed Clayton how to take a chunk of eel, score it with a knife, then tie it onto the line with a clove hitch. He left a space of about six feet between the pieces of bait. The dog had jumped into the boat and stretched out in the shade under the bow. From time to time Theron threw her a scrap of eel skin, which she chewed steadily with half-closed eyes.

When the trotline had been baited from one end to the other, Theron loaded it back onto the *Leda* and they got aboard. A light breeze had come up. Clayton cast off from the dock and the canvas sail bellied out. Theron steered the *Leda* along the canal, past the boats at their docks and the men working on eel pots, mending nets, and fixing rudders. At the river he nosed up into the wind and tightened the main sheet. The *Leda* shivered, listed, and picked up speed. Clayton sat on the windward side and leaned out over the water. He breathed in deeply, loving the smell of marsh and mud, the spray on his face. He felt a wild spasm of affection for Perry's little sister; without her toothache, his friend would have been at the boatyard the day before and might have been chosen instead.

They sailed toward the mouth of the river, to a small indentation in the bank called Rose's Cove. Clayton had been there once before in a rowboat, looking for marsh wren nests. Theron came up into the wind, and they anchored one end of the trotline and marked it with a yellow buoy. Then he worked slowly back across the river under sail, and Clayton played out the trotline as they went. Near Long Point they anchored the other end. The sun had come out from behind the clouds and the water shone. Out on the bay a white powerboat touched its reflection as it bounced along. The hull and its image met and parted, met and parted, cutting the water like a pair of shears.

They sailed back to Rose's Cove, giving the crabs time to find the bait. There they picked up the line on a shiver attached to the gunwale; the shiver lifted the line and dropped it back down, bringing the bait close to the surface. Theron pointed with his chin toward the flat net, a skimmer made of chicken wire. Clayton took it and stood in the bow. Below him on the trotline a piece of black eel swam into view. He breathed in, to steady himself. No crab on that bait. The boat sailed slowly, almost drifting. It was quiet except for the lapping of waves along the hull and the barking of the gulls. Clayton stared down into his own distorted reflection. A crab appeared briefly, then faded into the murk. Clayton plunged the net, far too late. "Look lively," Theron said sharply from the stern, and Clayton jumped, almost dropping the net. He felt his eyes sting with shame. In another instant a second crab rose toward the surface, and this time Clayton plunged the net into the water. Up came the crab, gripping the chicken wire. Clayton flicked it into the basket in the bow, waking the dog. He turned back in time to see another crab hanging on the line. Down went the net, breaking the undulant gloss of the water. Twice he missed the basket and the crabs scuttled into the bilge, brandishing their pincers.

When the bait gave out and the yellow buoy appeared, Clayton looked up, surprised by the blue sky. He felt like a swimmer coming up for air. His eyes hurt from staring into the bright water, and he realized he'd been grasping the pole of the net so tightly his fingers ached. "Ready about," Theron said, and the *Leda* pivoted neatly in the water.

By the end of the fourth run, the basket was full and Clayton's technique had improved. A few of the crabs looked too small to keep. Clayton gripped them one by one with the tongs and glanced back at Theron. When he shook his head, Clayton flung the crab in question out over the water. Next he retrieved the two from the bilge and added them to the basket. Now that he'd acquitted himself well, he felt filled with happiness and relief. Beyond Long Point the salt marsh stretched, a haze of yellow green bordered by the darker green of high-tide bush and mallow. A marsh hawk flew low over the spartina. On the bank toward the boatyard a heron stood without moving. In the boat, the crabs clicked and bubbled, pinching at each other. The tide had begun to turn. They hauled in the trotline and returned for the other end, winding the line back on the spool as they went. The line would be stored in a barrel and covered with salt to keep it from rotting; they could use the same bait for several days.

Back at the boatyard Clayton learned how to pack the crabs in seaweed in small barrels, using a pair of tongs to keep from getting pinched. With a hatchet, Theron chopped out pieces of the barrel stays for air. They covered the barrels with burlap tops and tagged them. Theron did not own a car, so Jimmy Starke drove them down to the Fire Neck train station in his truck. Clayton rode in the back with the crabs. In his mind he played over the afternoon, the net gripped in his hands as he waited for the bait to come into view. At the station, he and Theron loaded the barrels onto the platform, where others already sat, waiting for the next New York train. The price for crabs was three dollars a barrel.

Theron held out his hand, and Clayton, confused, started to shake it. Then he felt the coins jingle into his palm. "Tomorrow at three," Theron Greaves told him. He turned and whistled for the dog. Clayton clambered onto the truck for the ride back to the boatyard. He stood up against the window, clinging to the roof. The wind whipped around him as if he were flying. It had been, he felt, the best day of his life.

Waiting at the train station, Nancy fought a rising panic. Over the last month and a half she had collected a small pile of envelopes with Boston postmarks. On days when there was nothing for her at the post office she affected nonchalance and bought a bag of Red Hots for Clayton. One day a letter came that was only a page: *I've convinced our director that the New Guinea psittacine in the Washington aviary demands closer study. I'm packing my calipers and my camera and will be returning to your exotic island in two weeks. I look forward to seeing you again.*

At the end of the platform a friend of Roy's whose name she couldn't remember picked at his teeth with a toothpick, a folded newspaper under one arm. Washington's driver was waiting with the car. Nancy tried to keep from pacing. She was making a fool of herself for a man she hardly knew. Maybe she'd misjudged his interest, she thought, maybe he was amusing himself at her expense. She remembered reading the letter on the bench beside the post office, and how, when she'd finished, she'd raced Buckshot down Old Stump Road at a reckless gallop. She worried now that Robert would think she was too forward, meeting the train like this. At the side of the building Buckshot stood tied to a post, flicking his tail at the flies. The train whistled in the distance. She glanced back at the horse, calculating the time it would take to unhitch him and mount. If she left now, she thought, Robert wouldn't see her. The whistle sounded again. Nancy imagined riding home. In the house on Salt Hay Road, her grandfather would be dozing over his cards while Mavis and Captain Kelley carried on another endless discussion about the nature of the divine.

The train pulled in, brakes squealing, and there was Robert stepping out of it three cars down from where she stood. He looked younger than she remembered, his hair sticking up in the back, his gray suit rumpled from the trip. She felt a momentary uncertainty, as if this might not be the man she'd been writing to for all these weeks. He blinked, dust in his eyes, and scanned the platform. Nancy stepped out from the shadow of the station wall and their eyes met. The happiness on his face was unmistakable. She felt herself smiling.

"Mr. Landgraf!" Washington's driver was hurrying over. Robert turned toward him with a groggy look, like someone torn from a deep sleep. "Mr. Landgraf, the car's over here."

"You can take the luggage on ahead," Nancy said boldly. "I'll bring Mr. Landgraf myself."

"Yes," Robert said. "Thank you. I need to stretch my legs." The driver looked unsure. Robert fumbled in his pocket and handed over a tip. The driver pocketed it, then picked up Robert's bags and turned in the direction of the car.

The train was pulling out again, and they moved away, toward Buckshot. Nancy unhitched the horse. "Where are you leading me this time?" Robert asked.

"To the lodge, like I said." She grinned at him. "On horseback."

Robert took a step backward. "Better not. I fell off one of those as a boy. Never learned to work the brakes."

"You'll be fine," Nancy said. She saw the hesitation beneath his mock alarm. "Leave it to me." For weeks she had wondered what it would be like when she saw him again, haunting the post office while she waited for his letters. Now she understood that it would be hard for him to refuse her. She felt a burst of reckless pleasure.

The station had emptied except for a small gang of boys playing marbles. She led Buckshot to the horse block at the edge of the road.

"Observe," Nancy said. She held the reins and put her hands on the horse's neck. Grasping the mane in one hand, she swung herself onto Buckshot's back, aware of her own easy grace. She looked down at Robert, who was watching her with a gratifying expression. "Your turn," she told him. "Put your left hand here." The horse whinnied and shuffled his back legs.

"Why don't I walk beside you instead?" Robert asked without moving from where he stood. "I have a lovely view of you from here."

"But you'd never keep up with me." Nancy reached toward him. "Hold on with this hand and raise yourself on your arms." Robert looked up at her, shaking his head. He was wearing black leather shoes, city shoes. After a long moment he moved forward. Nancy watched his foot step onto the white-washed horse block. He put his hand on the edge of the saddle and lurched toward her. Buckshot tossed his head and began to sidle away, and Robert stumbled back, his face flushed.

"I'm going to break my neck," he said. Nancy considered taking pity on him. But he had already grasped the saddle again. Buckshot sidestepped, head bobbing, as Robert swung himself up in a single desperate assault, nearly unseating Nancy. She felt his body pressed abruptly against hers, his legs on either side of her own. Goose bumps broke out along her arms.

Robert laughed in surprise. "I'm a cowboy!"

Nancy felt him shift behind her in the saddle as he tried to give her more room. "Sorry," he murmured. She lifted her hands, and without being told, Robert put his arms around her to grasp the horse's mane. He smelled faintly of camphor. The ride had been an idle impulse, a way to tease him. Now his man's hands lay in front of her, his fingers stained with black ink, the veins and muscles showing under the reddish hair. What had she done? What was she doing? She could feel him breathing behind her. She had crossed a border into foreign territory.

"Here we go," Nancy cried, clacking her tongue and giving a jab with her heel. The horse started with a little jump, and Robert's arms tightened around her. Buckshot, unused to the extra weight, stepped with a nervous prancing motion. They turned off the road, taking a path through Kozlowski's back field. The air was thick with pollen and the smell of honeysuckle.

Nancy wondered what would happen when they reached the lodge, how they would act toward each other with their feet on the ground. She thought of Danny Traphagen; how childishly flattered she'd felt when he asked her to dance at a party the summer before, how clumsy he was in his car afterward as he pulled at the strap of her dress. Her curiosity had given way to annoyance, and she told him she had to get home. He drove sullenly, without speaking, and Nancy was glad to reach Salt Hay Road and get out of his car. When she saw him again, at the beach four days later, he'd made a point of ignoring her.

"All right back there?" Nancy tried to keep her voice light.

"Never better," Robert said, his mouth close to her ear.

There was a soft explosion ahead of them as half a dozen bobwhite quail shot out of the grass and scattered, wings whirring. Nancy's hands tightened on the reins and Buckshot drew up, ears pricked forward. She felt Robert's breath on the back of her neck. The birds disappeared, leaving a swirl of dust in the air, and after a moment the horse wheezed and reached down to crop the grass at the edge of the path. Robert's hands still gripped the mane in front of her. Nancy watched his ink-stained fingers disengage from the coarse black hair. Slowly he opened one hand and lifted it over hers. With the smallest movement of her foot, Nancy thought, the horse would start forward. Robert's warm fingers laced around her own. She held completely still, barely breathing. Through the fabric of her blouse she felt his beating heart.

Clayton's friend Perry lived with his family on Carman Street. Like most of the roads south of Old Purchase, Carman dead-ended in the Great South Bay. At low tide Clayton and Perry were sent to the little margin of beach to collect eelgrass to mulch Mrs. Gilpin's garden. "Don't forget your sister!" Mrs. Gilpin called from where she stood beside the henhouse with a scrap of chicken wire. Perry rolled his eyes. His sister was nine. She was the youngest Gilpin and the only girl out of seven children. Mrs. Gilpin had named her Pearl, she said, after the pearl of great price. Her brothers called her Pearl the Girl.

Clayton studied the Gilpins furtively, like a field biologist. He was fascinated by the way Perry and his brothers spoke to their mother and how she answered them, exasperated and affectionate, and by Pearl, who was so little like his own sister. She had no authority over her brothers at all.

"Mo-ther!" Perry complained now, kicking the side of the wheelbarrow. "She'll get her shoes wet!"

"See that she doesn't! Stay out of the water, all three of you!" Hearing Mrs. Gilpin include him in her order, Clayton felt a flush of gratitude.

Perry and Clayton each took a handle of the wheelbarrow. The rakes rattled against the side. "Come *on*, Pearl," said Perry.

On the way to the water, on the other side of the street, was the Fleming Tree Nursery. Because Pearl was with them, they had to stop at the nursery to look for Molly and Dolly, the two big mares that pulled the nursery wagon. Pearl called to them across the field and they lumbered over and breathed heavily into the children's hands, searching for lumps of sugar.

Farther along lived Chicken Jackson. It was rumored among the neighborhood children that he was one hundred and one years old. Chicken Jackson raised white leghorns and Rhode Island Reds and sold eggs and pullets from a shed in the back of his house. In the spring he went around town in a goat cart and caponized roosters at ten cents apiece. The goat was a billy with yellow eyes and a heavy, musky smell that clung to the cart and also to Chicken Jackson.

At the end of the road the seaweed had washed up along the narrow beach in dark snaking ridges. Fire Island shimmered in the distance, looking as if it had broken into pieces that floated on the horizon. "Come on," said Perry. He lifted a huge armful of black eelgrass into the wheelbarrow.

Pearl sat down on a high ridge and waved a cattail like a scepter. "I am the queen!" she announced. Her brother pitched a clump of seaweed at her and she screamed.

That night on Salt Hay Road Nancy came in half an hour late for dinner. Her cheeks were pink and her eyes shone. She looked feverish again, Clayton thought in alarm. Roy and Scudder stared up at her, their forks poised in midair. "Your plate's on the stove," said Mavis shortly. "I'm afraid the potatoes are cold."

"I'm engaged!" Nancy burst out. "I'm going to be Mrs. Robert Landgraf!" She threw her arms around Clayton's shoulders and gazed out at the others with a brilliant smile.

No one spoke. Clayton sat as stiff as a rabbit under his sister's embrace. *Mrs. Robert Landgraf*: it was the name of a different person, someone he didn't know. She was marrying the man from Boston. *Boston*. The syllables brought to mind a cold grayness. A city crammed with buildings and concrete and strangers. It seemed at that moment farther than Peking, a world away from the landscape he knew. *Boston, Boston, Boston.*

At the head of the table Scudder frowned down at his plate, the announcement a wave of icy water down the neck. What was the girl thinking? Marriage, at her age, and to a stranger from another state! She would take herself off, after all they'd done for her. Did the girl have no family feeling? He couldn't bring himself to look at her. She was shameless, he thought angrily, like a cat in heat.

Roy turned from his niece's gaze. He had been that age once; how long ago it suddenly seemed. For the first time in years, he recalled the despair that had led him to that unconfessed moment of folly on the bay. Had he really loved a girl so badly he'd believed he couldn't live without her? He felt a grudging admiration, as if, in the extremity of that youthful grief, he'd elevated himself above the mere unhappiness of the rest of the population. Plenty of people suffered in love, but how many went out of their heads like he had? What surprised him most, looking back on it, more even than the astonishing fact that she'd loved him, was the ferocity of his own emotion. It seemed hard to credit. Now he barely remembered what she'd looked like. She had faded in his mind, like the Cheshire Cat, leaving only her gap-toothed smile.

Mavis was remembering the view from Madame Sonya's dress shop on Old Purchase Road. As her mother and Madame Sonya discussed adding a panel to the train of her wedding gown, Mavis stood idly looking out the window. A large black fly crawled back and forth along the bottom of the pane. Outside, a Liberty truck loaded with pine caskets rumbled past along the road. It was 1918, and the soldiers at Camp Upton were dying of the Spanish flu. Behind her Mavis heard her mother's voice: "Our last girl . . . I want it to be perfect . . ." A second truck passed. It seemed to Mavis now that there had been an omen in the casket-laden trucks; she had sensed it at the time, but had ignored it.

Nancy let go of her brother's shoulders and stood up, her face cramped. "Can't anyone say something? What's the matter with you all?"

Mavis cleared her throat. "It's very sudden. And right in the middle of dinner . . ."

"Doesn't anyone care that I'm happy?" Tears glittered in Nancy's eyes.

Boston, Boston, Boston. In the hush punctuated by Nancy's choked breathing, Clayton stood and pushed back his chair. With a vague nod he made for the door. He walked deliberately, like someone who has received a blow to the head that he is unwilling to acknowledge, or of which he is not yet fully aware.

An hour later Nancy tapped on Clayton's door. Inside his room, the floor was littered with glass specimen jars. Nancy remembered how, the summer before, he'd collected over one hundred beetles and insects. First he sketched them, and then he stored them in jam jars in the barn, each one wrapped in tissue paper and carefully labeled. At the end of the summer he stayed up past midnight arranging them on a corkboard with pins. Under each specimen he wrote the Latin name and the date it had been found. That night while he slept the barn mice found the board, and by morning the beetles and insects had been eaten. All that was left were the pins in the corkboard, each with a scrap of white paper beneath it, and, along the floor, a jumble of brittle legs and wings.

"Clayton," Nancy said. He sat on the rug by the bed with a glossy black beetle in one hand. She disliked his fascination with dead animals and insects, the way he would crouch for an hour beside a chipmunk covered in ants, drawing it from different angles. Sometimes she wondered if it had something to do with their parents, if her brother was trying to understand the meaning of that loss by studying the mechanics of decay. At other times she thought perhaps it might be a kind of strange comfort to him to feel that death was all around them, though on a manageable scale. Either way, she found his interest macabre and wished he would grow out of it.

Nancy moved aside a sketchbook and sat down beside him on the floor. Another wave of impatience with the others downstairs coursed through her, the way they'd all stared at her when she told her news. They couldn't bear change. But Clayton would see her side of it. Trying to meet his eye, she realized that she wasn't sure what he was thinking. He was closed off like a turtle in its shell. He used to follow her around, after their mother died, unwilling to let her out of his sight; now he disappeared all day with Perry Gilpin and came home smelling of mud and bait fish. He had his own spending money from his job at Washington Lodge and used it on books of natural history and collection jars that arrived in the mail from a supply company in South Carolina that he'd found who knows how. Nancy remembered when his greatest pleasure had been the sticks of black licorice she brought him from a candy store in Drowned Meadow.

"I should have told you first," she said at last. "I planned to, but then I came in and everyone looked up at me and I couldn't keep it in. I'm so happy!"

Clayton said nothing. He fiddled with the top to one of his jars.

"I told Robert I couldn't go anywhere without you too," Nancy said. "Of course he understands. He likes you already, Clay. And you two have so much in common."

Clayton picked up another jar and moved it from hand to hand, as if judging its weight. "Why do you want to get married?"

Nancy laughed. "We love each other! Come on, Clay. Most people get married."

He lifted his head and met her eyes. His face seemed leaner, less rounded, his stubborn jaw more pronounced. "No, they don't. Roy never did."

"The point is," said Nancy, "I'd never, ever leave you. You're my brother, Clay."

Clayton looked back down at the beetle. Nancy stood. "I know you're going to like it." She bent down quickly, before he could shift away, and kissed him above the ear. His hair smelled brackish, unwashed. She remembered how, as a child, he'd presented his bumps and scratches to her for kisses. It had been easy to reassure him then. Now he seemed almost sullen in his self-possession. Sometimes she looked up and saw him watching her from the doorway. Yet he would hardly let her pat his shoulder.

"And Robert works in a museum," she added, at the door. "He'll be able to show you how they mount the exhibits. Think of all the specimens you'll get to see."

Clayton frowned down at another label, his pen in his hand. "I don't want to go to Boston."

Nancy shook her head at him fondly. "Wait till you see it."

He would come around, she reassured herself in the hall. He would get used to the idea. But she felt an uneasiness about the way they'd all reacted, staring at her in that awkward silence, the dinner congealing on the plates. Why should it be so surprising? She was old enough to know her own mind. Was she supposed to put off falling in love until her brother finished school? Did they expect her to stay here forever? Didn't she deserve her happiness, after everything she'd been through?

She and Robert had been in the aviary, among the cages and his instruments and reference books. Robert held a little brown-and-white bird with bright, seedlike eyes, its pink, scaly legs tucked firmly between his middle and forefinger. As he tried to measure it with a pair of calipers, it jabbed its small beak fiercely and repeatedly at his gloved hand. Robert laughed, rueful, glancing up at her. "The stuffed ones are easier to handle." Finished, he slipped the bird back into a cage near the table and pulled off his leather work gloves. The light in the room, tumbling through the large windows with sudden brilliance, illuminated the bits of fluff that hung in the still, guano-scented air like dust motes. Turning to her, Robert's face grew serious. Around them the bright, darting birds trilled and screeched and sang. "That's how I feel about you, Nancy." She leaned forward so she could hear him above the din, distracted by a white spot on his right eyebrow. A piece of down, she realized, caught like an unmelting snowflake. Without thinking, she moved her hand to brush it away, and then stopped herself, afraid it was too intimate a gesture. Robert misunderstood and fumbled for her hand. "Being with you, and being apart. It's like the difference between these birds and the dead ones I work with." Nancy caught, at last, the change in his manner. She stared hard at his eyebrow, uncertain and confused. How was she supposed to respond? The asymmetry of the white fluff gave Robert a startled look, and it struck her that he was as unsure of what to do next as she was. And then he said, "I don't suppose you'd ever want to marry a man like me?"

Of course that was what she wanted. Of course. There was no need to feel confused. How easy it would be, after all. She raised her hand and gently brushed the fleck from above his eye.

In her room, Nancy opened the window and leaned out into the warm, dark air. They would all be happy in Boston, she told herself. She felt her future billow out before her like a kite on a string, pulling the three of them forward.

The day after Nancy announced the move to Boston, Clayton sneaked onto the roof, using the remnants of his grandmother's wisteria trellis for a footing. From the yard he was screened by the pine tree. No one knew where he was, and this was what he valued most about the spot, even more than the view. On hot days in the summer he and Perry climbed up here often. Looking south over the marsh to the bay, they could see the flat ribbon of Fire Island in the distance. They'd try to guess which boats were docked by the position of the masts at Starke's Boatyard, whether the one with the blue-and-white pennant belonged to the *Comet* or the *Foam*. Sometimes they brought the thick heads of cattails from the marsh and smoked them like cigars; they'd hold the stem between their teeth and light the other end with a match filched from the kitchen, cupping their hands against the wind. The cattails smoldered, giving off just the right amount of smoke. Below them the world seemed to shimmer. When they tired of their cattail cigars, they'd pick at gobs of tar along the seams and chew them. The tar tasted like something that was probably good for you, like Malt and Iron, or the castor oil mixed with orange juice Perry got a nickel a week for drinking.

To the north, between the house and Starke's Boatyard, stood Captain Kelley's squat, one-story cottage. At five o'clock in the evening, Clayton saw the Captain step out of the door with his brown cap and his bow tie, ready for his constitutional. He took off briskly around the perimeter of his house, trailed by six or seven cats. At intervals he stopped to do his exercises. The air was still and Clayton heard his reedy, old-man's voice carried up on the evening air: "Arms in! Arms out! Arms in! Arms out!" After a few circles, the cats grew bored and wandered away, except for a gray one, which stopped when the Captain stopped and sat beside him, delicately scratching its neck with a back leg, until he resumed his walking.

At six the fish wagon made a delivery. Clayton saw the fish man in his white apron knocking at the cottage door. Then the Captain stood outside his little kitchen, gutting and scaling the fish on a plank of wood. When he finished, he threw the remains to the cats, which rushed with them into the overgrown garden, dragging the entrails in the dust.

Later Mavis came out and called Clayton's name, close enough so that he could hear her mutter "my best East India salad too" in the silence after he didn't answer. She and Nancy had been airing out the house; the clothesline was hung with wash and the lawn littered with linens and bedding. As Clayton watched, they were gathered in, sheets and blankets, lawn-chair pillows and tablecloths, and then the doors and windows were shut, the house like an enormous flower furling itself for the night. The darkness seemed to seep upward as if from the ground. Fireflies blinked in the field. Clayton smelled the warm, rotten scent of the pond, where low tide had exposed the peaty mud.

He thought of the birds at Washington Lodge, his scapping job with Theron Greaves. It made him angry that Nancy expected him to leave this all behind because of her. She wasn't his mother; she couldn't force him to go anywhere. Tears prickled his eyes and he wiped them roughly with his sleeve. Let her go to Boston if she wanted, he thought fiercely. She could move to China for all he cared. He sat looking out toward the dark marsh with his arms around his knees. The first stars came out and the moon hoisted itself over the river, lopsided and bruised.

Even now, as angry as he'd ever been at her, it was hard to imagine his sister going so far away. It was like trying to convince himself that he could walk with only one leg. Perched on the dark roof of the house, he felt a coldness seep into him. His biggest fear had always been that Nancy might die, like their parents had, and leave him alone. He remembered waiting up for her in secret when she went out to dances in Southease, unable to sleep until he knew she was safely home. It hadn't occurred to him then that there were other ways to lose someone.

But it was her fault, he thought. She was the one who'd decided to get married. His chin poked forward in the dusk. He had other family besides his sister. Why should he have to go to Boston? He would live in Fire Neck, in this house, for the rest of his life.

The morning after his granddaughter announced her engagement, Scudder woke with an ache in his left knee. Over the course of the day the pain lessened, but he couldn't shake a morbid fascination with it. He found himself probing the spot with his fingers, the way once, after a tooth extraction, his tongue had sought the pulpy hole in his mouth. Seventy-nine years old, he'd never allowed himself to dwell on minor aches and pains before, convinced that cosseting would only encourage them. And sure enough, within days of the first pain in his knee, other troubles followed: his shoulder felt sore, his hip made a sound like a squeaky boom, he grew short of breath after climbing the stairs. Acknowledged at last, his body clamored for attention.

He realized bitterly that he had wasted his last good season of sailing, like a sentimental fool. That spring he and Clayton had found a nest on the mast of the boat, on one of the spreaders. Scudder borrowed a boathook to knock it down, but as he returned, a swallow darted overhead. He couldn't bring himself to destroy the nest, not with the boy watching. "I don't think there's enough wind, after all," he muttered. Clayton nodded, looking relieved.

After that, every time Scudder wanted to go sailing, he looked up at the nest and the swallow peered back down at him. He'd turn around and leave the dock, cursing swallows and birds in general. George Rowley began to call the boat *The Incubator*. Ten years, even five years ago, he would have cleared the nest off the spreaders without a thought. Now he couldn't help but think of his daughter Helen, dead in her prime. He was going soft in his old age, he berated himself, as maudlin as his late wife. But he'd spared the nest once, and after that, it seemed ungentlemanly to change his mind.

Finally, one afternoon, there was no bird on the nest. A lively southeast wind was blowing and Scudder stepped on board and uncleated the lines. He'd reached the channel marker at the mouth of the canal when he noticed two birds darting frantically after him. The eggs had hatched, he realized, and the chicks were in the nest above him, hungry and cold. Scudder sighed, came about, and sailed back to the dock, the swallows fluttering around the mast.

Now, sitting on the porch nursing his sore shoulder, he remembered how hard it had been even then to move around the deck, the way his arms had ached from holding both the tiller and the mainsheet even that short distance. He would never sail alone again. The realization pierced him.

As soon as Roy came back from dropping Mavis at the lodge, Scudder told him he wanted to haul the boat. Roy pointed out in surprise that it was early in the season. Scudder declared he was through with sailing. Saying this, he thought of his granddaughter, who seemed hell-bent on throwing her life away, moony female that she was. He'd expected more from her. Now it pained him to have her around. "I'm swallowing the anchor," Scudder told Roy. Then he added unkindly, "It's not as if you have any use for a boat." There was nothing Roy could say to this. He went down to the boatyard after feeding the dogs to make arrangements with Sam Burnett.

By afternoon the boat lay upside down on blocks along the privet hedge. Clusters of dirty-white barnacles and rot showed on the faded red hull. Scudder wanted everything properly stowed, and had dismayed Mavis by putting two cans of varnish in the icebox, insisting that it had to be applied cold. Mavis felt sure it would affect the taste of the butter, but something in her father's manner kept her from objecting. Scudder and Captain Kelley took over the yard in front of the porch, littering it with tackle, rags, spars, red and yellow cans of turpentine and polish, scraps of sandpaper worn supple as chamois.

Nancy sat on the porch behind them, writing a letter to her friend in Brooklyn on her portable typewriter. Scudder, his back turned toward her, could hear the clacking of the keys. In the pauses he imagined her playing with the envelope, tapping it against her chin while she thought of new ways to express her happiness in prose. He pressed hard against the spar in his hand, smoothing the rough bumps and making a cloud of dust that hung in the air and sifted onto his trousers, fine as flour.

"Remember the body Randall found in the bay?" he asked the Captain suddenly. Behind him the typewriter keys clattered.

"A sad affair," muttered the Captain. "I wish I remembered that sight less clearly."

"Such a young girl," Scudder said. "Only nineteen or twenty." He spoke a bit loudly, telling himself the Captain had grown hard of hearing. "Beached in the reeds without a stitch on her."

The Captain shook his head and reached for another scrap of sandpaper. "It doesn't bear thinking about."

"They held a gentleman friend for questioning," Scudder went on, ignoring this last remark. "But they couldn't prove he'd done it." Behind him a chair squeaked against the floor, and a moment later the porch door slammed.

"I heard he moved out West," the Captain said. "That always seemed a bit suspicious."

But Scudder had lost interest in the drowned girl. The spar was nearly smooth now, and he needed to find a clean brush for the varnish.

Nancy began mucking out Buckshot's stall in the horse barn in the early evening, giving her a clear excuse for missing dinner. She knew her brother was avoiding her and understood he needed time to get used to the thought of moving to Boston. But no one else in the house seemed willing to look her in the eye either. She shoveled violently away at the manure-heavy straw, frustrated with all of them. She wondered about her friend Enid's engagement and thought uncomfortably about her own coolness on the subject. Even though Robert was completely different from her friend's pompous husband, she wished now that she'd been less critical. The horse rubbed his head against her shoulder as she finished shaking fresh straw onto the floor.

It was nearly dark when Nancy stepped into the kitchen. Roy and Scudder sat at the table, an empty dish before them. The eggy smell of bread pudding hung in the air. Mavis was at the sink, washing up, and Clayton stood beside her with a tea towel in his hand. Like a boy helping his mother, Nancy thought resentfully. The room was strangely hushed, and Nancy felt sure they'd just been talking about her. "You're going to need help packing all your odds and ends," she told Clayton briskly. "You won't be able to bring every specimen jar; I hope you realize that."

Her brother looked away from her. The room seemed very quiet. "I can help you sort your things," Nancy added, sorry already for the way she'd sounded. She wished the others were somewhere else, that she'd waited to talk to her brother alone. "Those glass jars should be wrapped in newspaper."

"I don't want to go." Clayton spoke softly but clearly.

For a moment she saw him as a toddler again, a boy in blue flannel pajamas jutting out his little chin at bedtime as he announced that he wasn't tired. She almost had to bite back a smile. "Don't be silly. You're going to love it. You'll see."

"I want to stay here," her brother said. Nancy was dismayed to hear tears in his voice. She stepped closer to him, but he held up the dish he was drying, as if to ward her off, as if she were going to haul him north to Boston this very moment. "I'm right in the middle of school."

"There are schools in Boston." As if school mattered to him. "Robert's job is there. We have to go. I've already told you."

Clayton was no longer looking at her. She was surprised to see him glance beseechingly at Roy, who sat at the table with the paper in his hands as if there were no sound in the kitchen but the radio news. Scudder, beside him, polished a spot on the table with the frayed sleeve of his shirt. Nancy felt sure he was enjoying her discomfort.

Clayton looked at their aunt. "*Please* could I stay?" He was asking Mavis, not Nancy, as if Mavis were in charge.

Mavis straightened up with a sigh and turned, a soapy wooden spoon in one hand. The suds ran onto her wrist and dripped to the floor. "You know there's always a place for you here." Her eyes met Nancy's. "I don't see why he needs to go, just because you want to."

Nancy felt a sudden heat, as if she were standing in front of a furnace, the door to which had been wrenched open. Her dislike of her aunt flared, white hot.

"We're all family," Mavis added blandly. She turned back to the sink to rinse the spoon she'd been holding, as if to indicate that it was all the same to her.

"He's *my* brother!" Nancy said, more loudly than she meant to.

Roy put down the paper, rustling the pages. He looked up for the first time in the conversation. "It's his choice, don't you think?" He said it reasonably, as if he were merely pointing out something they would all agree was obvious.

"But *I'll* be in Boston, Clay," Nancy said. It had happened so quickly. How had she come to be pleading with him? "Please, darling, you want to be with me, don't you?"

Carefully, Clayton set down the dish he'd dried and picked up the next one. Only then did he look up at her, apologetic and pained. But his face was set in that way she knew. Shocked, Nancy saw that he had already decided. He'd only been waiting to make sure Mavis and Roy would allow it.

"Think about it first," she cried. "There's no need to hurry! We can talk about it later, after we've all calmed down!" Her voice rang in the low-ceilinged room. Her heart pounded. The others stared, taken aback.

"I'm staying here," her brother said.

"But why shouldn't he?" Robert asked. They were in the aviary at Washington Lodge, surrounded by the chirping, rustling birds. Robert had set down his camera. He was looking at her with concern and a little confusion.

Nancy struggled to control her tears. She'd been up most of the night, veering between fury at her brother, at Mavis and Roy for being party to his decision, and her own horrible uncertainty. She thought of how much easier it must have been for her mother at her age, with no one to take care of but herself.

"He's happy here, isn't he?" Robert went on. "Your aunt and uncle will take care of him."

They don't know him the way I do, Nancy wanted to say. They'll let him run wild. He'll play hooky, neglect his homework, and no one will notice. "It's not the same," she said, after a moment. She tried to put her feelings into words, but nothing sounded reasonable. Clayton should be with her because he was her brother and she loved him. She'd take care of him. Why was everyone making it so hard for her? She supposed Clayton would be safe with Mavis and Roy. But she didn't want him to end up trapped on Salt Hay Road, like they were. Clayton didn't see it this way, he was too young to understand, but she did. Leaving Clayton behind felt like consigning him to something dreary. She wanted to pull him with her into her own bright future, and he was making it so difficult; she felt as if she were trying to heft him bodily, the way she'd done when he was a child throwing a tantrum, unwilling to leave the park or the beach, and he was making himself into a dead weight in her arms.

Robert was still gazing at her, his forehead creased. Nancy chewed her lip. "My mother expected me to take care of him," she said desperately. "Mavis is his legal guardian, but *I'm* his sister . . ."

"It's not like you won't see him, sweetheart. He can visit us anytime. He might decide to stay, once he's been there and seen it."

Nancy felt the lump in her throat swell like a sponge. She wanted to believe Robert was right. She knew Clayton was mulish and she couldn't bully him into changing his mind. Maybe if she let him think he was getting his way, he'd like it when he visited.

The moment of her defeat in the kitchen came back to her with its smell of eggs. The family had united against her. She gripped Robert's hands. His green eyes, flecked with brown, stared into hers, and she remembered the bit of white fluff caught in his eyebrow on the day he'd proposed. Around them in the aviary the birds warbled in their cages. Could she marry Robert and move to Boston if it meant leaving her brother here? She felt suddenly afraid. Clayton seemed determined to stay behind, and this made everything tenuous. She and Robert had to marry soon, she thought, before the summer was over. In that moment, there seemed only two possible fates for her: to marry and move away, like her mother had, or to end up on Salt Hay Road forever. She wouldn't let her chance for happiness slip away. In a flash, she saw how she would seal this decision. Today, before her courage failed her.

"I've never seen the rest of this house," she cried suddenly. "Would you show me around?"

Robert looked surprised. "If you'd like . . ."

Agitated, Nancy glanced out the window. Clayton stood under the copper beeches, his back to her. He was bringing the cockatoos in for the evening. Above him, the hook on the end of the pole swayed and fumbled before it caught against a metal hoop. The cockatoo flashed its white wings and squawked, lunging at the pole as Clayton lowered it to the ground, where others already rested, the hoops obscured by the grass, the birds preening themselves or prancing, bowlegged, at the end of their chain tethers.

She stepped to the open window. *"Clay!"* Nancy called. Beyond him she could see the figure of the gardener, bent over a clump of greenery. Mavis had already gone home. "Clay!" she called again, as loud as she dared. He turned, and Nancy waved him over, staying just inside the doorway, where she hoped the gardener would not be able to see her.

"Do me a favor when you're finished and take Buckshot home. You can ride him if you like. It'll save you some time. Just don't let him go faster than a trot."

"Why?" Clayton asked.

"Because we're walking into town soon." The lie came out smoothly, if a little fast. "I don't want him to be spooked by the traffic, and besides, he's been out all day. Put some hay in his stall and make sure he has plenty of water, would you? I owe you one."

"I mean, why shouldn't he go faster than a trot?"

Nancy felt her cheeks flush. "I don't want you falling off. If he gives you any trouble, slap him on the neck with the reins."

"I guess," said Clayton.

Nancy studied his face for signs that he believed her. Since he'd told her he wasn't moving to Boston, they had treated each other carefully, with a certain distance. "You don't mind? It's not too much of a bother?"

But Clayton had already lost whatever interest he'd had in her plans and was turning back to the beeches and the few birds still in the branches. He shrugged. "I can do it."

The absence of the horse did not commit her to anything, Nancy thought. She swallowed. "Thanks. Make sure Mavis doesn't hold dinner. I'll be home later."

Robert stood waiting for her on the landing with a bemused look. "Clay's taking Buckshot back," Nancy said as casually as she could. She thought again of how Robert had proposed, the way his eyes had widened when she'd said yes. She would marry him and live with him in Boston. She clung to her resolve, like a tow rope.

Down a long corridor hung with prints of birds and flowers, they came to the room where Robert was staying. He opened the door with a little smile. "This isn't my natural habitat." The room was nearly the size of the entire upstairs of the house on Salt Hay Road. There were three arched windows through which the late-afternoon sun streamed, warm and buttery, like the light that fell in churches. Nancy was aware, without looking directly at it, of the canopy bed, its pale, glossy coverlet gleaming like icing on a cake. The carpet was thick under her feet, and she wished she had on pumps instead of her riding boots. She stared at the walls, covered halfway up in a light green brocade, and at the white marble fireplace. Beside the fireplace was a dark leather armchair. A mahogany desk stood under the window. Robert's sketch pads and charcoal pencils were jumbled on one side. A wardrobe carved with a pattern of leaves sat against the far wall, opposite a matching dresser.

"I keep expecting to hear someone coming up the stairs," Nancy said, trying to account for her jumpiness.

"We could stow you in the wardrobe," Robert offered. "Until the coast was clear. Or else in here." He opened a door on the other side of the fireplace, revealing a closet the size of a small bedroom. It smelled of cedar. Three or four of Robert's shirts hung close together near the door, as if for comfort. The back wall was mirrored, and Nancy stared at the reflected image of herself, dwarfed by the room behind her, her face small and pale.

"There's a nice view from the window," Robert told her, closing the closet door. Nancy was relieved to leave the mirror behind. There was no reason for the opulence of the room to cow her, she thought. She had grown up in a house that, if not quite as grand, had not been so very different from this one. Her chin rose, ever so slightly, at the thought of being intimidated by a brocade wall. Out the window the flat surface of the pond shone in the late-afternoon light. They stood in silence, peering down. The gardener was pushing an empty wheelbarrow along one of the gravel paths toward the white gardening shed.

Nancy wished that it were dark. Why hadn't she foreseen the difference this would make? Robert was still staring down at the lawn. She realized that she could comment on the loveliness of the room and then ask him to show her something downstairs, the library or the dining room, and he would escort her down the hall politely. It was probably what he expected. She wondered in a sudden panic what he had attempted before and with whom. Someone should have prepared her better for what she was about to do. She thought of her mother telling her after Clayton was born that they'd found him at a florist's shop in New York City, beside the potted gardenias. Nancy, seven years old, had understood that this was both absurd and not to be questioned. She studied the freckles on Robert's neck. He glanced toward her, his eyes patient and amused. Nancy felt her determination ebbing. Taking his hand quickly, she spread it open and pressed his palm to her cheek. His fingers smelled faintly of charcoal.

They kissed on the edge of the gleaming bed, and Nancy waited for the breathless urgency she'd felt before, kissing Robert on horseback, but it was different here, in the stately, impersonal bedroom, prearranged. She felt anxious to get it over with. Robert seemed to sense this and to hesitate. Nancy worried again that she would lose her nerve. She lay back and flung out her arms. The glossy bedspread was slippery under her fingers. Robert watched her. "Nancy," he began. She turned toward him and kissed him hard on the mouth, aware that she was close to tears. He began to unbutton her blouse, his fingers cold. She felt his hand on her stomach and shivered. His belt buckle pressed against her hip and he stopped to unfasten it. It seemed to take a long time for him to disengage from his pants. Nancy glimpsed his legs, pale and unprotected, and his undershorts tenting out above them. She squeezed her eyes shut. After a moment she felt him fumble with the zipper of her riding breeches. Blindly, she helped him peel them down her legs.

Approaching the bird feeder where Nancy had tethered the horse, Clayton was careful to stay clear of Buckshot's enormous hooves. He had nothing against Buckshot particularly, but he found horses unsettling, a fact he tried to conceal from his sister. The animal snorted. His huge head bobbed up and down, reminding Clayton of Captain Kelley nodding at Mavis. He wonders where Nancy is, Clayton thought. He remembered Roy saying that poker cards and horses could both sense fear, and forced himself to pat Buckshot's side. His hand seemed insubstantial against the muscle heaving beneath Buckshot's sleek coat. It would feel, to the horse, like a fly landing. He patted harder, and Buckshot's black tail swished around and whisked him in the face.

He felt bad for the way he'd told his sister he was staying; he should have done it in private, he realized now. But he'd needed the rest of the family there in order to say it. She wanted to boss him around, and this time she couldn't. He was sorry for her, but she was the one who'd decided to go. A part of him hoped she'd give up the whole idea, but last night she'd sat for hours at the kitchen table with a map of Boston in front of her, measuring distances with a ruler. He hid his unhappiness, more determined than ever to stay on without her now that he understood he was one of the things she was prepared to leave behind.

He wondered if the horse would miss her. There wouldn't be a place for Buckshot in Boston. It had always impressed Clayton how fearlessly Nancy handled him, pushing him aside to load hay in the feed bin or prying a hoof off the ground to check for stones, as if Buckshot were an oversized dog, a good-natured Labrador. Clayton untied the reins from the base of the bird feeder and pulled. He was gratified when Buckshot lurched forward. Clayton held the reins under the horse's chin, like he'd seen Nancy do, and Buckshot's head bobbed beside him, one enormous eye visible. Clayton could feel the gusty breathing in his ear and on his face. Buckshot's black, rubbery lips moved, showing teeth as long and yellowed as piano keys. The black lips reminded Clayton of the movement of a caterpillar's back feet, but a caterpillar of monstrous size. Bristly hairs stuck up from the soft flesh of Buckshot's nose. The horse heaved a noisy sigh and, swinging his head toward Clayton, nudged him hard on the shoulder. "Whoa," Clayton said, side-stepping quickly. "Easy."

In the upstairs bedroom back at Washington Lodge, Nancy opened her eyes. She was surprised to feel the pain diminishing, the sharpness of it giving way to something more like an ache. Robert rocked awkwardly on top of her. She felt the muscles of his chest straining. He made a gasping sound, his face pressed against the side of her head. Above her the white canopy arched. Nancy tried to think about the wedding, tried to imagine the flowers and the dress, but she couldn't escape the ebbing pain and the weight of Robert's body pressing and pushing. All his habitual self-possession had been stripped away. He seemed to have disappeared, leaving her alone in her awareness of this interminable moment. It had never occurred to her that it would take so long.

She felt a warmth on her neck. Robert kissed her jaw, the lobe of her ear, his mouth moving with a wet, steady urgency. The ache intensified. Suspended inside it, she felt it shift to a glimpse of something almost familiar. It was like approaching a jump on horseback, anticipating that surge of muscle and then the effortless feeling of being airborne. Nancy moved toward it. A feral noise escaped her throat.

Immediately Robert stopped. Nancy stiffened as he pulled away, his weight on his hand, until he was looking into her eyes. For a moment they stared at each other like frightened strangers. Nancy felt the blood pound in her head. "Did I hurt you?" he asked hoarsely. His cheeks were flushed, his eyes anxious. Nancy shook her head and pulled him closer, until he couldn't see her face.

Five weeks later, Nancy Poole married Robert Landgraf in a small ceremony at the brown-shingled Presbyterian church in Southease, overlooking the bay. Robert's oldest brother, attending from Maine as his best man, nearly fumbled the ring at the crucial moment; Nancy tried to hide her alarm, but Robert noticed it, and apologized later on his brother's behalf, explaining that he grew flustered around beautiful women. Nancy flashed him a smile and bent her head over her bouquet of yellow roses. She wore a simple cream-colored dress in a halter style, cut on the bias, without a train, so that she could dye it for later use. Stepping out of the darkened church, the bride and groom were pelted with rice by Clayton and Perry. Nancy held the roses up to shield herself, laughing. Beyond the sloping church lawn, the water of the bay shone in the August light, so bright they had to avert their eyes.

On Salt Hay Road, the house had been scrubbed from top to bottom and hung with white and pink streamers for the reception. Mavis served a fruit punch and a molded Kentucky salad, and a wedding cake layered with figs and citron. Enid Snow had come from Brooklyn with her husband; marriage had softened him, Nancy felt, and Enid herself looked plump and happy. Nancy made a point of charming Robert's brother, forgiving him his moment of clumsiness with the wedding ring and his cheap suit, and the fact that he had none of his brother's easy banter. Like Robert's, his hands seemed slightly too large for his wrists. He stood by the end of the dining-room table, placing molded salad on his flowered china plate. Robert glanced over at them, and she felt his worry; perhaps his brother embarrassed him, the way she sometimes felt about her aunt. "Thank you again for being here," she told him, putting a hand on his brown wool sleeve. She felt a fresh admiration for Robert, who'd grown up in the same household and yet forged a different life. "It means so much to both of us."

"None of us get away much," Robert's brother said. "Because of the farm." He glanced down at the salad and seemed to remember something. "We hope you'll be very happy together," he added gruffly, and it was clear to Nancy that he was speaking for the entire somber Landgraf clan, and that they had their doubts. She nodded, a little shaken, and moved on to attend to the other guests.

A hush hung over the house when Nancy came for her things. She and Robert had spent a rainy weekend on Shelter Island for their honeymoon. Inside the house on Salt Hay Road the rooms were dark except where a ray of sunlight shone on the stairs and illuminated a pair of muddy shoes. Clayton had set them neatly on the stairs with the laces folded in. Now he would be crabbing barefoot on the river. Roy had gone out after rabbits with his gun and his dogs; Mavis was working at the lodge. Only her grandfather was home. He sat on the porch, feigning sleep in his chair, as if she would believe he'd fallen asleep with a pipe in his hand. She had never guessed before her engagement that he could be so childish. She'd expected that it would be sad to leave, but now she couldn't wait to be gone. The air itself seemed to strangle her. If only Clayton's shoes weren't perched like that on the stairs, so muddy and so precisely arranged. For a moment she imagined snatching them up and bringing them with her. She dashed back up for another look at her room. The white walls were bare, the bed stripped down to the mattress. The typewriter sat on the table, its black keys furred with dust. She had no use for it now. Out the window the leaves of the pepperidge trees shook in the wind. Her husband called her name. Nancy clattered down the stairs, past Clayton's shoes, and grabbed at the handle of her suitcase. There came Robert, smiling at her as he strode across the lawn. She turned, but the porch was empty. Even the smell of pipe smoke was gone.

"Goodbye!" she cried to the empty house, hefting her suitcase behind her.

In all the years Captain Kelley had lived across the field, Scudder had visited him only half a dozen times. He knew the Captain enjoyed seeing Mavis, and the light at his own house was better for cards. Besides, Scudder was not fond of cats. Now, as the Captain opened the door, blinking, several of them thrust themselves forward as if attempting to trip Scudder up.

"Come in, come in," the Captain exclaimed. He pulled the door open, and more cats emerged and twined themselves around Scudder's legs. Inside, Scudder could barely see. The light outside had been blinding, and here the shades were all drawn. Scudder stood just inside the door, hobbled by cats. He felt the Captain's hand on his elbow. "What a pleasant surprise. Will you have some tea? A drop of brandy?"

"Brandy," Scudder said. His own voice sounded odd to him, a croak. He let himself be led to a small table cluttered with books and dishes, feeling suddenly feeble: an old, broken man. A cat hopped up beside him and rubbed against his shoulder. Something rose in his throat. It threatened to choke him. He coughed hard, smothering what might have been a sob.

The Captain placed a jelly jar in his hand. "Good for the heart."

Scudder drank it down, and the reassuring warmth of it spread over his chest. The Captain began to shuffle a deck of cards, and he found the sound soothing, like the lapping of waves against the hull of a boat. The Captain dealt. Scudder reached across the table almost without thinking. He picked up the cards and fanned out his hand.

Later Scudder thought he heard the rumble of a car pulling away down Salt Hay Road. But he had drunk several jars of brandy by this point, and perhaps, he told himself, it was only the purring of Kelley's cats on the crowded table.

PART TWO

Honey in the Walls

The August that Nancy married Robert Landgraf and moved to Boston, Clayton was invited to stay with Perry Gilpin's family for a week at their house on Fire Island. There Mrs. Gilpin and the children lived each summer. Clayton walked through the boatyard with his knapsack to the ferry dock, nodding to Sam at the boat shed. There were two ferries to choose from, the *Okalee* and the *Westaway*, their schedules posted at the landing. Clayton waited for the former; the captain, an old bayman and friend of Theron Greaves's, sailed instead of using the engine whenever possible. Clayton and Nancy had always preferred the *Okalee*.

Clayton made his way quickly to the bow and found a seat. Around him crowded families with picnic hampers, a boy with a melting ice cream, a man in a straw hat carrying only a mandolin. The *Okalee* motored past Rose's Creek out to the mouth of the river, and then the captain hoisted the sail. In the quiet after the motor was cut, Clayton heard an osprey's high-pitched call. They were retracing the route, Clayton thought, of his great-grandfather's house, from the Terrell River all the way to

Starke's Boatyard along this same stretch of shore. He stared out at the green spartina, the pepperidge trees, and high-tide bush, wondering how much it had changed since the house had floated past.

In the distance, Clayton could see the bridge where the bay narrowed and the contours of the barrier beach dipped toward Long Island at Taffy Point. There were nearly a dozen houses along the shore to the west. Most were summer houses for people from the city. A few of the smaller ones belonged to local families like the Gilpins who'd bought the cheaper land on the bay side and done some of the work themselves. As they drew closer to Fire Island, Clayton could make out the figure of his friend, barefoot on the dock. Perry waved his arms in mock semaphore. Clayton signaled back.

The Gilpins' beach house was yellow, with a wide front porch that faced across the bay toward the Barto River. Perry's mother had named it Beach Plum, he told Clayton, after the tart little fruits that grew wild nearby; the others called it Off Plumb, because of the way the front porch had settled in the sand, listing toward the west. There were three low-ceilinged bedrooms upstairs, one with bunks for the boys, one for Mr. and Mrs. Gilpin, one for Pearl the Girl, and a kitchen and living room downstairs, all with plain wood floors worn by the sand. The outhouse had a water tank on top for outdoor showers.

Every Friday after work, Mr. Gilpin joined his family at the beach, bringing the mail and fresh supplies. The evening of Clayton's arrival, he lit a bonfire on the shore and they roasted potatoes in the embers. In the past Clayton had sometimes seen bonfires on the beach from his upstairs room on Salt Hay Road and the sight had made him feel like a sailor on a ship at sea, glimpsing the lights of a port along the horizon.

Charlie, Perry's oldest brother, who worked for the South-ease Hook and Ladder, was there on a rare visit. He claimed to have been knocked low by the news of Nancy's marriage. "We flew the station flag at half mast," he teased. Clayton sat on the sand, holding his steaming potato, and stared into the glowing ashes. Since his sister had left Fire Neck, he himself had felt off-plumb, a three-legged dog.

It was easier, at the Gilpins' house, for Clayton to put Nancy out of his thoughts. Here at least he didn't half expect to see her every time he entered a room. Sometimes he pretended to himself that he and Perry were brothers and that he'd always lived in the noisy, affectionate Gilpin household. Lewis and Fred had finished high school and now worked on the bay, saving up for their own boat and clamming gear. They were brown and freckled, the skin on their noses eternally peeling, and their arms and shoulders bulged with enviable muscle. Donald, two years older than Perry, was obsessed with bicycles. He considered Fire Island a form of exile, a wasteland of boardwalks and sandy trails, and spent as much time as he could on the porch poring over bicycling advertisements and dreaming of macadam.

Clayton slept in a sleeping bag on the floor of the room Perry shared with his brothers. Long after they'd finished talking about boats and fishing and plans for the following day, and after the breathing of the others had deepened and grown regular, Clayton lay awake. He listened to the unfamiliar roar of the breakers out the window and felt a sharp stab of homesickness, not only for his room on Salt Hay Road, but also for the house with his sister in it. He thought of reasons that would make her return, and drifted off to sleep imagining himself in the hospital with rheumatic fever and Nancy hovering over him, full of self-reproach.

In the morning the mood had passed completely, like a fall of rain that evaporates within the hour. He woke to someone stepping on his foot. The house smelled like sausages and coffee. "Hurry up," Perry hollered. Clayton pulled on his clothes and followed the other boys as they trooped loudly down the hall. On the way they passed the small room Pearl had to herself. Darting in, Perry and Donald pulled the blankets off her bed. Pearl shrieked and threw her pillow at them.

"You leave that girl alone!" Mrs. Gilpin bellowed from the kitchen. "You'll spoil her disposition!"

After breakfast Clayton chased Perry along a path through the beach plum and bayberry, swatting at the mosquitoes. They crested the low hill of dunes and there was the ocean, hurling itself at the sand. The warm air felt damp and salty on Clayton's face. With a whooping cry, Perry hurtled down the face of the dune, ignoring the wooden steps. Clayton followed. Down on the wet margin of the shore, sand fleas exploded around their bare feet, as if the beach itself were effervescent.

They plunged into the surf and porpoised through the breakers. When the water finally became too cold, Clayton flopped on the sand, rolling over until the sand grains covered him. Perry and his brothers called this "breading" themselves, after their mother's manner of dredging fish. As the sun heated their skin, the sand grains dried and could be brushed away. The sand worked itself everywhere. Before dinner they rinsed off quickly outside the kitchen door, taking turns holding the hose, and still their sheets and pillows were always dusted with a layer of sand.

One afternoon, splashing out of the surf, they heard a familiar voice call their names. Blinded by the sun, it took Clayton a moment to realize it was their teacher, Miss Collier. She stood before them in a bathing suit, her hair around her shoulders. Clayton felt a deep, reflexive panic. Miss Collier usually wore her thick blond hair pulled back and loosely pinned. When she turned to the blackboard, the nape of her neck was exposed, and he had relished the view of that patch of bare skin. Now most of Miss Collier was bare. Clayton had dreamed of her many times since school let out, in much the same state. "Enjoying yourselves?" she asked. Perry said something about the beach house while Clayton stared at Miss Collier's bare shoulders and bare arms and bare thighs and knees and legs. Roy had told him once that when he was a boy it had been considered a thrill to catch a glimpse of a woman's ankles as she stepped up to board a train; at the time, Clayton had wondered at anyone having the slightest interest in an ankle. Now the sight of Miss Collier's bare feet in the sand made his head pound. Instinctively, he put his hands down to cover his wet shorts. But he had nothing to hold in front of himself, no towel, no chair to hide behind. Miss Collier, listening to Perry, had turned to look in the direction of the Gilpins' beach house. In a moment she would turn back and see Clayton with his thin, clinging shorts angled toward her. His face hot, he turned and flung himself into the surf. The cold water surged mercifully over him. He waved in the direction of the beach and dove below the surface, his entire body tingling.

At dinner, Clayton sat next to Perry at the Gilpins' crowded table. Mr. Gilpin was a short, energetic man who spoke loudly from the constant need to make himself heard over the noise of his household. He had grown up in Fire Neck and remembered the beach twenty years earlier, when the soldiers from Camp Upton used to arrive on their days off. The soldiers, he told them over dinner, were huge, strapping boys from the Midwest who'd never seen the ocean. They yelled to each other all the way across the boardwalk. "You could hear them a mile away," said Mr. Gilpin. "They swarmed over the top of the dunes, making war cries, shucking off their clothes. They'd tear down the beach in their undershorts and charge at the water as if it were Lake Michigan. The surf just scattered them like ninepins. We'd sit on the dunes and laugh. They'd come up spluttering and coughing. Didn't know what hit them."

Mrs. Gilpin was passing a plate of bluefish. "You know," she said, her voice unusually quiet, "some of them never made it home."

"Well, you're right," Mr. Gilpin answered, chastened. He was silent a moment. "I guess the war surprised some of those boys worse than the Atlantic."

Clayton, reaching for another ear of corn, caught the glance that Mrs. Gilpin cast around the table at her own boys, while Perry licked his fingers and Donald and Lewis kicked each other under the table. It was a maternal look, full of love and worry.

That night, in his sleeping bag on the floor, he found himself thinking of his mother. Toward the end she had lost interest even in the sailboats on the Sound. She had rested during the day in a downstairs room with tall windows where a white-clad nurse admonished him to lower his voice. The light seeped in around the edges of the curtains, and when he thought of his mother now, he saw in his mind those dark curtains edged with light. He remembered the softness of her palm on his cheek and the dry, floral smell of talcum powder as he inclined his face to receive her kisses. He'd felt oppressed, not only by the silence and the still, close sweetness of the air, but by the understanding that no matter how long he stayed, it would never be long enough. Lying in the dark in the Gilpins' beach house, he wondered for the first time what his mother had thought about during those slow, hushed mornings and afternoons. He wished now he'd asked about the polished sailing trophies lined up along her bureau, or about his father, or her childhood on Salt Hay Road. But he had not been interested. Or rather, it had been hard for him to believe that she'd once existed outside the heavy silence of the room with the velvet curtains. He had visited her mostly for the butterscotch candies she kept in a glass jar with a fluted lid, each wrapped in a square of waxy paper, and he wondered now if she had kept them for precisely this reason. It hurt him to think how clearly she must have seen into his greedy little heart.

At the house on Salt Hay Road, Scudder and Captain Kelley had been playing cribbage since nine o'clock. Scudder, distracted, had lost almost every game. It was past midnight, warm and still. The tide would be ebbing, he thought. He could smell the salt marsh and the mud. June bugs and moths bumped against the screen door, drawn to the electric light. The rest of the house was dark and silent, as if he and the Captain were the only ones left, marooned in the kitchen with a deck of cards. At the table the Captain finished shuffling. He licked his thumb and began to deal.

"Remember the *Margaret Harte*?" the Captain asked, pushing the cards across the table. This was another game they played, quizzing each other out of nostalgia and the need to prove they still remembered. Seven surfmen and the keeper lived at the Smith Point Station back when they'd worked together on Fire Island. They had a wreck pole near the station to simulate a mast and practiced rescues on it, trying to get someone off in the breeches buoy, a life ring run on a pulley, in under five minutes. They learned the international signal code and the colors of the Coston flares: Red, *You are seen*; blue, *Do not attempt to land*.

Scudder leaned back in his chair, fanning his cards in front of him. "The *Margaret Harte*? Eighteen eighty-nine. Her cargo was whiskey and peanuts."

The Captain's bow tie bobbed as he nodded. "Every fisherman from here to Moriches was trawling for bottles."

Scudder remembered crowds of barefoot children, their pockets stuffed with waterlogged peanuts. "Remember the *Chippewa*?"

"She was the one with the ostriches—1908. Ostriches, watermelons, yellow pine."

"What about the *Clementine*?" Scudder asked.

The Captain grinned. "Still got my fork." The *Clementine*, bound for Boston from Jacksonville, Florida, had struck an outlying rock one morning in a thick fog. The sea was calm and they reached her easily in the lifeboat. The ship seemed safe enough, and when the captain, profusely apologetic, invited them into his cabin for breakfast, they accepted. Kelley had just speared a piece of ham when a wave smashed through the cabin door and swirled around them. He fought his way on deck and into the dory. There, reaching for an oar, he'd found the fork still clutched in his hand.

"And the cargo of shoes?"

"The *Geoffrey Manning*," said Scudder, and he recited:

"There were shoes galore along the shore
  In assorted styles of leather,
  But the undertow had scattered them so
  There wasn't a pair together."

"Bravo," said the Captain. "You always had a head for verse." Scudder snorted, though it was true. At night, patrolling the beach, he used to keep himself awake with poems he'd learned as a schoolboy, "The Highwayman," "Gunga Din," and another called "The Bell Buoy."

The Captain played an eight on Scudder's seven and advanced his ivory peg with a flourish, winning the game. Scudder shuffled while the Captain took out his tobacco pouch and filled his pipe. "I remember one night," the Captain said, pausing with his fingers in the tobacco. The aroma drifted across the table. "The sea was full of phosphorus. You've seen it like that. Pitch black, and the waves glowing as they break on the bar. Spooky." The Captain bobbed his head again. "I don't mind admitting it. And about halfway to the hut, near the hulk of the *Bethany D.*, I heard a clapping noise. It sounded like two flat sticks slapped together. My hair fairly stood on end. I kept going and met up with the other patrol, Jeb Scheibel, I think it was. I didn't say anything. I was hoping I'd imagined it. But on the way back I heard it again. And you know what?"

Scudder had filled his own pipe. Now he struck a match and lit it, leaning back in his chair. "Your hip flask was dry?"

"No, you old sinner." The Captain lowered his voice. "The next day it blew from the north and the *Sun Dog* went aground."

"The *Sun Dog*," repeated Scudder. "That was 1903. Turpentine, cotton, and tobacco. We got everyone off just fine."

"It was a warning," the Captain insisted.

There was a noise on the stairs and they broke off talking. Scudder looked up as Mavis appeared in the hallway wrapped in a blue flannel robe. His heart flooded with a ridiculous gratitude; since Nancy had left them, he'd realized that he was an old man, and it comforted him now to have what remained of his family around him.

"Oh," Mavis said, startled to see them at the table. She rubbed her eyes. "The moon's so bright, I couldn't sleep." She bustled into the pantry.

Scudder watched as the Captain stared fondly after her, ignoring his cards. He and Mavis shared an interest in spiritualism and religion. They traded books on mesmerism and had attempted to contact the departed Mrs. Scudder through the use of a Ouija board. Mavis lifted down the flour and the sugar and began to measure them into a bowl. The smell of cinnamon drifted from the counter. Molasses cake, Scudder thought. He had long since finished dealing and was regarding his hand with a severe look, because it was a good hand finally, kings and fives, and he didn't want the pleasure to show in his face. The Captain chatted with Mavis while she mixed the batter with a wooden spoon.

With a clatter, Mavis set the cake in the oven. She stood by the table and looked down at the cribbage board. Her face was pink and her dimpled hands dusted with flour. She pushed a strand of hair from her forehead. Scudder sat with his cards fanned out, waiting to resume the game. "Your turn, I believe."

The Captain fingered a card, considered it, examined another. "Oh, I meant to thank you," he said, addressing Mavis again. "That was an interesting pamphlet you loaned me."

Mavis brightened. "Do *you* think of God as a righteous will? Or more as absolute energy?"

Scudder cleared his throat, a bit loudly, but the other two

didn't take any notice. The smell of molasses filled the room. One o'clock struck on the hall clock. He heard Mavis telling the Captain, "It's so important to be scientific."

The Captain nodded. "Yes, by all means. By all means." Scudder watched with disappointment as his friend absently laid his cards face up on the table in order to fiddle with his tie. "Although," the Captain added, "there's also faith to consider." He rose and, with a stilted gallantry, picked up a dish towel and offered to dry the dishes.

Scudder rested his cards on the table. In the same way that his body had finally mutinied, revealing its aches and pains and demanding his attention, his mind had also grown peevish and fitful. He found himself returning to memories that pained him. Now, as the others talked about belief at the sink, he remembered with harrowing precision exactly how he had lost his own faith half a century earlier. This was something he'd carefully hidden, from his wife, Genevieve, when she was alive, and now from his grown children and his friends. He lived with it like a secret illness that was fatal but not contagious. It had happened during a rescue, one that neither he nor the Captain ever spoke of, though Scudder was sure they both remembered it more clearly than any of the others.

In 1890, a storm had hit during the worst winter any of the Life Savers had seen. William Bryden, patrolling the beach, sighted a three-masted schooner aground on the outer bar. It was late afternoon and bitterly cold. Scudder and Mapes had been playing gin in the station house when Bryden came in with the news. They dropped their cards and pulled on boots and oilskins.

Outside, the wind howled around them, tearing at their caps. The sand was frozen in hardened mounds beneath their feet. They followed Bryden to the shore, where a strong surf was running. Ice clogged the waves and the spray froze as it fell, stinging Scudder's face as he stared out at the ship. The schooner had hit a sandbar about four hundred yards out and was being pummeled by breakers. White water frothed over the listing deck. Scudder could see the forms of sailors who had climbed into the rigging. He counted eight. "Mother of God," Mapes said beside him. Randall and the others arrived with the cart, hauling the Lyle gun and the surfboat.

They got the Lyle gun pointed at the schooner and King fired it off, an incredible shot. The wind cleared the smoke, and the men's eyes followed the line as it looped over the pounding waves. Randall slapped King on the back. "I think that took." They'd all seen lines fall short, especially in high winds, but King was one of the best.

Now they waited for someone on board to climb out of the rigging and make the line fast to a mast or a spar; with the line secured, the surfmen could send out a breeches buoy and bring the sailors off one at a time. They watched from the beach, straining their eyes. But the line was either too far out of reach or the men too weak to climb to it. King shot another line aboard. "Come on, boys," he muttered, willing the sailors to move. "Come on, haul her in." Finally, there was a movement in the stern. Scudder caught his breath. The figure swayed for a moment, like a drunkard about to break into song. Then it dropped from the rigging and vanished in the surge.

"Sweet Jesus," said Mapes. "Sweet Mary and Joseph."

"Man the boat!" Randall bellowed. In seas that rough, the surfboat was a last resort. Scudder scrambled into the dory and took his place with Bryden, Miller, and King. Mapes and Kelley waded into the icy wash, holding on to the gunwales and trying to point the bow directly out from the beach. The boat pitched and pulled. The men in the water waited for a receding wave, then pushed the boat through the surf. The oars iced over in Scudder's hands; he could barely grasp them. He felt the blades skitter on the water. A wave broke over the bow and knocked him sideways. He came up, wiping his eyes, and heard Miller yelling over the roar of the breakers. Looking down, he saw water gushing through a hole punched by the ice. The next wave hammered the surfboat against the sand. Randall and the others grabbed it before the water could suck the boat away. The hull was bashed in like the shell of a hard-boiled egg.

Kelley was sent west to the Southease station, Bryden east toward Lone Hill for more men and another surfboat; this was before each station had a telephone. The others stood on the beach beside the ruined dory. A crack appeared in the clouds and lit the figures caught in the rigging like flies in a web. Scudder thought he saw the shape of a woman, her dark skirts whipped by the wind, her arms wrapped around the aftermast. The light began to drain from the sky. King shot four more lines out onto the ship, until all they could see was the dirty white on the crests of the breaking waves. Driftwood littered the upper beach and they built a fire to warm themselves. Sometime during Scudder's watch the wind shifted. For two hours, he listened to the crash of the waves against the ship and the grinding thump of the hull on the bar. It was brutally cold. He tried to pray. All night, over the shriek of the wind, he kept hearing human cries.

In the first dawn light they made out six figures still clinging on. It was a miracle, Kelley said. The stays of the mainmast had snapped in the night, and now the mast swayed out in a broad arc each time a wave pounded the hull. Randall paced along the shore. The fire had died down to embers. Mapes came up, dragging flotsam, and started it blazing again.

That morning Scudder watched helplessly as another figure

pitched forward and was swallowed by the waves. Volunteers from the Southease and Lone Hill stations arrived soon after dawn with a horse dragging another surfboat, but it was only after the wind had dropped a notch that they were able to launch it. Scudder sat in the bow, waves breaking over him, as they maneuvered through the floating ice. When they came up under the lee of the tilting hull, it grew strangely quiet. Scudder was the first into the heaving rigging and made for the closest figure, on the jibboom. He saw with shock that it was a boy. He was hunched down, very quiet, but he was still there, he hadn't fallen. Scudder spoke to him, cupping his hand against the wind. The boy did not stir. Scudder thrust out his hand and touched the boy's cheek, but his fingers were too numb to feel. He grasped a halyard and leaned forward, pressing his mouth to the child's forehead. A slick film of ice melted under his lips. The boy's eyes stared past him, frozen open.

The word that Kelley had used that morning caught in Scudder's throat. A *miracle*. He fought the urge to retch over the side. His belief in God he'd carried unthinkingly, a smooth white stone in his pocket; only now, when he felt how completely it gave under the pressure of his fingers, did he see that it had been hollow, like an egg, all along.

The woman was dead as well. He helped Randall wrench her arms free of the mast. Her black hair had frozen wildly to her face. On the mizzenmast, sheltered slightly by the topsail, two men were unconscious but still alive. The surfmen got them into the dory with the bodies of the boy, the woman, and a thin sailor found frozen in the stern. One of the survivors was a bearded giant it took three of them to lift. He wore seaboots that had filled with water; the water had frozen solid. He died a few days later at the Marine Hospital on Staten Island after the doctors amputated both his legs. The other survivor was a

Swede named Magnus Carlsson. When he came to, warmed by the fire in the station house, he narrowed his pale blue eyes. "I'm a tough one," he rasped. "It'd take more than that to do me in." Scudder, who was piling him with blankets, bent closer to hear, and the Swede fixed him with a malevolent stare. "I could have hung on all night," Carlsson said, raising his voice. "With a can of beans. And my pipe." Later that week he was taken to Amityville to an asylum for the insane.

"I told you," Mavis said to Captain Kelley. She stood at the kitchen counter, lifting a square of molasses cake out of the tin. She set pieces on three plates, careful of crumbs, and the Captain helped her carry them to the table. "He's not interested in the divine." Mavis bent forward and Scudder smelled her lilac perfume. "You'd rather talk about shipwrecks, wouldn't you?" She set a piece of cake before her father and smiled. A large dark moth, more shape than substance, fumbled against the screen. Steam rose from their plates, molasses-scented. The Captain stood and held out a chair. Mavis settled into it, and the three of them began to eat.

The house with Nancy gone was not, outwardly, so different. Clayton, back from his visit with the Gilpins on Fire Island, still sneaked onto the roof and smoked the odd cattail cigar. Without Perry, or the possibility of being caught by his sister, it was not as much fun as it had been. Mavis complained to Roy about the dogs in the kitchen, and Scudder and the Captain played cribbage on the porch and discussed the many ways the world was going to hell, starting with the ill-advised merging of the Life Savers with the Revenue Cutter Service a dozen years earlier and ending with the Italian invasion of Ethiopia.

In the evening, Mavis cooked blue claw crabs Clayton caught with Theron Greaves, and Clayton felt a satisfaction in seeing the family sit down to eat food that he'd provided. It made him feel a little like his uncle, who brought home ducks and rabbits and the occasional squirrel for dinner. Maybe this year, he thought, Roy would take him hunting when duck season started.

It was at night, long after the dishes had been washed and the downstairs lights turned out, that Clayton felt that the house with Nancy gone was irrevocably changed. Lying in bed, kept awake by the insistent mosquitoes, he listened to its muffled creakings. The house seemed less substantial, as if a flaw in its construction had been revealed by his sister's departure. Down the hall the door to Nancy's room yawned open, and its emptiness merged with the darkness until the house around him seemed hollow, even flimsy, little more than a skiff or a raft. In those moments of loneliness he imagined he could feel it bumping slightly against the ground beneath them, like a beached dinghy on an incoming tide, and it seemed to him that the house was in danger of floating away.

From below him, faint but distinct, came the pinging sound of a spoon against a bowl and then the creak of a cupboard door. His aunt was also awake, moving quietly in the kitchen with its solid chairs and table, the stippled lampshade, the white enamel stove. Reassured, Clayton felt the house settle firmly around him once again. In another moment he had fallen asleep.

On the marsh, the pepperidge trees were the first to redden, bright against the tawny reeds and the green high-tide bush. In September, Clayton and Perry went back to school. On afternoons when the tide was right, Clayton continued to scap for

Theron Greaves. Once a week Mavis made him sit down at the kitchen table and write a letter to Nancy in Boston. His letters were short: *Today me and Perry caught three toads near the pond. Thank you for the sweater.*

Nancy wrote long letters poking fun at herself in Boston. She'd taken a wrong turn coming back from the market, "like the rube I am," and found herself in a narrow street where a throng of people waited in line for food. "Some had their shoes tied on with rags." She'd asked a short-tempered policeman for directions. She wanted to know if Clayton was keeping up with his schoolwork. Did he remember the promise he'd made her not to play hooky? Reading this, Clayton felt annoyed; she was still trying to tell him what to do. And she wanted Boston to sound important. He thought of the far-off places Washington's birds arrived from, the Solomon Islands, the coast of Madagascar. If he ever left Fire Neck, it would be for somewhere halfway around the world.

Scudder spent more time at Captain Kelley's. When he wasn't playing cribbage with the Captain, he liked to sit in his chair on the porch, smoking his pipe or dozing. He never mentioned Nancy, nor did he show an interest in her letters, but when he said to Roy, "The winters are much colder up north, you know. I bet they get plenty of snow," Roy guessed that he was thinking about her. Her marriage still felt to Scudder like a personal affront. It would probably fail, he told himself, with a certain grim satisfaction. *Marry in haste, repent at leisure.* She'd come home again eventually, just as Mavis had. At the thought of Nancy suffering, he felt a thawing in his chest, and had to remind himself that she was still married and, as far as any of them knew, entirely happy.

———

Nancy stood at the counter of the small kitchen that was now hers, breaking eggs into a blue glass bowl. Beside her Robert measured coffee with a spoon. They had stayed in bed too long, and now he had to hurry to get to the museum on time. She felt shy and a little clumsy, bumping his elbow as she handed him a plate of scrambled eggs. He ate them in a few bites, then laced up his shoes as she packed a cheese sandwich for his lunch. At the door he kissed her tenderly on the mouth, and she smelled the camphor and naphthalene under his aftershave, stronger here in Boston because he used them every day at the museum to protect specimens from the dermestid beetles. Then he hastened out into the street. From the window she watched him until he disappeared around the corner.

Nancy turned, feeling slightly at a loss. The smell of the coffee, rich and bitter, hung in the air. From the street came the squealing of a trolley and the shouts of children playing ball. The apartment itself was hushed. In the narrow kitchen, she washed and dried the breakfast dishes. Arranging the blue-and-white teacups on the shelf above the stove, she smiled at the memory of Robert saying he drank from a saucer. Their apartment was on the first floor and overlooked a small yard that might once have been a garden, now hung with clothes and linens from the laundry next door. The incongruous smell of soap permeated the rooms and the dingy yard, as if they were actually squeaky clean. Empty stockings dangled side by side, like the shed skins of snakes. The oddness of the image made her think of her brother, and she wondered what he was doing at that moment.

She glanced at the clock. It was only nine forty-five. A few months ago she would have been practicing her typing. Of course, she had left her typewriter behind. She imagined Buckshot, grazing idly in the field beyond the barn, then pushed the thought away. There were stables in the city and she'd hoped to ride here from time to time, but hiring a horse turned out to be far too expensive. From a few doors down she heard the muffled barking of a dog.

Walking into the small sitting room, she surveyed the faded brown curtains. The apartment was rented furnished, a euphemism, Nancy thought, for cluttered with hand-me-downs. She would stitch up some pretty ones to replace the curtains, she decided, and fresh pillow covers for the mole-colored sofa.

Beating the pillows in the small backyard, she raised a cloud of dust and earned a nasty look from a red-faced laundry woman in a white blouse flecked with suds. "Sorry," Nancy murmured, abashed. She didn't know what rights, if any, she had to the space where the laundry hung. But she could hardly beat the pillows on the front steps. She felt the city suddenly pressed tight on either side of her, block after block of crowded buildings where tenants squabbled over cramped and weedy yards. She threw the pillows on the couch, amid a puff of remaining dust, grabbed her handbag, and went out to look for material for curtains.

In October the director of the Museum of Comparative Zoology threw a party for the benefactors and the board of trustees. Nancy took pains deciding what to wear, wanting to make Robert proud. She was afraid that the nicest dress she had, an A-line in rose-colored silk, looked girlish, and besides, it was too late in the year. In the end she decided on a navy crepe gown that felt more sophisticated. She put on red lipstick and a pearl necklace that had been her mother's, and scanned the mirror in their little black-and-white-tiled bathroom, pleased with the result.

Entering the wide front doors of the museum with her husband, she felt the first flutter of uncertainty. Ahead of them, a blond woman in a calf-length white fur coat leaned on the arm of a man who carried himself like a film star. Smiling to keep her anxiety from showing, Nancy moved closer to Robert. She'd visited him at the museum before, down in the basement room smelling of sawdust and tobacco where he painstakingly removed the flesh from dead birds to make study skins at a table overflowing with cotton batting and cornmeal. She realized now that she had expected to see the same white-haired men in moth-eaten jackets and earnest, flat-chested secretaries in dark skirts and white blouses she'd come to associate with his work. This was another world altogether.

They made their way inside, moving within a throng of well-dressed people. Nancy noticed a woman in black velvet, draped in diamonds. Flocks of bright, motionless birds behind glass lined the long hallway. "From the Pennand collection," Robert said. He hurried her along, nodding to people he knew, unconcerned by the finery around them. She wished he'd thought to warn her.

In a high-ceilinged room hung with chandeliers, the diamond-draped woman gazed reverentially at the paintings on the walls. "Audubons," Nancy heard someone murmur. "Originals."

A moment later Robert exclaimed, "There's Dr. Peters!" Nancy caught sight of a tanned, scruffy gentleman across the hall, mobbed by admirers. "He's just back from Mexico. Let me see if I can get a quick word with him, darling."

Nancy found herself wedged between two lepidopterists who were discussing South American moths. Snatches of other conversations reached her: *When we were last in Greece . . . Not with the market what it is . . . German submarines, they told us . . .*

The lepidopterist on her left had eyebrows that poked out in front of his face like the feelers of an insect, and she wished she had someone to share this observation with. She imagined Clayton on the floor of his bedroom, his vials and specimen jars spread out around him, his inexplicable urge to collect the dried husks of beetles and give each one its proper Latin name. He'd always been a quirky kid. She remembered how, as a toddler, he had been scared of sneezes. She'd never found out why. It wasn't the noise alone, because even a picture of a sneezing frog in a book had frightened him. She'd completely forgotten that. It had lasted only a month or two, at most. And now he was thirteen years old. He probably wouldn't believe this if she told him. She wished suddenly that he were with her, and scanned the room as if he might somehow be spotted among the crowd of sophisticated strangers.

Beside her, the lepidopterists waved to someone they recognized and moved away. Nancy stood by the display case, hemmed in by a paunchy man with a beard who was telling a small group about an expedition to Argentina. "Twelve hundred specimens in a single year," he announced triumphantly. "Peters is already planning the next one."

She glanced down, into the yellow glass eyes of a stuffed crocodile. The room bustled around her. *Caiman crocodilus, El Salvador*, the sign beside the crocodile read. *New Bride*, she thought, *Long Island*. Robert had told her how the museum organized research and collecting parties to places across the globe. She knew he hoped he'd be asked to take part in one. But wives weren't invited along, she was sure of that, and she hadn't thought to ask how long these expeditions lasted. A month in Florida would be one thing. But what if it was somewhere far away? Would Robert abandon her for a year to shoot birds in Tibet? She realized that given the opportunity he probably would, and a panicky feeling gripped her at the thought of being left behind in a city where she had no one.

Across the crowded hall she caught sight of Robert, now standing beside a tweedy gentleman who gestured excitedly as he spoke. Robert was looking directly at her, and she realized he'd been watching her. He would be concerned that she was bored. Quickly, so that he wouldn't worry, she waved her hand and smiled. He smiled back, over the heads of the crowd. Then the tweedy gentleman pulled a passerby forward and Robert turned as he began to introduce them. Nancy stood beside the crocodile and wondered how long they were expected to stay.

On Long Island, the pokeweed had turned from green to red, and duck hunting season had started. Clayton, home from school, lingered in the kitchen. He knew Roy would be out on the marsh with his gun and the dogs, and was hoping he'd return before Mavis came home from Washington Lodge. He missed his sister, though without her here he was free to sketch the dead bat he'd propped against a bowl on the kitchen table. Clayton had found it in the hayloft, and now he was sketching the delicate bones and the webbing of its wings, putting off the more difficult job of drawing its wrinkled, inscrutable face.

He heard his uncle whistling first, then the snuffling of the dogs. Roy came through the door sideways, bearing a cluster of ducks, their limp heads strung together, their orange feet dangling. Seeing Clayton with the dead bat at the table, he gave a conspiratorial wink: Mavis wouldn't want undressed game in her kitchen, either. Clayton, who longed to hunt with Roy, knew the names of all the local waterfowl: canvasback, scaup, black duck, brant, bufflehead, and goldeneye, the mergansers that tasted of low tide no matter how long Mavis soaked them in milk. Now he admired the blue-winged teal while Roy patted his face dry with a striped dishcloth. Outside, a light rain had begun to fall, and Roy smelled of marsh mud and wet dog. "Ugly out," he said, lighting a burner on the stove for coffee.

Clayton wondered for a moment if he should save up for a gun instead of a boat. No, a gun wouldn't be as good. The boat changed frequently in his mind, sometimes a runabout, sometimes a clinker, most recently a flat-bottomed scow, built for the Great South Bay. It struck him as odd that his uncle didn't keep a boat at Starke's. Scudder had practically given the family sailboat away to a friend of Dr. Thayer's, which broke Clayton's heart, though he hadn't let it show. Roy didn't have a boat at all. Clayton glanced up at his uncle, leafing through the paper. Tall and deliberate, with the same spare build as Scudder, Roy hunched his shoulders slightly. Standing motionless, lost in thought, he reminded Clayton of a heron. The rain drummed on the roof, making the kitchen somehow more private.

"Wouldn't you like a boat?" Clayton's voice sounded squeaky. He cleared his throat. "I mean, a boat of your own."

Roy looked startled, as if he'd forgotten Clayton was there. His eyes took a moment to focus. "No." He shook his head. "I don't really care for the bay."

Clayton felt taken aback. Not care for the bay? It was like claiming not to eat strawberries and cream. But when he thought about it, he realized Roy never came sailing; it was always Scudder who took them. Roy seemed to sense his amazement. "Your mother loved it, of course. She was the sailor in the family. You've got it in your blood."

But she was your sister, Clayton nearly said, and then thought of Nancy trying to interest him in riding, his schoolwork. Still, he wished he could prove his uncle wrong, or talk him into changing his mind.

"You know all about engines," he protested. "What about a motorboat?"

Roy shook his head, folding up the paper and finishing his coffee. He filled a large pot with water and set it on the stove. The ducks lolled on the drain board, giving off the heavy smell of damp feathers and blood.

Sailing, Roy thought: he'd rather sit under a clothesline strung with bedding and have cold water splashed in his eyes. His nephew sat at the table with a crestfallen look. The water was boiling on the stove. Roy picked up the first of the ducks by its limp feet and scalded it. Steam rose from the pot, and the smell of wet feathers overwhelmed the kitchen. The boy seemed to be waiting for something. So after a moment Roy said, "I've never been much of a swimmer."

The boy stared at him, then glanced down at the floor as if embarrassed on Roy's behalf. Roy felt again that he disappointed the kid, who clearly wanted something more from him. He tried to imagine how he would appear through a boy's eyes: lonely, middle-aged. A man with the stuffing knocked out of him. He was gripped by a spasm of self-disgust.

He pulled a clump of wet feathers loose with a practiced jerk. An urge came over him to prove he hadn't always been like this, and he thought of how wildly he'd once gone out of his head, the day he had sought the water out. "There was a girl I knew," Roy said, "when I was younger." His back to the boy, eyes on the folded feet of the duck in his hand, he began the story he'd never told before.

He'd come downstairs late for breakfast. It was a Sunday. His mother and Mavis were at church, his father at the boatyard. Helen was married by that time and living in Connecticut. Roy had picked up the paper idly, a slab of bread and butter in the other hand. And there was the headline, DEBUTANTE KILLED IN TRAGIC ACCIDENT, and there was her name, Grace Elizabeth Perdue, underneath her picture. It was a posed photograph, done in a studio, and though she looked beautiful, her mouth was closed, hiding the little gap between her teeth.

When he looked down, he'd been surprised that the table was still there, as if nothing had happened. The walls stood, the ceiling held. He forced himself to read on: *rain and fog, Merritt Parkway, family inconsolable.* He had a sudden image of her father, red-faced in a white linen suit, leaping to his feet with a roar at the sailboat races, and then Grace glancing over at Roy. She hadn't liked sailing either; that was how they'd met, bored at the Southease dock watching the races. He had been staring abstractedly at her pale straight hair, so unlike the carefully scalloped curls the other girls favored, unable to help himself. When the race ended and her father launched himself off his seat, their eyes met and she smiled with a little shake of her head.

He looked back down at her photograph. *The victim had recently broken off her engagement to the son of Mr. and Mrs. Alfred Kehlenbeck of Albany, New York . . .*

Her family had come out from Manhattan for the summer and were staying at the Pattersquash Inn. Her fiancé was up in Albany until September, she said. He was the son of family friends, Roy gathered. He didn't care. The next day he borrowed a horse for her and they rode together all the way to Drowned Meadow and back. Her father nearly had a seizure.

The poor girl, Roy found himself thinking now, so many years later. He hadn't given her a moment's peace. One morning, when he knew her parents had planned a trip to Fire Island, he walked all the way from Taffy Point to the Southease beach as the sun came up and wrote her name in clamshells across the highest dune. Recklessly, he played his ukulele outside her hotel window until the lights went on in the downstairs office. He brought her to Salt Hay Road and walked with her through the humid, rose-scented greenhouse to the quail pen. Into her soft cupped hands he slipped a single brown-speckled chick, no bigger than the first joint of his thumb. How could her fiancé not seem a cold fish in comparison? The night before she went back to New York City, Grace whispered that she would end her engagement. That had been the last he heard from her. He'd been afraid that she had changed her mind.

Roy left the note on the white enamel stove, where his family would find it when they came home from church. He didn't remember walking, though it was nearly a mile to the end of Carman Street, only the light on the water as he moved toward it, the way it seared his eyes. He could see Fire Island, shimmering and broken by the distance into a string of islands floating within the meniscus of the horizon. His mind was entirely clear.

The road ended, and Roy kicked off his shoes. The Great South Bay lay flat and calm under the undulating light. Far out, a single black cormorant flew low over the water. It was late September, but the water hardly felt cold. The light on the bay was so bright it was like walking into fire. He felt a stern exultation: he was going to drown himself in the brightness of the water.

He walked and walked and walked. His foot came down on something that scuttled away, and he jumped instinctively before continuing on, more gingerly. The exultation faded. He walked some more. He looked back, and the sand at the end of the road was a smear of white in the distance. The water reached only to his thighs.

He stood in his wet socks in the middle of the Great South Bay, dry from the waist up and entirely alive. Of course he knew the bay was shallow, everyone knew the bay was shallow. But *this* shallow? What a joke! Even now, more than twenty years later, the memory of that moment made him wince. He'd let out an inarticulate howl of misery. A flock of gulls rose from the surface of the water and flew off toward the Southease dock. He dropped to his knees. The salty water soaked his shirt and filled his mouth with the taste of tears. Now he was kneeling in the bay with his head protruding like a turtle's. He should have stayed home and slit his goddamn wrists.

Roy had taken engines apart and put them back together, and later he felt as if something similar had happened to him in the still middle of the Great South Bay. In that moment of personal disassembly, a small part of him went missing; he almost believed he'd heard the muffled plunk of it hitting the water. It was something almost insignificant, like the washer off a bolt, not observable from the outside at all. But he had never worked the same again.

He stood and, after a moment, turned around and began the long walk back. Emerging gradually, the water coursing down his legs, he saw his black shoes on the white sand at the end of Carman Street. They seemed to be waiting for him, with the patience of the inanimate, as if they had known all along that he wouldn't actually go through with it.

His wet clothes stuck against his skin as he limped home with his shoes in one hand. The gravel bit into his feet. In the kitchen he was relieved to see the note still on the stove. He tore it up and threw it on the coals. When the family came home, they found him in bed, listless with an illness he didn't specify.

Roy felt the boy's eyes on him after he finished, but did not turn. The ducks lay on the drain board, stripped of their feathers. He was here at this moment, he thought, as the result of his own ridiculousness.

Mavis woke from a dream in which she'd been screaming. She struggled in the tangled sheet. Any moment she expected to hear her husband's tread on the stairs, his voice thickly singing, *"Fare thee well, Polly m'dear, I must be on me way."* She fumbled for the electric light beside the bed, and her own room on Salt Hay Road sprang up around her. Breathing as steadily as she could, she tried to calm herself. It had been years since she'd dreamed about Ramsay. Her nightgown clung to her skin, damp with sweat, and she went to the window and opened it to the cool air. Outside, nothing stirred. The full moon showed the tide at dead low. Mavis, still rattled by her nightmare, had a vision of the entire field molded under aspic.

She had received two more letters from the lawyer in California. The last one threatened her with "legal action" if she failed to respond. She had meant to write back, and went so far as to purchase an envelope and two sheets of writing paper at the post office. But she couldn't match the formal language the awful lawyer used. Standing at the counter at Washington Lodge, brushing her teeth before bed, she tried to find the words that would explain how little she knew and how none of it was her fault. In the end, she'd given up, ignoring the letters in the hope that they'd stop coming.

Now, standing at the window, the menacing dream came back to her. It hadn't been the fist-shaped cloud this time.

There had been something tightening around her. It was the ring she still wore on her right hand, an opal ring her husband had given her before they were married, claiming it had once belonged to the French grandmother who'd been a childhood friend of her own Granny Chaffey. They'd been on the porch alone after dinner. The ring was in a little blue velvet box, slightly worn around the edges. He held it out, and she'd exclaimed over it, surprised and flattered. She remembered how he had put his two hands out and drawn hers toward him. And then he took the ring and slid it onto her finger, working it over the knuckle.

In a flash of rare and perfect clarity Mavis saw that the ring itself was cursed. She had to steady herself against the windowsill. For all this time she'd been carrying the curse on her right hand. Before he'd given her the opal ring, her life had been innocent and good. After the ring had come her unhappy marriage, the death of her mother, her childlessness, her sister's cancer. Even the explosion of the fireworks factory, and her niece decamping with a man nobody knew! She stared down at the thin band and the opal like a blind eye on her finger. It seemed to be poisoning her bloodstream. She pulled at it. But her hand had grown plump; she couldn't get it over her knuckle. In a frenzy she gouged her skin, drawing a bead of blood. The pain made her pull herself together. She found the washbasin. The soap stung the cut, but she worked the ring up and down in the lather until she could wrench it off.

Holding it in her palm, she marveled at its smallness. It looked so malignant to her now that she couldn't believe how long it had taken her to realize the truth.

Mavis grabbed her robe and her shoes. Carrying the ring in one hand and the shoes in the other, she made her way quietly down the hall. Anyone hearing her would assume she was just going downstairs to bake. In the kitchen she lit a kerosene lamp and laced up her shoes. Again she forced herself to breathe deeply and steadily. She opened the kitchen door. The night air was chilly. The moon outlined the trees still heavy with leaves, the spiky reeds along the edge of the pond. Mavis walked down the path toward the road, studying the ground. Where the gravel ended there were flagstones. She placed the ring on the flat slate and stamped on it hard, over and over, nearly losing her balance. When she was through, she bent down. The ring was flattened, the metal crumpled like a ribbon found between the pages of a book. The opal had turned to fine grit that sparkled in the moonlight. Mavis gathered it into her palm, using the flat of her thumb to pick up the last of the opal powder. Cupping the ruined ring in her hand, she flung both metal and dust over the low fence. Then she turned back to the house, exhausted and relieved.

In the kitchen she took off her shoes, carefully wiping clear the place where the opal had left a dusting as of flour. Blowing out the kerosene lantern, she made her way upstairs by feel. She climbed back into her narrow bed and fell into a sleep so sound that Clayton had to wake her in the morning by tugging at her arm. She had prepared a story about losing the ring in the sink at Washington Lodge. But as it was, no one noticed it was gone.

Three days later Mavis received another letter from the lawyer in Fresno, California. This one stated that unless her husband could be located she would be held responsible for his debts. How could that be true? She hadn't seen him in over nine years. Even when they were together she had had no control over their finances.

Dear Sir, she wrote back. *Believe me, I am not responsible for my husband's debts. You have to understand that my husband can be unreasonable. In fact, I will tell you frankly, he is a difficult man.* The rest of the page yawned whitely before her. But she felt there was nothing more to say. When she showed the letter to Roy, he was silent for some time. He tapped the paper against the table.

"I tell you what," he said finally. "Let's talk to Al Donner. He's a lawyer. He'll know what to do."

The next afternoon, Mavis changed into her black wool dress and put on her best hat. She had not slept well. In her hand she carried a loaf of potato bread as a gift for the lawyer. Roy escorted her into the small office. He looked ill at ease in a stiff white shirt and brown jacket and stood behind Mavis's chair, fiddling with a button on his cuff.

Mr. Donner did not seem, to Mavis, particularly sympathetic. He read the letters and turned to face her across the polished oak of his desk. "Mrs. White," he said, "I understand you and your husband are separated." Mavis nodded. "Has your husband attempted any communication with you since you last saw him?"

Mavis felt goose flesh stand up along her arms. It occurred to her that maybe Ramsay *was* dead. Maybe, she thought, he had been sending her messages from beyond the grave. She gaped at Mr. Donner. "Communication?"

The lawyer leaned forward to indicate that he was being patient. "Has he sent you any letters, Mrs. White? Any telegrams? Has he contacted you by telephone?"

"Oh no," said Mavis. "No, he hasn't."

Mr. Donner asked a few more questions and promised to look into the situation further. He would take over all correspondence with the lawyer in California. But he cautioned her that he was not optimistic. "In the eyes of the law," he explained to Mavis, "you and Mr. White are still man and wife."

Mavis feared for a moment that he meant the law could force her back to him. "How do you mean?"

"If your husband has failed to honor his financial obligations, the injured party or parties will look to you for restitution."

"Restitution?"

"You will have to pay his debts."

Mavis turned her wide, pained eyes to her brother. Roy shuffled his feet. "Hold on now, Al," he said. "I don't see how that could be right. The man deserted her."

Mr. Donner rose. "I'll see what I can do, of course. But you should be prepared for that eventuality."

Back on Salt Hay Road, Scudder headed across the field to Captain Kelley's for a game of cribbage. The November wind had turned sharp, and the yellow leaves of the locusts fluttered like fish in the net of the bittersweet vines. Scudder knocked. When no one answered, he pushed open the door. Inside, he was surprised by the cold. The fire in the woodstove had gone out. Cats seethed across the kitchen table and across the floor. Scudder called for the Captain. The dark house was silent.

He stepped through the tiny kitchen into the sitting room. The couch with its threadbare arms was empty. Scudder called again, "Kelley? You home?" The cats mewled and pressed against his legs.

Scudder looked in the small back bedroom only as a last resort. It felt strange to open the narrow door; he'd never been through it. A pale rectangle of sunlight fell from the one high window onto the brown bedspread, and in the light a gray cat slept. The Captain lay in the bed staring fixedly at the ceiling.

Scudder knew in an instant that his friend was dead; he had seen eyes open like that before. The Captain lay flat, with his arms at his sides. He must have died in his sleep, Scudder realized. He swallowed, his mouth dry. He thought of the men he'd found dead in the masts of wrecked ships, their hair stiff with ice, and of the bodies washed up on the beach after winter storms.

Once, as a boy, Scudder had misjudged a breaker at Old Inlet while playing in the waves. Instead of cutting through the water as it broke, he'd been snatched and pummeled by it. The wave came down on top of him like a train. He had tumbled for what seemed like hours between water and sand. When he finally fought himself free and had finished retching up salt water, he sat for a long time staring at the crashing waves. He mastered the trick of riding them that summer, but he never forgot the raw strength of the water or its colossal indifference. It was as if the sea were pure brawn, muscle with no reason behind it. He didn't believe, then or later, that there was anything malicious in the sea. Shells, pebbles, ships, men; it was all one to the flexing waves.

Now he felt that same dizziness, the sting of salt in his eyes. He sat down on the only chair, displacing a heap of socks and sweaters. The walls of the room were hung with fly-specked maps and magazine illustrations of sailboats and the insides of cathedrals. To the left of Scudder, above the chair, was a curled photograph of the men of the Smith Point Life Saving Service. They stood in their uniforms, the station house behind them. Scudder remembered the year Kelley joined the station. He himself must have been twenty-six or -seven then. Kelley had seemed younger than he actually was, gawky and painfully shy. A few days after he'd first arrived, somebody's sister, maybe it was King's, had brought a cake out to the station house. Kelley came in from patrol and got halfway across the room before he noticed her. The sight of the girl so flustered him he walked into a chair. It crashed over with his foot caught in it, and he'd gone down hard on the floor. Kelley had simply lain there, and they feared for a moment he'd knocked himself out. But he was too embarrassed to move. The men laughed hard, Scudder with them. Mapes nearly choked with laughter. King's sister told them all to let the poor man alone, but it did no good. For the rest of the season they threw the word "girl" into every other sentence, just to watch Kelley's ears turn red.

Scudder studied the grainy black-and-white faces. They stared back at him, young and serious in their white uniforms, their bristling mustaches. He thought of the unofficial Life Saver's motto: *You have to go out, but you don't have to come back.* In the photo only Mapes was smiling, his head tossed back. Kelley stood very straight, as if being measured for a suit. In the middle sat Randall on a chair, his hands on his knees, not knowing that one day he'd be lost over the side of the lifeboat, his body never recovered. And Bryden, who died not long after that of stomach cancer. Miller outlived his wife and two of his children. Scudder heard it was pneumonia that finished him. And Oates had hanged himself, years before Miller's death, from a rafter in his father-in-law's barn. Scudder sat on the chair by Kelley's bed with his hands over his face and cried for all of them. And for himself, an old man whose last friend was dead, whose wife and daughter were dead, whose granddaughter had left to throw in her lot with a stranger up in Boston.

———

Mavis and Roy drove back from the lawyer's in silence. Once or twice Roy shook his head and patted his sister on the knee. Mavis sat slumped beside him. She was too stunned to cry. She wished now that she knew where her husband was. Before, she had felt better not knowing, as if it somehow made him less real, less menacing. Now it occurred to her that as long as she had anything he would find a way to take it from her.

She remembered that her father had once complained of Ramsay's boots. This was after he'd first been invited to dinner at the house on Salt Hay Road. They'd had a woman who came in to help then, who drank too much but made perfect, airy soufflés. Mavis came back into the sitting room after wishing Ramsay good night in time to hear her father say ". . . boots like that."

"What could you possibly mean?" her mother asked.

"They're too tight," Scudder said. "You can tell by the way he walks. I never trust a man who doesn't know his own shoe size."

At the time, Mavis had been affronted, though she pretended not to have heard. She took it as an example of her father's lack of breeding.

Lost in thought, Mavis didn't see the crowd gathered in the field beyond Salt Hay Road until Roy gestured toward it. A figure, seeing their car, broke free of the group and ran toward them. It was Clayton. He waved his arms, and Roy brought the car to a crunching stop in the driveway. "It's the Captain," Clayton stammered. His face shone with importance and horror at the news he was delivering. "He's dead."

Roy wrote the letter to Nancy as plainly as possible, telling her the Captain had died in his sleep of a weak heart. *He was a good friend to all the family*, he wrote, *and will be deeply missed here.* This was the first letter Roy had ever written to his niece, and he found it difficult to compose. He was not a man to elaborate, but he felt bound to acknowledge his sister's strange behavior. In the end he added, *His death has hit your aunt especially hard.*

Roy found himself wishing that Nancy were home; not that she and Mavis had ever been chatty, but maybe another female could have somehow reasoned with her. Because Mavis had completely astonished him by running into the house and locking herself in her room as soon as she'd heard the news. Roy had to talk to her through the keyhole.

"Open the door, there's my dear girl." There was a strange gasping, as though she was having trouble breathing. Then he heard her voice, but she didn't seem to be speaking to him. It sounded like some dreadful chant.

Roy tried again. "Please, Mavis, come down to the kitchen with me. Come have a cup of coffee."

"Oh God, ohgodohgodohgod." Her voice sounded muffled, as if she had buried her face in a pillow.

"Pigs!" muttered Roy, under his breath.

He had to drive up to Washington Lodge that evening and tell them she'd been taken ill. He couldn't say when she might be back to work. A sudden onset, he explained. Roy concluded privately that the shock of Captain Kelley's death, on top of her anxiety about her husband's debts, had unhinged her. The sound of her weeping kept him awake that night. Lying in bed and listening to her strangled sobs, he wondered, embarrassed, if perhaps the Captain had meant more to his sister than he'd previously thought.

The Captain's funeral was held at the sprawling Catholic church in Southease on a day of driving rain. Afterward, Scudder developed a bad cold. For three days, he stayed in bed, and when he was strong enough to come downstairs, he seemed to have aged ten years. His eyes were hollowed out and his face had sunk, leaving his nose protruding more than ever, like a rooster's beak. Clayton, helping him down the stairs, was surprised by the skin of his hands, as brittle and dry as the yellowed paper he found wrapped around the pears Mavis saved for the winter in a dresser in the attic. Scudder had never been a large man; now he seemed puny. Clayton was sure he could have carried him down the stairs himself, though he would never have offended the old man's dignity by suggesting it.

Downstairs Scudder sat in an armchair close to the living-room fire, a red-and-black-checked blanket wrapped around his legs. His illness had left him with a harsh cough. Mavis made him nettle tea with honey to ease it, and the smell of the tea lingered in the kitchen and hall. Roy tried to interest him in patience, since no one in the house played cribbage and it was a game he could play alone. But before the round was half over, Scudder had fallen asleep with the cards tumbled in his lap.

Scudder's cough eventually faded, and Mavis stopped brewing nettle tea. But even after he recovered, he spent most of his time in the chair by the fire. Some days he never left the house. He kept *The Collected Poems of Rudyard Kipling* on the table by his chair and read it methodically, from start to finish, and over again. Many of the poems he already knew by heart. Roy brought him other books as well, Edgar Allan Poe and the detective stories of Arthur Conan Doyle. Scudder leafed through them disdainfully, and then returned to Kipling.

Captain Kelley's death had aged Mavis too. She spoke infrequently and her face looked worn. She baked more and ate less, and donated food to the Relief Center in Patchogue. On Sunday she went to church in Southease, wearing her black wool dress and her hat with the feather. On the way to the car she shocked Clayton by suggesting he come with her. When he shook his head, she crushed him painfully against her and he heard her whisper above her choke hold: *Take pity, Lord!* Skittish afterward, he tried to avoid her unless her arms were full.

The following week, Clayton was in the kitchen, where the bread was still warm from the oven, when his aunt mentioned Kelley's cats. "We should take the poor creatures in, Roy."

Clayton watched his aunt's dimpled hand on the handle of the knife, cutting into the smooth crust. The heel pulled slowly away, steaming, exposing the pale inside of the loaf.

"No," Roy said. "You know the old man hates them."

"We can't leave them to starve!" His aunt's chin trembled. "I think one's died already." Clayton wondered if he should leave. He stared hard at the loaf of bread. "It's un-Christian not to help them."

"*People* are starving. All over the country!" Roy sounded exasperated. There was a charged pause. Then he said, more kindly, "They're half wild, you know they are. The dogs would only chase them out again."

"*Please*, Roy." His aunt sounded so desperate, Clayton almost hoped his uncle would give in. He glanced up quickly. Roy's expression was set. In that moment he reminded Clayton of Scudder.

"Do you want our house smelling like that cottage? Leave them where they are, Mavis. I don't even want you feeding them."

Mavis sniffled as she passed Clayton a slice of bread. He

smeared it with cream lifted from the top of the milk jug with the flat of the butter knife. The cream was yellow with fat, thick as leather. Clayton sprinkled sugar over it and then crammed the slice into his mouth. The grains of sugar pressed against his tongue.

Later he saw Mavis taking dishes of milk across the field when she knew Roy had gone out. "I'm not *feeding* the cats," she told Clayton sternly. "I'm giving them something to drink."

November continued, cold and windy. From the end of Carman Street, where he and Perry had collected eelgrass, Clayton saw a flock of broadbills in a dark line like a false horizon. Staring out at the gray, metallic surface of the bay, he tried to imagine his uncle wading into it. Disturbed by the story itself, Clayton was still awed that his uncle had confided in him. "And damned if that water wasn't too shallow to wash a dog in!" Roy had said. Clayton hadn't known how to answer. He wondered now if Roy had meant it as a lesson, making a joke out of something that pained him.

He walked home along the edge of the marsh. Surely his uncle hadn't really wanted to drown himself, he thought. On the pond, the last of the maple leaves were tumbling onto the choppy water and capsizing like flimsy boats. Clayton was surprised to see, beyond the maples, a figure in front of the Captain's cottage. A tall woman stood surrounded by a haphazard collection of bags and boxes. She wore a frayed gray coat that whipped in the wind. There was no indication of how she and her meager belongings had arrived, and Clayton let himself believe for a moment that she had parachuted into the field. One of Kelley's cats sat on top of a cardboard box and yowled pitifully.

When he told Mavis that someone was moving into the Captain's house, his aunt put her black hat on her head and took Clayton with her across the field. She brought a fresh loaf of bread and made Clayton carry a pie. The pathway worn by the Captain's feet had begun to grow over with grass. Clayton hadn't been into the cottage since the day the old man died. Once or twice Perry had tried to interest him in a dare, but he'd refused to rise to the bait.

The door opened and a smell assailed them, the smell of cats and the stale, ammoniac urine of cats. The tall woman greeted them cheerfully. She had dark, untidy hair and an angular face. "I'm trying to air it out," she told them, "but as soon as I open a window, they come back in." She glanced over her shoulder, into the room, where a thin cat scratched at the kitchen floor. "I suppose I'll have to drown them," she said distractedly. "The poor things."

"We live in the house across the field," Mavis explained, and they introduced themselves. The woman, Judith Purlowe, was a widowed niece of Captain Kelley's. At the time of his death she'd been living with her sister-in-law's family in Pennsylvania. She seemed delighted to have inherited the house, the cat problem aside. "I'd love to have you in," she said, waving toward the dark, low-ceilinged room. The small living room and the smaller kitchen were piled with bags and makeshift luggage. They continued to stand in the doorway. "I could brew some tea . . ." Judith Purlowe began to riffle through a brown paper bag, producing a shoe with a broken heel and a scrap of cloth that might have been a pillowcase.

"Another time," said Mavis. "Once you've settled in."

"I'm sure I have tea *somewhere*." Judith Purlowe squinted toward the sink.

Clayton had stood through this conversation with the pie grasped firmly in his two hands. Now Mavis set the loaf of bread carefully on top of it. "I'll leave my nephew here," she said. "He can help you unpack your things."

Judith Purlowe turned from her search and smiled a quick, wide smile that illuminated her face, making her suddenly pretty. "Thank you for the things to eat, Mrs. White. I'll bet you were a blessing to my uncle."

Clayton was mortified to see tears appear in Mavis's eyes. But Judith Purlowe had turned toward the kitchen, loaf in hand, and was looking in vain for a bread knife. "Make yourself useful," Mavis told Clayton on her way out.

Clayton set the pie gingerly on the counter. Judith Purlowe had abandoned her search for a knife and stood in the center of the kitchen, holding the loaf of bread. "I'm not sure where to begin," she confessed. "I guess I'd better clear out the cupboards." She handed Clayton a paper bag. "You can start in there." She pointed to the small living room with the sway-backed sofa. "Once we empty out the cabinets, we'll sort through it all."

The dresser was covered with a layer of gray dust and cat hair. The top drawer squealed as Clayton pulled it open. Compacted inside lay pieces of string and twine and colored yarn, rolled into balls and knotted, crinkled sheets of cellophane and shiny paper, tinfoil carefully peeled from packs of cigarettes, lengths of bent wire, jars of buttons, and others of screws and nails. One corner of the drawer was heavy with bottle caps. Clayton began to extract objects in groups to arrange on the floor. It was like taking apart a mouse's nest; pressed together for so many years, the cellophane maintained the drawer's rectangular shape as if molded.

The third drawer stuck. Reaching his hand inside, Clayton felt the sharp corner of a box and bore down with his fingers until the drawer popped open. Mixed in with odd shoelaces were backgammon boards, cribbage sets, and playing cards. Clayton had cleared nearly all of them when he found, beneath a chess set with a broken hinge, a deck of playing cards with worn edges. The deck was held together with a rubber band the color of putty that fell to pieces in his hand. The card on top showed a dark-haired woman with her back to the viewer, looking over her shoulder, her pale, dimpled buttocks exposed. Clayton felt his heartbeat quicken. He glanced toward the kitchen. The tips of the widow's shoes were visible on one of the rickety kitchen chairs. Quickly he fumbled through the deck. Every card showed a half-naked woman. Sirens in old-fashioned hairstyles reclined on sofas, half dressed, or lifted their skirts, smiling coyly. The Ace of Diamonds rode a rocking horse, pitched forward, her heavy bosom grazing its mane. The Four of Hearts winked at him, a hand propped behind her head.

From the kitchen came the thump of a cabinet door. Guiltily, Clayton crushed the cards into his pocket. He couldn't let the widow see them. What if she'd been the one to find those pictures? The thought appalled him. He imagined her gasping for breath, collapsing in a faint. He kept the deck in the front pocket of his pants, where it pressed uncomfortably, distracting him as he sorted through more piles of frayed papers, books on mesmerism and the spirit world, empty tobacco tins. Against his thigh it seemed to generate a faint, illicit heat.

An hour and a half later, lifting a pile of yellowed handkerchiefs from a dresser in the Captain's bedroom, Clayton felt something between the layers of worn cotton. He shook the handkerchiefs onto the bed and out fell a wad of paper money.

Clayton peered quickly through the small bedroom window. Judith Purlowe was outside, beating the striped kitchen rug with a broom. Clouds of dirt and dust swirled around her. Clayton sat on the bed and counted the crumpled bills. It was a small fortune, thirty-two dollars in all. Who would know if he kept it for himself? he thought. His aunt and uncle did not keep track of how much he earned, though Mavis told him every payday at Washington Lodge that he should "put something away." His sister would have noticed if he suddenly had more spending money. She might even have sensed something just by looking at him. But Nancy was in Boston. He felt that it would somehow serve his sister right if he took money that wasn't his.

He stood and pressed the bills into a pile. Trying to stuff them into his pocket, his hand was brought up short by the indecent playing cards. There wasn't room for both. Outside, the dull thump of the broom on the rug had stopped. He could see the widow set the broom down on the grass. He pushed the bills into the other pocket. Now both pockets bulged, like the face of a chipmunk with acorns in either cheek. It seemed clear to him in that moment that he would have to choose between the money and the deck of filth and pleasure. He felt a rush of shame.

Judith Purlowe came back into the house with the kitchen rug draped over her arm just as Clayton dashed out of the dark back bedroom. The cards hidden in his pocket thumped against his leg. He held out the creased and folded dollars. "Look!" he called. "Look what I found for you!"

Mavis knew she was responsible for the Captain's death: she had thrown the remains of the opal ring over the fence onto his property, and four days later he was dead. That she had done this unwittingly, that she would never have wished him any harm, that he was one of her oldest and dearest friends, only worsened the horror of it. She knew that curses do not take intention into account.

There was no one she could talk to. Roy would never believe what she knew was the truth. She considered her brother's understanding of these things limited, at best; he would fall back on scientific fact. No one at her church would be able to see past what they'd call superstition. The only one who would have listened to her and sympathized was the Captain himself.

Mavis took an instant dislike to his slatternly widowed niece. But this in no way lessened her acts of charity. She returned the following afternoon with a pot of soup and found Judith Purlowe washing her hair. The house was in the same wild disarray and the smell still overpowering. Nothing seemed to have been cleaned or organized. Back at home Mavis asked Clayton what he'd done to help the day before. He told her Mrs. Purlowe had had him emptying drawers. "And I found money. A heap of it."

"Money?!" said Mavis. It seemed obscurely unfair that a strange woman, especially such an untidy one, should come into a windfall. Though it was clear, thought Mavis, that she had need of it, judging by the state of her coat and shoes.

"Thirty-two dollars." Already it seemed to Clayton that he'd never hesitated to hand the bills over. The cards he'd needed to keep to protect Mrs. Purlowe. He would throw them away, he told himself, or burn them, but he had to wait until he was sure his aunt wouldn't see them. In the meantime, he'd found a hiding place under the mattress in his room.

———

Guilty over the Captain's death, Mavis tried to interest Roy in helping the widow. "We need to be neighborly. She'll never get that gutter back up on her own." A gutter over the kitchen window had collapsed months before. Now it listed across the window itself, giving the small house a drunken look. Roy complained that he had enough to do maintaining their own property. The greenhouses were becoming unsafe, the barn roof leaked, he needed more oats for the horses.

The next day, while Mavis was at work at the lodge and Clayton at school, Roy noticed the widow hauling a ladder around to the front of the house. He stood and watched her from the porch as she climbed the rungs. At the top, bracing herself with her feet, she tapped at something with a hammer. Then she pulled a piece of wire from her coat pocket. It took her several tries to hook the wire around the gutter. Roy felt a prick of conscience. But he stayed on the porch. Not out of laziness or unkindness; he simply wanted to keep watching her. She was going about the repair entirely wrong, wrapping wire around the gutter and attaching it to a hook instead of nailing the gutter itself directly to the wall. He wanted to see how she would manage. After about ten minutes, she climbed down from the ladder and surveyed her work. The gutter hung straight above the window, bisected by a line of wire. Judith Purlowe picked up the ladder and disappeared around the back of the house. Roy found himself grinning. When Mavis came home, he pointed out that the gutter on the cottage across the field had been fixed without his interference.

One morning in early December, Scudder didn't come downstairs for breakfast. Mavis was getting ready to leave for the lodge when she realized he hadn't appeared. "Run up to your grandfather's room," she told Clayton. "He must have overslept."

Clayton found the old man collapsed on the floor of his bedroom in his nightshirt. Terrified, he stood frozen in the doorway. His grandfather had always seemed invulnerable. Now Clayton saw the spindliness of his bare, old-man's legs, one thin, ropy arm spread out across the rug. Scudder's eyes were closed, his stern face half pressed against the floor. Clayton made sure that he was breathing, then ran for his uncle.

Together they got Scudder back into bed and made him comfortable. He seemed more affronted than injured and pretended not to understand why they were fussing over him. Dr. Thayer was summoned, at Mavis's insistence. "Nothing's broken," he reassured them. "He's bruised his hip, that's all. But he's an old man and his bones are fragile. A break at his age could lead to complications."

That evening Roy and Mavis decided it would be safest to move Scudder from his upstairs bedroom to a corner of the living room. Out in the barn Roy put a rough daybed together out of spare lumber, finishing by the light of the kerosene lamps that Clayton helped carry out. Back inside the house they made space downstairs for Scudder's bureau and his bookshelf.

"We've set up a bed for you downstairs," Roy told Scudder. It sounded like an apology. "So we can keep an eye on you."

Scudder fixed his son with a clear, fierce gaze. Clayton, standing in the doorway, was reminded of an injured hawk. In a hoarse voice, not addressing them but rather a point on the far wall, Scudder spoke: *"And he risks his life for others in the quicksands and the breakers. / And a thousand wives and mothers bless his name."* It was a poem about surfmen that Clayton had heard once or twice before. No one moved for a moment after Scudder broke off. Finally, Roy stepped forward and put his arm carefully under his father's back. Clayton hurried to help him. "It's warmer downstairs," Mavis said with false cheeriness. "You'll be right near the stove." Scudder didn't answer. He held himself stiffly between Roy and Clayton and did not in any way assist them, allowing his feet to brush the floor without supporting his weight. His bones under Clayton's arm felt brittle, a bundle of dry sticks. Tentatively they made their way down the stairs.

Once in place, Scudder made no complaints. The daybed was near the fire, and from it he could look out the window onto the marsh. Soon the entire downstairs smelled of pipe tobacco. He was often asleep, and to keep from disturbing him, the rest of the family spent more and more time in the kitchen.

Clayton watched with fascination as his grandfather turned slowly into a bird. Not the rooster or hawk he had at times resembled, but the hatchling of some altricial species, a blue jay or a mourning dove. Scudder's eyes were often shut, so that the closed lids veined with blue seemed not to have opened yet. His white hair stuck up from his head like tufts of down. His nose looked more than ever like a beak, but a fragile one that had only recently pecked its way out of a shell.

It was Clayton who asked Mavis if they should bathe him, when the sour, rotten smell began to permeate the room. He used a sponge and a basin of water while Mavis held her father under the arms and primly averted her face. Seeing his grandfather's spindly legs and soft, extended belly made Clayton think of a hatchling again. When the wet sponge hit Scudder's groin, the old man's eyes opened in alarm and he struggled. Mavis kept him from falling as she tried to reassure him, but the bath was considered a failure and they did not attempt it again.

And it was Clayton who most often remembered to feed him. Mavis alternated between furious bouts of baking and trancelike states during which she sat at the kitchen table and stared up at the ceiling as if attempting to read something in the cracks in the plaster. Clayton fed the old man oatmeal, because it was easy to chew.

Standing over his grandfather with the oatmeal bowl, Clayton thought of the shipwrecks the old man had told him about: the *Lucy Norton*, the dark-eyed figurehead of which stood at the entrance to the Southease town hall; the rescue divers who worked for weeks to salvage bolts of cloth and bags of mail off the *Belle of the Isles*. Since before he could read, Clayton had known the names of ships that sank fifty years before he was born. He imagined those lost cargoes strewn across the shores of Fire Island, buried like treasure in the sand.

"Time to eat." He rattled the spoon in the bowl. His grandfather's eyes were closed. Clayton watched his chest, relieved when it rose with the old man's shallow breathing. "Time to eat," he said again.

His grandfather couldn't just die, he told himself. Not a man who had lived through so much. Scudder knew more about Fire Neck than anyone. He loved the history of the roads they walked on and had told Clayton the stories behind the names. Fire Neck, for the signal fires the Indians burned on the banks of the river to guide whaling parties through the inlet and back across the bay. And he had mapped in his mind the shifting cartography of the south shore. It was not as solid as it looked, he'd told Clayton. Back in the 1700s the ocean burst through narrow Fire Island and made an inlet across the Great South Bay from Southease. With a single storm, the town became an ocean port. Scudder had described the shipyards, the wharves that reached into the bay, the mansions with cupolas and widow's walks that went up along the shore. Then, in another storm, a ship loaded with grindstones sank in the channel. Underwater, sand swept and settled around the wreck. The next ship that foundered there carried a load of salt. Together the two wrecks closed the inlet.

Clayton remembered how, as a little boy, he'd believed what his grandfather told him: that this second ship was the reason the Great South Bay was salty. Out east, Scudder had explained with a poker face, out near Shinnecock, the water tasted sweet: that was where a ship bound to Boston from Havana went down with a cargo of molasses.

Reaching out with the tip of the spoon, Clayton tapped his grandfather gently on the lower lip. Please eat, he thought fervently, *please*. The old man's eyes stayed closed. But at the pressure of the spoon his mouth opened, like the mouth of a baby bird.

Roy was up on the roof of the horse barn patching a leak when he noticed Judith Purlowe heading across the field. She carried a burlap bag at arm's length and moved slowly but grimly, her neck bowed. It was not yet six-thirty in the morning and the gray sky sagged with clouds. Roy was anxious to mend the roof before the rain or snow hit, and had come out before he'd had his coffee. At the edge of the pond Judith Purlowe hesitated. She set the bag on the grass, where it began to writhe. Roy watched her run a hand through her hair. Standing by the pond in her ancient overcoat, the dark clouds massing in the sky behind her, she looked forlorn beyond bearing. Roy abandoned the roof and set off to intercept her.

She slowed down when she saw him and waited till he reached her before she began to explain: "I can't keep them out. The whole house smells. I tried taking them to Southease one night, but they were back before morning. You have no idea what it's like. They're all over me every time I sit down to eat. I can't possibly feed them through the winter." As she talked, she kept up a steady, resigned shaking of her head. "It's taken me days to get them all together. You should see the scratches on my arms."

The thought of scratches on her skin offended Roy. "Do you have a brick in there?"

The widow shook her head again. "I've never done this before." She said it like a confession. Her bottom lip was chapped, and Roy found himself wondering if she chewed it. "Is the brick required?"

"I understand it speeds things along."

They regarded the bag beside them on the grass. It had gone strangely still, as if the cats inside were listening. The silence stretched on. Even the clouds seemed to be waiting.

"Why don't you let me take care of this," Roy found himself telling her. It seemed the obvious thing to say. It was, he realized, why he'd left the roof in the first place.

Judith beamed at him. She had a bright, surprising smile. Roy smiled back, to lessen her embarrassment. They stood grinning at each other. "Thank you," Judith said. "You have no idea . . . I appreciate it . . . You're so kind." Her brown eyes glistened. She reached forward quickly and pressed his hand with a warm, strong grip.

Roy felt the blood rush to his face. Before he could speak she'd moved away, walking back across the field toward the Captain's cottage. It had begun to rain, a cold, spattering rain. The burlap bag struggled blindly at his feet. He picked it up, feeling light-headed but purposeful. He looked toward the marsh. Could he really let it drop into the river, knowing it would float for some time? He was a man famous for his squeamishness, a man who had failed at his own self-destruction. Should he fight against his essential nature? His hand tingled where Judith Purlowe had touched it.

Roy carried the wriggling bag to his car and spent the

morning driving to Wading River. There he opened the bag in the woods outside of town. He backed away quickly as the cats tumbled out, their fur matted, scratching and spitting. Roy watched as they disbanded, hightailing it into the bushes. It was a cowardly act on his part, and he knew it. The cats would slowly starve, or attack a stranger's chickens. He could not defend himself. He drove home in great spirits, singing loudly out the window into the freezing rain.

One Saturday morning Perry arrived with the news that the canals had frozen at Starke's Boatyard. He carried his older brother's eel spears. Clayton borrowed a hatchet from Roy's toolbox, and the two boys walked down to the boatyard with a bucket on the end of the long-handled spears. Out on one of the frozen canals they smashed the surface with the hatchet and cleared the broken ice away to make a hole. Clayton's fingers smarted in his wool mittens. Into the hole they thrust the eel spears, each with its row of barbed hooks. Somewhere in the mud below them the eels lay curled against the cold. At the first hole the boys plunged and plunged without any luck. "Pigs," said Clayton, feeling grown-up.

They moved the gear farther out on the ice, toward the opening at the mouth of the river, then used the hatchet to smash another hole. "One, two, *three*," called Perry. Standing at the edge of the hole, they poked into the dark water. "Got one!" Perry yelled, in the same instant that Clayton felt the handle jerk in his own hand. They hauled their spears to the surface. Caught between them like a thick black rope writhed a single eel. The boys shouted with triumph. Working their spears free, they pushed the huge, dripping eel into the bucket.

Then they watched, transfixed, as it thrashed its sinewy bulk against the sides.

They caught three more, adding them to the black tangle in the bucket, but none could match the first. "Go on and take the big one," Clayton told Perry when, hands stiff with cold, ears stinging, they'd finally decided to head back. "There are only four of us." Around them the canal was pocked with the rough holes they'd made in the ice, as if a rain of meteors had fallen. Along the shore the docks rose at odd angles like enormous insects, the pilings pushed up out of the mud by the grip of the shifting ice. Perry dared him to climb the tallest dock and Clayton ran to it, sliding on the ice. He clambered out on the gray planks as if the dock were a ladder, egged on by the urge to impress his friend and by his own agility. At the top he felt the dock sway under his weight like a pair of stilts. He could see over the wild privet hedge to the field beyond and the roof of the Captain's cottage and the house on Salt Hay Road. By their woodpile, his uncle was chopping wood. Clayton suddenly wished he hadn't offered the monstrous eel to Perry.

"Come on," he told Perry, jumping down off the dock so that the planks clattered. "I've got to get home."

They carried the bucket between them. Clayton, trying to get back before his uncle finished with the wood, sloshed frigid water onto their legs in his hurry. They clambered over the fence, the eel spears tangling in the privet, and Clayton was relieved to see Roy still by the woodpile. Intent on his task, Roy didn't notice them until they were nearly beside him. They set the bucket down on the brown grass, and he looked up, startled. Clayton, abashed by his own eagerness, couldn't think of anything to say.

"We caught the great-grandfather of all eels," Perry announced. He pointed into the bucket. "Clay said I could take it." He glanced up at his friend, to make sure the agreement still held. Clayton was watching his uncle from the corner of his eye.

Roy stepped forward and peered into the bucket. He let out a low whistle. "That's the biggest eel in Christendom," he said solemnly.

Clayton felt his chest expand with pride. "We speared it at the same time," he explained.

That night he sat at the kitchen table under his aunt's stern eye to work on his weekly letter. *Dear Nancy*, Clayton wrote, *Today me and Perry caught the biggest eel and Roy said . . .* He knew even as he wrote the sentence that it wasn't something that would impress her.

In Boston, Nancy shopped for Christmas presents alone. Robert was working extra hours at the museum to catalogue the new birds from the Mexico expedition and often didn't come home until after eight. They had agreed to stay in town over the holiday in order to save money, and it had seemed to Nancy at first like a romantic idea. But in the days leading up to Christmas, as she returned with bags and boxes to a dark and empty apartment, she often thought of the house on Salt Hay Road. Robert had asked if she wanted a tree, and she'd stoically said no, thinking of the cost, and instead bought a few pine boughs and put them behind picture frames to bring a little greenery inside. On Long Island, Clayton and Roy would have gone onto the marsh and brought back a small red cedar, and Mavis would tell them not to get sap on the rugs. In the past, she and Clayton had decorated the tree with white paper stars and red paper flowers, and popcorn strung on thread, and with the two dozen green and red glass ornaments from their grandmother Genevieve, stored in tissue paper in a box in the attic. It would be warm in the kitchen, and it would smell of the rum cake Mavis made each year especially for Scudder and the gingerbread Clayton loved to eat with cream.

On Christmas morning, Robert brought her coffee and toast in bed. "I blackened it specially," he said.

She sat up, smoothing her hair. "Is this a Landgraf Christmas tradition?"

He laughed, and the coffee sloshed onto the tray. "Hardly. I spared you the sweet onion sandwich."

"No!"

Robert nodded, climbing back into bed beside her. "My father eats one every morning. Christmas, Easter, Fourth of July. He says it's good for the teeth."

Robert didn't speak much about his family. Nancy knew they hadn't approved of his going away to college, and that his mother had died during his freshman year, so that he'd never had a chance to convince her he'd made the right decision. "Do you miss them?"

He was quiet for a moment, and she worried her question had pained him. But when he spoke, he sounded merely thoughtful. "Only my uncle. He used to let us ride with him on the snow roller. That was a treat. You probably don't have those on Long Island. They're for packing down the roads after a snowstorm, some planks bolted to a frame like a drum. He's a potato farmer. The black sheep of the family, till I came along. If you ask him what he grows on his farm, he says *rocks*."

Nancy raised herself on her elbows and looked down into Robert's face. He smiled at her, ink smudges on his chin. She thought happily that he would be home with her the whole day. "You don't wish we were there?"

"Good God, no," he said with feeling. "All they'll talk about is cows, and the diseases of cows, and which is better, Holsteins or Dutch Belted, and silage, and who's joined the Dairymen's Association." A bitterness she'd never heard before crept into his voice. "If I hadn't gotten my scholarship, I'd have gone to work canning corn. Anything else."

Nancy, her head on his shoulder, thought of how much she appreciated her own family since moving away. "I'm sure they miss you, though."

"They'll manage." He put his arm around her. "I forbid our sons to be dairymen," he said solemnly. "Dogcatchers, sure."

The thought of a son seemed oddly disloyal to her brother. "I'm only having daughters," Nancy declared. "We can name the first one Helen, after my mother. Or maybe Helena."

"Helena," Robert murmured, kissing her shoulder. "Helena handbasket."

They opened their presents on the sofa, under the largest of the evergreen branches. Nancy had found him an illustrated book of parrots of the world in a bookstore on Washington Street and was gratified by his awed whistle as he unwrapped the brown paper. Heavy, gilt-edged, with tissue paper between each of the exquisite plates, it had cost quite a bit more than she should have spent. The money would have to come out of her housekeeping allowance, and the thought of the gifts she'd sent to Long Island as well made her nervous.

"My mother loved Christmas," Nancy said, remembering a time when money hadn't mattered. "We always had a big tree in the front hall, and she'd decorate it in blue and silver, and there'd be candles in all the windows. The cook made marzipan farm animals every year, they looked just like toys. One time when Clay was little, he tried to eat a painted lead pig in the nursery because he thought it would taste the same."

Robert was silent. When she picked up the small box with her name on it, he grimaced. "I don't know, Nancy." He put his hand out to stop her. "I'd rather get you something else, something better."

"Don't be silly." She laughed, opening the box. Inside was an olive-green bracelet of large square beads. They looked to Nancy like Bakelite. The ugliness of it took her aback. Recovering quickly, she thanked him and put the bracelet on her wrist, where it gave her skin a sallow cast. It didn't matter at all. She thought of the thin blond girl with dirty hands and a baby in her arms who'd asked her for money on the street just the other day, avoiding her eyes. She didn't care a fig about a bracelet. Only it surprised her that he could misjudge her taste so completely.

She glanced up, smiling, but Robert didn't meet her gaze. He took the discarded wrapping paper and stood with it balled in his hand, as if judging its weight. Outside, it had begun to sleet. Later, it seemed to Nancy that in that moment she felt the day veer off its course with a lurch, like a horse that stumbles mid-stride on a stone. Without the normal workaday bustle of the street the apartment seemed eerily quiet. Even the neighbors with the terrier were gone. A musty dampness hung in the air; the laundry had closed for the holiday week, revealing the apartment's underlying smell. Robert turned and walked into the kitchen, and Nancy sat on the couch, confused and hurt. Was it her fault that her gift had been perfect and his hadn't? Was it fair of him to blame her for that? She had spent too much on the book, but only out of love for him. Going over it in her mind later, in the house on Salt Hay Road, she would wonder what she could have done differently.

Down on Long Island, Roy accompanied Mavis to church in Patchogue, while Clayton stayed home to look after Scudder. For dinner, Mavis served ham with potatoes and leeks, and rice pudding for dessert. They unpacked the box from Nancy, full of oranges and chocolates for Scudder, socks for Roy, real vanilla in bourbon for Mavis, and a new jacket for Clayton. It was blue with brass buttons, and it reminded him, in its color and its vaguely military cut, of the little sailor suit he wore as a child in the photo Nancy had of him. After trying it on, he hung it carefully at the back of his closet. When Mavis asked later where it was, he claimed it was too nice for everyday. In his heart he felt that it was the jacket of a city boy, a boy who could never catch an eel or smoke a cattail cigar, someone he would despise instantly, should he ever come across him.

One morning in January, after three days of rain, Clayton woke to find the world dismantled in the night and replaced with a reproduction in ice. The sun gleamed on ice fields and ice trees, and there across the field stood a small ice cottage. At a fair in Riverhead he and Nancy had once seen a life-size statue of a cow, sculpted in butter. This was a thousand times better. Maybe the bay itself had frozen, he thought; he would find Perry and see. They couldn't possibly waste a day like this at school, no matter what he'd told his sister. Downstairs, he heard Mavis talking gently to Scudder in the sitting room. Stealthily, he grabbed a biscuit from the kitchen table and crept outside. The light stung his eyes.

It took him an eternity to walk to the end of Salt Hay Road; it was so bright it was hard to see, and he slipped and fell, slipped and fell. No one else was out. On Beaver Dam he passed a car abandoned along the side of the road. It had swerved into a low stand of bushes. The branches, encased in ice, clacked in the light wind against the windshield. All around him he heard a sharp cracking and clattering. There were no other sounds.

At the Presbyterian church he turned onto Carman Street. Here the trees that lined the road staggered under the weight of their ice-slicked limbs; they bent nearly double, the branches of each tree entangled with those of the tree across the road. It was like entering a long, glittering tunnel. He walked slowly, to keep from falling. Distorted images of trees and sky shifted on the gleaming surface beneath his feet. The cold air seemed to burn his nose and throat. By the Watsons', he heard a tearing crack and then, ahead of him, a large branch tumbled down and shattered like a crystal chandelier.

He had nearly reached the Gilpins' house when he heard a new sound, a steady scraping. Behind him, incongruous beneath the trees, sailed an ice scooter. The west wind blew behind it. It sailed on a reach, and the white canvas billowed out over the road, just clearing a gray mailbox. Clayton stepped back and it glided past, silent except for the scrape of the runners against the ice. The bundled figure at the tiller nodded to him with polite formality as the scooter swept by. Clayton stood staring after it as it sailed down the road, headed for the bay. It must have been the Coles' boat, he told himself, rigged at their house at the head of Carman Street. The lone scooter dwindled soundlessly in the bright distance. He thought of the ghost ships that his grandfather and Captain Kelley used to speak of in low voices, late at night when he was supposed to be asleep.

At the Gilpins' he learned that school had been canceled. Mrs. Gilpin made him sit down at the table and eat a plate of eggs with Perry before she'd let them out of the house. Slithering and laughing, the boys made their way down the ice-encrusted road to the bay. It shone like an enormous mirror. They walked out onto it, glancing back at the shore as it receded behind them. By the Southease dock scooters gathered on the ice, their sails like white wings, darting and settling like a flock of skittish birds.

Exposed on the frozen bay, they felt the wind scrape at their hands and faces. They pressed on, past the humped shape of John Boyle's Island to the east, toward the low dunes of Fire Island and the dock at Old Inlet. Here too the ice had pushed the poles up out of the mud. Planks hung like broken teeth. The boardwalk was silent, the landscape brown and bare. It felt, Clayton thought, as though they had returned many years later to a place that had been abandoned. Trying to shake the eerie feeling, he ran to the top of the dune and stood looking out over the beach where the waves had cut away the shore. There was no sign of another living soul. The ocean pounded against the sand, and it seemed unbelievable to Clayton that they were looking down on the same stretch of land where he and Perry had dug trenches and splashed in the water less than six months before.

They walked back down the slope of the boardwalk and returned across the bay in silence, feeling as if they were coming back from the moon. Already the light had changed. The sun had gone behind a bank of clouds and the ice seemed to emit a cold radiance.

At the end of Carman Street, a man in a red knit hat was skating. He moved, intent and graceful, in a series of turns and flourishes, as if through the steps of an archaic dance. Clayton and Perry passed him with their eyes averted, unsure what to make of him.

Later that week Clayton spotted the man in the red knit hat again, near the mouth of the river at twilight. He mentioned the skater to Roy, and his uncle nodded. "He likes to skate the Lord's Prayer on the ice."

Mavis had grown accustomed to scanning the mail for the lawyer's embossed return address. When a thick brown envelope came from Canada, she carried it out of the post office and rode all the way home with it on her lap, unaware of what she held. Only after she set the mail on the kitchen table at Salt Hay Road did Mavis notice the familiar handwriting with a feeling of vertigo. She sat down abruptly with the envelope in her hands. She hadn't heard from her husband since the day he left her. The blue stamps showed a picture of a steamer and a seaplane, the return address a post office box in Manitoba. He was not close by, Mavis thought, and he was not dead. He could pay his own debts.

Heartened by the thought of the distance between them, Mavis ripped the flap of the envelope. There was a sheaf of folded papers and a four-page letter on thin airmail stationery in Ramsay's rough, impatient hand. In places words and even whole lines had been crossed out, tearing the paper. *Mavis . . .* The letter began as an apology and veered almost immediately into a confession. He had been a bad husband, he wrote. He'd made a joke of the state of matrimony. Mavis realized she was holding her breath and stopped reading to steady herself. A miracle had been worked on her husband, she thought, awed by the power of God. And she felt a pinch of fear. She was still his wife, and he might expect a reconciliation. With a certainty like a stone inside her, Mavis knew that she would never go back to him. Not if he became a deacon, she thought fiercely, or even the Pope himself. Not if he were canonized.

She picked up the letter again and read the details of his unfaithfulness. He had been a drunkard and a fornicator. Debts from playing dice led him to clean out their bank account and disappear. First he'd gone to Michigan to stay with a lady friend, then to California, to Washington state, and from there to Canada. *I drifted like a bum*, he wrote, *stooping lower and lower.* And then, at a church supper in Manitoba three years ago, he had been saved by an angel. Mavis, a literalist, read several sentences describing her before it dawned that the angel Ramsay meant was the daughter of a potato farmer. Ramsay had found a job and rented a house. He married Gretchen Holgersson without anyone guessing that he already had a wife back in the States. Four months ago, he wrote, they had been blessed with a son. Here Ramsay had taped a photograph to the paper. It was barely larger than a postage stamp and showed a baby with a head like a turnip, its mouth open in surprise. *He's smart as a whip*, Ramsay wrote. *I can see it in his eyes when I talk to him. Also, he squeezes my thumb.* Holding his son, he'd realized how deeply he'd wronged the boy's mother. He was writing to ask Mavis to grant him a divorce, so that he and the mother of his child could be properly married. The enclosed papers had been drawn up by a lawyer in Canada. *I imagine you'll be happy to be quit of me for good*, he wrote. *I'm sorry for the things I did. I truly am.*

Mavis sat in the kitchen while a numbness spread out from her chest and radiated down her arms. There had been some mistake, she thought. She turned the letter over in her hands; a few scraps of paper with the ink bleeding through it. She picked up the envelope. The writing was familiar, and the name, but the man she thought she knew had been someone else. There was so much she didn't understand. Her head throbbed. The numbness revealed itself as pain.

For as long as she could remember, Mavis had lived with the fear that something important eluded her, like an object hovering just outside her peripheral vision. At times she resented the certainty and purpose other people seemed to possess. Life seemed to her like one of those French examinations that had caused her such misery at school; she could never be sure she understood the questions she was trying to answer. She remembered a small, dark-haired girl who'd sat at the desk in front of her in French class, how easily she seemed to rattle off verb conjugations, like a bird singing. Mavis felt her own tongue awkward in her mouth, the taste of bitterness like a rotten tooth. How could Ramsay be living happily in Canada, with a wife named Gretchen and a baby who pulled at his finger, when all this time she'd lived in terror of him showing up on Long Island? How could God allow good men like Captain Kelley to die and men like Ramsay to be saved by fertile angels? She gripped the packet of papers and felt the stiff envelope first resist and then crumple in her hands. She'd write back to the lawyer, but not to Ramsay. Let him wonder what had become of her for a change, she thought. He needed something from her now. He could go on needing it. She looked at the tiny photograph again. The baby stared back at her, homely and astonished. "You little *bastard*," Mavis said out loud. The vehemence in her own voice shocked her.

Nancy woke to the clinking sound of a spoon. She was alone in bed. The clock showed it was ten minutes to seven. Confused, she pulled herself up and threw on a robe. In the kitchen there were black coffee grounds on the counter and scattered across the floor. "Are we out of bread again?" Robert looked up from the bread box.

"What are you doing?" Nancy asked.

"Peters is coming in early. Didn't I mention that last night?" He drank the last of his coffee, standing at the sink. Nancy could tell by his face that his thoughts were already on the possibility of a collecting expedition, the endless cataloguing and correspondence that waited for him at the museum. Putting down his cup, he moved toward the hallway. Nancy followed.

She watched her husband putting on his coat and hat, and he looked different to her, as if the angle from which she observed him had changed. The feeling of remove unnerved her. She put out her hand and touched his shoulder. Robert patted it with one hand while rummaging in his pocket with the other. He seemed, in his ignorance of her condition and the obliviousness with which he jangled his keys, to be a thousand miles away.

"Don't forget to pick up some bread." He kissed her on the side of her head and stepped outside.

For twelve days now Nancy had suspected she might be pregnant. She hadn't said anything to Robert yet, because she didn't know for sure. She wanted to wait until her instinct was confirmed. The possibility both excited and scared her. Everything around her seemed to recede to make room for it.

Nancy sat down on the sofa. Outside, she could hear the yapping of the terrier. She had been dreaming something when the sound of the coffee spoon had woken her; the dream itself had melted away, but it left a bitterness behind, a residue of ashes. Her secret felt suddenly too big to bear alone.

She wouldn't wait to see the doctor, after all, she decided.

She'd tell Robert that evening. Resolved on this, she felt a pressure lift from her shoulders. She went back into the bedroom and lay down. She thought of the day the fireworks factory had exploded, the day she and Robert first met. They'd walked to Salt Hay Road from Washington Lodge, and she'd led him on the shortcut that ran past Scheibel's Creek. On the marsh they found a solitary tree. From a distance it had looked at first like a flock of strange birds had perched on the branches. As they drew nearer, they saw it was peppered from the explosion with scraps of yellow bunting and tiny American flags. What she remembered now, more than the strange sight of the tree festooned with flags, was the way Robert had gazed at her in amazement, as if she were somehow responsible. "I think we've discovered a new species," he'd teased. She hoped, when she told him about the baby, that he would look at her with that same wonder on his face.

It was nearly ten o'clock when she woke again, disoriented and queasy. The dog was still barking next door. She stood up quickly and pulled on her clothes. The relief she'd felt after deciding to tell Robert had vanished. She remembered something he'd said in passing about a colleague at work, a man with seven children. "Poor Aldrich! His wife won't stop producing them." What was that supposed to mean, Nancy wondered, indignant.

She went into the kitchen and made herself boil and eat an egg. Trying to picture Robert with a baby in his arms, she felt an unease that reminded her of being seasick. Now she wondered what would happen if she needed bed rest during the last months, like her mother had with Clay. How would she manage to cook dinner and do the shopping and keep the apartment clean? Her mother hadn't needed to bother with any of this. Nancy remembered Clayton as a red-faced baby, crying inconsolably, and the matronly nurse in her blue uniform whisking him away.

Now it seemed stupid to tell Robert anything before she knew for sure. She would find a doctor and make an appointment, so that there could be no uncertainty. Then she would present the fact to Robert. It was too late to ask him now whether or not he was ready for a child or if they could afford one. She had to trust that he'd be pleased. Maybe, she thought, a baby would ease the tension she'd felt between them since Christmas.

Nancy finished her late breakfast. As she washed the plate, she wondered what she would look like in a few months' time. She had a memory of her pregnant mother, surrounded by pillows, in her silk bed jacket, flexing one bare foot and then the other and grimacing. "My ankles have turned into sausages," she'd said in a tone of resigned disgust. Nancy dried her hands and went to the mirror in the hall. Her hair hung limp, and there were shadows under her eyes. She smiled bravely, tipping up her chin, and the prettiness flashed back into her face and then faded as she held the smile too long.

On the apartment steps she ran into her neighbor, Mrs. Pelagias, a broad, stately woman with a dark mustache and twin sons who fought each other constantly, whom Robert referred to, privately, as Cain and Abel. Nancy asked if she could recommend a good doctor with an office nearby. "Not for anything serious," she said quickly, flustered. Mrs. Pelagias beamed. She knew just the doctor, a grand man with women and children, she said. Nancy felt her face redden. Mrs. Pelagias drew a map on a slip of paper, marking the streets and the route to the doctor's office in great detail. Giving it to Nancy, she patted her on the cheek with a rough, warm hand.

All afternoon Nancy was conscious of shielding her secret, cupping it like a flame. The small errands she had to run, mailing a letter to her brother, buying a loaf of bread and carrots and onions for the soup she'd planned for dinner, seemed to take hours. By the time she got back to the apartment it was already dark. She switched on the light and looked around for what felt like the first time, struck by the illuminated shabbiness. The paint had begun to peel in a section of the ceiling and on the radiator against the wall. All the little improvements she had dreamed up in her newlywed excitement seemed pathetic to her now; the flowered pillows she'd been so pleased with only emphasized the sofa's threadbare arms. She pulled the curtains shut with a feeling almost of shame.

In the kitchen she studied the recipe for vegetable soup in the Fannie Farmer cookbook her aunt had given her for a wedding present. She was determined to cook a good and economical meal. While the onion sizzled in the pan, she set the table, using the pretty calico tablecloth they'd gotten from her friend Enid. She took the candlesticks off the mantel and set them in the center of the table.

Robert came home half an hour later, his hat and coat damp with melted snow. He was whistling. "I talked to Peters," he called, unwinding the scarf from around his neck. "He says Greenland's out, but Peru's still possible."

Nancy felt something burst inside her, like a balloon. He came into the kitchen and put his hand on her shoulder. She shrugged it off, like a horse shaking away a fly. "What's the matter?" he asked in surprise.

"Nothing."

Robert looked unconvinced. Nancy stood very still and stared at the carrots on the cutting board. If he would just go away for five minutes, she'd be able to master herself. She felt like running into the bedroom and closing the door.

She saw for the first time that Robert had planned his life in a way that had never occurred to her. He'd gone against his father to go to college, and he was determined to succeed. The expedition meant more to him than a chance to travel. He longed to impress his boss, become a full curator, to discover a new species and claim it with his name. Falling in love had been an unforeseen departure, unscripted. She wondered with a flash of bitterness if he regretted it.

"What is it?" Robert asked finally, his voice concerned. "What happened?" Nancy turned away, clutching the knife. She'd reduced the carrots to orange matchsticks.

Robert stood watching her, waiting uncertainly, and she felt a burst of fury like a flame. He would consider the baby an inconvenience. She was not going to be tricked into confiding in him. "Nothing," she repeated.

She'd left behind her brother and everything she knew, she thought. An overwhelming homesickness washed over her. If only she could dig her heels into Buckshot's flank and ride away. She remembered trying to explain to Robert why she felt her brother belonged in Boston with them, and how he hadn't been able to see what she meant. Alone in a strange place, she felt unable to make herself understood.

Robert's equilibrium seemed maddening, suddenly. "You have no idea what it's like for me all day!" she cried.

"How do you mean?" Robert sounded startled. "You seem happy . . ."

"Here? Without any friends? Without my family?"

He glanced around the cramped kitchen, looking defeated. "You have me," he pointed out, trying to put an arm around her. Nancy moved away from him, biting her lip to keep from crying. Her arms were folded tight against her chest. She should tell him she was pregnant, she needed to tell him, but nothing had gone as she'd planned. The dinner wasn't finished. The onions sat shriveled in the pan.

A pained silence followed. Nancy could hear the drip drip drip of the kitchen faucet. Robert stepped back. He looked unsure of what to do with his farmer's hands. We can't stop here, she thought desperately, we can't go on like this! She moved unsteadily toward the bedroom. He couldn't wait to go off without her, she thought, and it made her long to hurt him. "When I was a girl," she found herself saying before she shut the door, "my room was the size of this entire place."

Two days later a telegram arrived from Long Island. Robert had already left for work. With a sense of the world collapsing around her, Nancy read that her grandfather was dying. "Not expected last week," Roy had written somewhat confusedly. Nancy began to snatch up clothing and stuff it into her suitcase as if she could save her grandfather if only she got to Salt Hay Road in time. The idea of talking to the switchboard operator and then waiting for someone to track Robert down in the basement of the museum was too much to bear. She didn't even know if she wanted to hear his voice. Writing him a short note, she could not help feeling, even in her anxiety and confusion, a sense of relief that she was going.

It was on the train between Boston and Providence, after a two-hour wait at the station, that she first felt the cramping pain. In the dirty, lurching bathroom of the train she cleaned the blood away as best she could. She didn't know now if she'd been pregnant or only a few weeks late. Back at her seat she hugged her suitcase to her chest and cried, pulling her bobbed hair in front of her face like a curtain.

She did not allow herself to think about her grandfather dying. She held him in her mind, suspended, as if she could somehow make him wait for her. Instead, she thought about her brother, the miracle baby who'd beaten the odds after all their mother's years of struggle. She remembered how, as a toddler, he'd liked to talk to strangers. At the beach, at parks and restaurants, he would approach unknown women in large hats and declare, "My daddy died." Nancy had an image frozen like a photograph in her mind of Clayton in his blue jacket with the white trim, his brow creased in a considering stare. She would smile and give his arm a little tug as the stranger asked Clayton how old he was. At the end of the conversation he'd announce, using his pet name for her, "Nennie loves me." As if he felt the need, before parting, to reassure the unknown woman in the hat that he would fare just fine in the world. As if the death of his father and the love of his sister were the chief facts of his existence.

Ashamed, Nancy thought of the small part of her that had been glad when Clayton decided to stay, the small part that had felt freed. The day the fireworks factory exploded, instead of hurrying home to check for him, she'd walked back so she could flirt with Robert. She had grabbed at her first chance to leave, even when it meant abandoning her brother. Remembering that moment in the kitchen when he'd told her he was staying, she stared down at her hands. There had been no soap in the little bathroom, and the skin under her nails was dirty with her blood. The bare landscape flung itself past the window. In the seat ahead of her, a couple argued interminably about the broken buckle of a shoe.

Clayton rode in the Ford with Roy to Drowned Meadow on the north shore, in a manly and companionable silence. A part of him worried that Nancy's visit would change the new camaraderie he felt with his uncle. Roy might go back to deferring to Nancy on anything that had to do with him. And yet he found himself bouncing a little on the seat of the car. As they turned into the dirt parking lot by the dock, he craned his neck to catch a glimpse of the boat that was bringing her home.

Together they watched Nancy step off the ferry in a neat, dark hat, carrying her little suitcase. The first thing Clayton thought was how much smaller she seemed. He had worked hard to put her from his mind in the months since she had left Long Island. Seeing her, he felt a painful dislocation. It was a cold, windy day in early March and her dress blew around her legs. She looked uncertain, out of place, like an arrival from another country. When she saw them, she hurried over, waving. She was thinner. Clayton felt it when she embraced him. For once he let her squeeze him close without pulling away. At first he was measuring himself against her to see how much he'd grown; in the months they'd been apart he had shot out of most of his clothes and he was now as tall as she was. Then he felt her breathing catch and he realized she was crying. He stood, clumsily shielding her. She seemed to have gotten younger while he'd grown up.

After a moment Nancy patted her face with her handkerchief and stepped back. "Look how big you are," she said. "Those pants are appalling."

At the car Nancy pushed Clayton into the front seat with her, so that he was crammed between her and Roy. She asked about Scudder. Roy assured her that he didn't seem to be in any pain. He was merely fading away, his hold weakening. "Don't expect him to know you," Roy warned. "He's not aware of much. A week ago he said something about a breeches buoy. He hasn't spoken since then." Nancy sniffled into her handkerchief. Her hand found Clayton's, and she held it.

Pressed beside his sister, listening to her voice as she talked with Roy, Clayton felt a spreading ache in his chest. It was like the feeling in his fingers when he washed them in hot water after being out in the snow, the tingling pain of the blood moving back into the veins as the feeling returned, and they began to seem like hands again and not like blocks of ice.

Stepping into the living room of the house on Salt Hay Road, Nancy thought at first that her grandfather had died before she could get home. He lay still under the red-and-black blanket, his face waxen. She turned to Clayton, her eyes filling with tears. "He's sleeping," Clayton said quickly, understanding her look. "He sleeps most of the time."

Nancy sat down and gingerly picked up Scudder's hand. The nails were long and yellowed with tobacco, though it had been over a month since Scudder had smoked his pipe. She remembered that they'd once collected black walnuts from under the trees at the end of the road and how their hands had been stained yellow by the juice after they worked to pry them open. Nancy put her other hand on Clayton's arm, gripping it. "What does he say about me? Tell me the truth."

"He doesn't talk much," Clayton told her, glancing toward the stairs. In fact, Scudder hadn't mentioned Nancy after she left them to move to Boston. Quickly he offered to carry her suitcase up to her old room.

Nancy stayed in the chair beside her grandfather, holding

his cool, limp hand. Looking over the familiar walls, the worn rug on the floor, she thought of her hurry to leave this all behind. Now she tried to take some reassurance from the faded red chair and the braided rugs, the painting of the lighthouse in a storm, as if nothing would change so long as the room remained just as it always had been. She leaned her head against the wall, exhausted. Her lower back still ached. Though she'd scrubbed her hands again on the ferry, she needed a proper bath, a change of clothing. When she closed her eyes, she had a vision of the close, swaying bathroom on the train, the blood on her underthings and thighs.

After a while, she heard the car in the pebbled driveway and then the familiar squeak and bang of the kitchen door. Her aunt, back from work, surprised her by rushing in and pressing her tightly against her bosom. Mavis's polka-dot dress smelled pleasantly of cream sauce. "You poor girl," she exclaimed. "You're skin and bones! Let me get you something to eat."

The unexpected kindness in her voice made Nancy's eyes prickle with tears. "I had eggs with Clay and Roy," she stammered. Her instinct had always been to refuse any solicitude from Mavis.

Her aunt waved her hand dismissively. "Is that all? After your long trip?" Mavis hurried into the kitchen. "I'll fix you a bowl of stew and some pudding."

The girl had obviously had a bad scare, Mavis thought; Roy must not have prepared her, and she had always been the old man's favorite. Her niece looked skinny as a wet cat, with smudges under her eyes like bruises; Mavis doubted the girl had learned to cook so much as an omelet. She heated up a big bowl of stew and buttered three biscuits. When she carried the tray into the living room Nancy's eyes were closed, as if she had drifted off to sleep in the chair. Mavis set the dishes down on the little table beside the bed and Nancy started. "Oh, thank you," she said. The steam rose from the bowl. Nancy put it in her lap, lifted a spoonful to her mouth and blew.

"Eat that all," Mavis told her. "I'll be back with the pudding."

It took Mavis longer to reheat the bread pudding because she decided to add some raisins softened in a bit of warm brandy. She piled the pudding with brown sugar and then filled the bowl with cream. Mavis had to step carefully to keep from spilling it. Just before the open doorway to the living room she glanced up. The small electric light was on beside the bed, the rest of the room in shadow. Mavis stood in the dark hallway and looked in. Her niece was eating, not nibbling the way Mavis remembered, but ravenously, like one of the Captain's half-starved cats. Her face shone with tears. She tore a biscuit in half, weeping, and wiped the bowl with it. The tears dropped off her chin onto the biscuit and the bowl. There was something utterly unguarded about the girl. Mavis backed away very slowly and returned in silence to the kitchen.

Mavis sat at the table with the cooling pudding, giving Nancy time to finish her meal in private. The girl had always seemed so jaunty in her youth and her confidence. Now she reminded Mavis of herself, many years earlier, married and deeply unhappy. She thought of Ramsay's letter, hidden upstairs in the top drawer of her bureau, and the familiar bitterness rose in her like nausea.

She put the bread pudding in the oven to keep it warm. After a quarter of an hour, she took it out and carried it back into the living room. She brought a clean dish towel from the cupboard. Nancy's eyes were closed again. The bowl and plate sat empty even of crumbs. Mavis set the pudding down, and Nancy opened her eyes.

Without thinking, Mavis reached out and brushed a strand of hair from Nancy's cheek. The girl didn't seem to mind. Her face was streaked and puffy from crying. "Here," Mavis said, and her niece thanked her, raising her hands greedily for the bowl.

The cats had not come back. Judith Purlowe thanked Roy every time she saw him. If she caught a glimpse of him across the field, she waved her arms exuberantly. Roy told himself it was best to keep his distance, but he found himself worrying about her. The money Clayton had found in the Captain's drawer would be running out, and she hadn't yet been able to start a garden. Roy wondered how much of a pension she got. Unbidden, an idea for a business scheme flickered in the back of his mind. Remembering the quail chick he'd placed in Grace Perdue's hands, he imagined raising game birds again. Maybe ring-necked pheasant that he could sell to gun clubs and hunting lodges. He thought of the wire pens and dusty incubators stored in the barn and wondered what pheasant eggs cost.

The next morning on the way back from the marsh he stopped at Kelley's old cottage to offer Judith one of the black ducks he'd shot. She beamed when she saw him. "Come in! I'm just making coffee."

"I won't intrude," he started to say, but Judith laughed and took him by the elbow. Roy stepped into the small kitchen. It was dark inside and he stood still for a moment, his eyes adjusting. He could see the orange glow of the flames through the chinks on the top of the cookstove. The room was warm. He slipped his jacket off and hung it over a chair, then felt self-conscious. Removing his jacket seemed too familiar. But he felt stifled by the heat even without it. "I love duck," Judith was saying as she poured the water from the kettle into the battered coffeepot on the counter. "Especially in a stew."

Roy's arms prickled. "Duck is good," he said stupidly. "Good for stew."

Judith turned toward him. "Milk?" She held a chipped white creamer in one hand.

Roy watched her mouth as it formed the word. Her bottom lip was still chapped, as if she bit it without thinking. He sat down. "Yes. I mean no. No milk. Please."

"Sugar's on the table. Would you like a slice of bread?" She moved toward him, holding a steaming cup. He felt as though he could measure out the distance from his body to hers to a fraction of an inch. The smell of the coffee rose toward him.

Roy shook his head, unable to speak. He took the cup from her, bumping against her hand and spilling hot coffee on his fingers. Gulping at it, he scalded his tongue. Judith had moved back to the counter and was pouring a second cup. Roy watched her body shift as she tipped the coffee from the pot. She wore an orange sweater and a dark gray skirt that hung past her calves. Roy found himself staring at her ankles, bisected by the strap of her shoes, and at the back of her stockinged legs.

He saw too late what a mistake it had been to come. "Thanks," he said. He grabbed his jacket. "For the coffee!"

"Wait!" Judith laughed. "You've barely touched it."

"I need to go." He rushed for the door like a sailor in a flooded ship making for the hatchway. But the latch was stuck. He rattled it helplessly.

"It's tricky," Judith told him. "I'll get it." He stepped back and Judith reached for the latch. Roy had a glimpse of the pale skin of her neck as she bent forward, before the door swung open and the daylight shone in his eyes.

"Come back for some stew," Judith said. He waved blindly and hurried across the field. The throbbing pain had spread throughout his body. He stumbled like a man on fire.

A bird was singing. Nancy opened her eyes, surprised; in her dream, she'd been in the apartment in Boston. Her suitcase sat on a chair under the window, looking temporary. The bird sang again, and the fluid, warbling notes seemed to pierce her. She got out of bed, and the floor was cold on her bare feet. Out the window the early light shone on the brown field and the muddy pond and on the roof of the Captain's dark cottage. Nancy had never thought much about Captain Kelley; his bow tie and his obvious crush on her much younger aunt had struck her as faintly ridiculous. Now his life in that small house seemed unbearably sad. She imagined him waking up alone every morning and going to bed alone every night, with only his cats for company. She thought of her husband. He'd be asleep right now in the creaky bed in the small room at the back of their apartment, and she wanted to be lying beside him, under the gray wool blanket, listening to his breathing and planning what to make for breakfast while the trolley passed in the street outside, squealing as it made the turn. Tears rose in Nancy's eyes. Her married life seemed like an island on the horizon, and she felt herself carried farther and farther from it. The feeling was more than she could stand. Grabbing her dressing gown, she ran downstairs.

In the living room her grandfather lay in the same condition. Nancy held his hand again, relieved that it was warm. She kissed his forehead. He smelled sweet with decay. She sat and stared at his face; the skin seemed heavy, congealed with age. Unsettled, she tiptoed into the kitchen and called softly for her brother, as if, by speaking too loudly, she might disturb the still form of her grandfather in the living room. There was no answer.

She was making a pot of coffee when she heard Roy on the porch, singing a song she'd never heard: *"I'm something of a sporting man, I'll always take a bet, 'cause I stand a chance of winning, though I haven't done it yet."* The door opened. He seemed startled to see her. "Up in the barn," he said. "Sorting through some old equipment." His face shone with the cold. He pulled off his boots, whistling the same tune under his breath, and Nancy poured him a cup of coffee. Roy sat at the table, sipping it. The clock ticked behind the stove.

Her uncle looked different, Nancy thought, but she couldn't decide how; he seemed more fully awake, perhaps. For the first time she wondered why he'd never married. Of the three siblings, only her mother had been happy in love. At least, she thought, as far as she knew. "Never tempted to get married, Uncle Roy?" she asked lightly.

Roy amazed her by flushing red from his throat to his ears. Nancy had never seen a grown man blush so deeply. She looked quickly down at her plate and began to press crumbs up with the tips of her fingers.

He finished his coffee and stood up. Nancy had not expected him to answer, but he said abruptly, "Not cut out for it, I guess." She glanced back at him and was relieved to see the blush had passed. He made a wry, pained face. "Too risky now, at my age. Like chicken pox. I leave it to youngsters like yourself."

Nancy spent the day in the living room with her grandfather. He didn't seem to know her, though she fed him oatmeal and later some broth. Worried that the spring air was too chilly, she got the fire going again. Bored, she picked up the volume of Kipling. The book fell open on her lap to a poem called "The Bell Buoy," and she remembered hearing her grandfather recite it:

> *I dip and I surge and I swing*
> *In the rip of the racing tide,*
> *By the gates of doom I sing,*
> *On the horns of death I ride.*

Nancy cleared her throat. There was no one else in the house. Clayton was still at school and Mavis was at the lodge. Roy had gone back to the barn. Nancy began to read out loud, hesitantly at first and then falling into the rhythm of the lines:

> *"They christened my brother of old—*
> *And a saintly name he bears—"*

The telephone rang and Nancy jumped. Who would be calling now, in the middle of the day? She felt a tremor in her stomach as she walked toward the hall and lifted the receiver.

"Nancy?" Her husband's voice, scratchy with distance, sucked the air from her lungs. She pictured him in the basement of the museum, a bird turned inside out like a mitten on the table before him. He cleared his throat, and when he spoke again, he sounded guarded. "How's your grandfather?"

She glanced at the still form on the daybed as her heart beat against her ribs. "Not well. About the same."

There was a pause. Did he miss her? she wondered. Was he hoping she was no longer needed? She listened to the clicking echo of the phone line. "How long are you going to stay there?" Robert asked.

"I don't know." Why didn't he tell her what *he* wanted? Why didn't he ask her to come home? "Until he's better, I guess. Or until . . ." She couldn't say it. "Until we know more."

"Well, they're sending me to the Smithsonian." It came out abruptly, harshly. "In Washington, D.C. For a month or two. A new species account . . ."

The floor of the hall seemed to open beneath her feet like a trap door. She felt herself falling and put a hand against the wall.

". . . with the U.S. Biological Survey," he was saying. "Mayr wants a holotype." She couldn't go back to Boston, Nancy thought. He wouldn't be there.

A crackling emptiness hung between them on the line. Then he added, "And you're busy with your family. You weren't happy here. I don't flatter myself you'll miss me."

You're leaving me behind! While my grandfather's dying! A buzzing like cicadas filled her head. She opened her mouth. Her throat felt clogged, as if with sand.

"If you need to get in touch," he said, "you can contact the museum."

Stunned, she put the receiver back in the cradle and stood in the shadowed hall with her hands slack at her side. The house seemed empty, hollowed out like her chest. After a moment she went back to her seat beside the daybed. She studied her grandfather's face. He lay as unmoving as before.

———

Scudder was sleeping when Mavis came home from Washington Lodge. Nancy left the chair where she'd spent most of the day and sat with her aunt at the kitchen table, waiting for the water to boil for tea. Mavis slipped her feet out of her shoes with a sigh. Her husband had left her in Ohio, Nancy knew, but she had never thought much about Mavis's marriage. She wondered now how Mavis had learned he was leaving her. Had he told her as he was walking out the door? Had he written her a note? Or maybe he had simply not come back.

Years before, when Nancy was a child and used to visit Fire Neck with her mother, a couple named Waldron had lived on Oyster Lane, near Starke's Boatyard. The husband raised chickens, breeds like Orpingtons and Black Minorcas, and a flock of guinea hens. The guinea hens were loud and shrieked at night when it was windy, and the halyards on the boats slapped against the masts. One night the Waldrons had a terrible fight. The wife marched out to the hen yard in her nightgown and rubber boots and shot the whole flock with her husband's shotgun. Nancy remembered the adults talking about it in scandalized, delighted whispers. The noise! The feathers! The gun! Until now, Nancy had never stopped to wonder what the husband had said afterward, back inside the house, and how the wife, in her blood-splattered nightgown, had answered him. Because the Waldrons continued to live there for several more years, before they moved somewhere out East. She hadn't left him, and he hadn't left her. People said they were always fighting about something. They had three children, younger than Nancy, with ash-blond hair, who played cheerfully at the boatyard among the wood shavings.

And there were the Whitneys, on Koos Neck Road, who supposedly hadn't spoken a word to each other in twenty years. They were rumored to eat every meal together at the dining-room table and to communicate through their housemaid.

Nancy hadn't paid much attention to her own parents' marriage. Expansive, good-humored, older than her mother, her father was often away on business trips. Nancy remembered sensing early on that her mother treated him a bit like a child. What had surprised Nancy most, the first time he took her to the big, gleaming office where he worked, was the deference everyone showed him. His secretary made a fuss over Nancy, giving her a pencil to draw with and a lollipop, while an important-looking man in a dark suit tried to interest her father in a sheaf of papers, bending toward him earnestly while her father laughed, not unkindly, and shook his head. At home, around her mother, he always spoke in slightly hushed tones, ceding to her wishes about the fountain she wanted built in the side garden, a trip she didn't care to take. Nancy realized now that he must have been concerned about her miscarriages, maybe even felt guilty. She'd seen him watch her mother brush her hair in front of the mirrored dresser; he had followed the sweeping motion of her hand with fond and anxious eyes.

Why hadn't anyone counseled her to wait? But she was the one who'd wanted to rush, she thought miserably. "Why is it so hard to be married?" she said out loud.

Mavis looked up with a shocked expression, and tea splashed from the flowered pot in her hands. Nancy wished at once she could take the words back. How stupid of her to say something like that, given her aunt's unhappy experience. Flustered, she rose from the table. "I'll check on the woodstove," she called over her shoulder.

———————

Mavis sat holding the teapot. So that was it, she thought. The poor, poor girl. She remembered her own husband, the wet tips of his mustache, his drunken mouth, his predatory nocturnal advances. There had been no one for her to confide in, no one to protect her. She thought of her niece's husband, who'd seemed so mild-mannered. But Mavis had learned that you could never tell, from the surface.

Roy found himself watching Judith Purlowe's house. He noticed when she opened the curtains in the morning and when the lights went out in the kitchen at night. From the house on Salt Hay Road he couldn't see the window of the back bedroom where he imagined she slept. For that he'd have needed to walk down to the pond, something he wouldn't allow himself to do. He had not been inside the cottage since he'd dropped off the duck and scalded his hand with coffee. When he saw that the woodpile along the side of her house was dwindling, he brought over a wheelbarrow full of split logs, first waiting until he knew she'd left for town. The next day she came across the field to thank him, and they stood looking at the barn together while he explained how he had a hundred pheasant eggs in two incubators and wanted to get chicken wire around the old dog runs before they hatched. Pheasants panicked easily, he told her, and he'd need to shade the pens with branches and matting to keep them from getting spooked. He rambled on too long, half afraid that she would ask him over for coffee. But she merely thanked him again for the wood and said she'd come back to see the chicks, before turning toward the cottage alone. Roy watched her ambling walk. She had on the same gray overcoat and long skirt. Her dark hair snaked in the wind, and he saw her hand go up to her face and brush it away. When she reached her door, he turned back to the barn so that she wouldn't see him staring after her.

The next evening, setting the table for dinner, Mavis said, "I see our neighbor has an admirer."

Roy's face grew hot. He turned away, toward the pantry, as if looking for more napkins. Was he so transparent? he wondered. He would have to give Mavis more credit. "I don't know what you're talking about," he muttered, stalling for time.

"Oh, Roy, of course you know Mrs. Purlowe. The Captain's niece. The widow. She has an admirer. Someone from the boatyard. They were chatting over the fence for nearly an hour yesterday."

Roy's chest tightened. He felt a coldness spread along the back of his neck.

"I don't see the appeal, myself," Mavis went on, setting down the salad bowl with a thump, "considering the way she wears her hair. But a man who guts fish all day can't be choosy."

All through the meal Roy found it difficult to concentrate. The food tasted dry and chalky in his mouth. "Pass the *salt*, Roy," Mavis asked him for the third time. After dinner he tried to read the paper without succeeding. Finally, he gave up.

Upstairs, he changed into a pressed blue shirt. Before leaving the house, he ducked into the pantry and scanned the shelves, looking for something that might serve as a pretext for visiting Judith Purlowe. The shelves were dusty, with wide spaces between the jars of preserves that Mavis had put up the summer before. Roy grabbed one at random.

It was dark as he started across the field, a night with no moon, and the stars seemed closer than he'd ever seen them. Behind him the clatter of dishes in the kitchen died away. He hadn't said where he was going, letting Mavis assume he was checking on the incubators before turning in. He felt ridiculous, sneaking across the field under cover of darkness. The smell of daffodils reached him as he neared the cottage. The glass jar was cool and heavy in his hands.

He knocked, and Judith opened the door. She did not seem surprised to see him so late at night. "Come in," she said, and Roy ducked into the cramped, familiar kitchen. The same mess of bags and papers was strewn across the table. The air smelled of strong coffee and faintly, still, of cats. He held out the jar.

Judith reached to accept it, and Roy felt the same prickling awareness of her hand almost touching his. " 'Chokecherry jelly,' " she read. "Thank you. I've never tried that." Roy remembered the flavor of the jam suddenly and why there was still so much of it. Mavis had scorched it slightly and it had a burned aftertaste that lingered in the mouth.

"I hope you like it," he said. "A bit of an acquired taste."

"Shall I make some toast to put it on?"

Roy nodded, determined not to run this time. Judith moved to the counter and began to slice a loaf of bread. He took off his jacket and placed it deliberately on the back of his chair.

"Are you settling in here?" His voice was scratchy. He cleared his throat. "Making friends?"

"Oh sure," Judith said. "Now that the cats are gone." She turned and smiled her wide, generous smile, and Roy's heart rolled over in his chest, a dog doing tricks.

They ate the jelly on toast, sitting at the kitchen table. Roy finished two slices very quickly, hardly tasting them. He stopped himself reaching for a third and looked instead at Judith, buttering a slice of bread from a butter dish covered in crumbs. Her fine-boned, narrow face was etched with thin lines. He realized he knew nothing about where she'd come from or what her life had been like before she arrived at the Captain's cottage in the dead of winter. He wondered most about her husband.

"You must miss the people you knew," he ventured.

She nodded. Roy's heart sank. He thought of Grace Perdue and his own insane grief.

"And your husband." It was a question. Roy felt it pulled out of him. He was hardly sure, for a moment, where the words had come from.

Judith tilted her head. "Yes. I was living at his sister's when I got the letter about this place. I don't miss that." She looked up and gave a small smile.

"What did he do?" Roy persisted. "I mean, what line of work?"

Judith sat back in her chair and sighed. "He wanted to be a sailor. But he ended up working in the mines, like his brothers. He wasn't lucky, that's how he saw it. He always drew the short straw." She looked down at her hands. "Six of them were trapped the day the tunnel caved in. Four made it out."

She glanced up, and her eyes caught his and held them, calmly but without smiling. Roy felt the room fold around them like a tent.

"I'm sorry," he said. He leaned forward as he spoke, and it was unclear whether he meant he was sorry about the loss of her husband or the fact that he was kissing her in spite of it.

In the house on Salt Hay Road Nancy sat by Scudder's bed in the living room, stoking the fire and reading aloud from his volume of Kipling. She wanted him to eat another bite of rice pudding, but he kept his mouth closed when she prodded him gently with the spoon. Nancy thought his face looked firmer than when she'd arrived. Perhaps, she cautioned herself, she'd only grown used to his changed appearance.

Packing for Long Island in a hurry, Nancy hadn't brought much besides her black wool dress and black shoes. No one at that point had expected Scudder to last more than a few days. That had been nearly six weeks ago, and now the snow had melted and water dripped from the eaves. For two days she hadn't been outside; it had been too wet and muddy. Nancy thought of her rubber boots and, more wistfully, of her riding clothes, unused in the closet of the apartment in Boston since the cost of hiring a horse had turned out to be so great. Now there was no one to ask to mail them. Robert had sent a brief note to let her know he'd arrived in D.C. Reading it in her up-stairs room, she thought of the letters he'd sent before they were married. She remembered the thrill she'd felt the first time she saw her name scrawled in his handwriting, how she'd hung around the post office, the drafts she'd gone through, perfecting her replies. And this was what it had all been leading up to, she thought miserably. In her mind she studied their courtship, looking for the flaw.

As a child, she'd loved to watch her father light the fire in the big living-room fireplace. There would be a layer of crumpled newspaper, one of kindling, and then the logs balanced on top. Her father always rearranged them once or twice, as if to align them in precisely the right configuration. Then he knelt down with the box of matches in his hand. It looked like a magic trick: her father held the match and flicked his wrist and the flame burst out, like a scarf from a magician's throat. One afternoon when she was supposed to be napping, she slipped out of bed and found the matches she'd seen her nanny hide in the bathroom. She crumpled a few pages of her drawing paper and set them in the middle of the rug. Two small chairs taken from her dollhouse approximated the kindling. Kneeling, she dragged the red head of the match across the scratchy side of the box. Nothing happened. She tried again, this time mimicking the flourish of her father's wrist. A tiny orange flame appeared, a genie conjured out of a lamp. Delighted, she watched the flame creep down the matchstick until it singed her fingers and she had to drop it. The next match she held close to the paper. She watched, immensely proud of herself, as the flame climbed the edge of one crumpled sheet and jumped to the next. The doll's chair blazed and blackened. Then the rug began to smolder. The smoke made her cough. A moment later the bed skirt blazed. Nancy backed toward the door. As her pillow began to burn, she left the room, careful to close the door behind her. In the hallway she stood still for a moment, wondering what to do next. She was playing on the swing set when the fire trucks arrived.

What struck her now was neither her irresponsibility nor her fascination with the sight of her bed in flames, but her certainty that, by shutting the door, she had solved her part of the problem.

Nancy remembered getting off the ferry at Drowned Meadow and catching sight of Clayton in his outgrown pants and Roy, smiling as they strode toward her, calling her name. Returning to Fire Neck had been an escape, a way to turn her back on the mess she'd left in Boston. As a child she had set the fire in her room deliberately before walking out and closing the door. Now her marriage felt like a burning house, but she couldn't understand how it had happened.

She felt angry with herself, restless. The kitchen was quiet; Mavis had finished putting away the dishes and gone upstairs to bed. Clayton would be asleep already, no doubt dreaming about beetles or the salt marsh. The clock ticked in the hall. The portable typewriter she'd brought downstairs sat on the little side table. Nancy aligned a fresh piece of paper along the back edge and cranked it into place. She glanced at her grandfather, motionless under the wool blanket; the sound had not disturbed him. She sat up straight and pushed back her shoulders. *Dear Sirs*, she typed briskly, *We are happy to inform you that in the matter of . . . Robert, in my dreams you stare out the window, missing me, and you eat your lunch sad that I am gone . . .*

She backed the carriage up and x'd out the words one by one.

The last day she'd spent in Boston the city itself had seemed hostile because of their stupid quarrel. There were people everywhere she turned and not one familiar face. The strangers looked through her, as if she were made of vapor, and she'd felt again, acutely, the loss of nerve she'd experienced at the museum party in October, the sense of not belonging. It was dark by the time Robert came home from work. She sat at the window, looking out at the streetlights and the dark figures hurrying past. When she recognized him, the way he held his face up to the night air, his stride, she ducked into the kitchen. She didn't want him to know she had been waiting.

She hammered on the keys again. *I'm sorry I told you I wasn't happy. I don't care about the apartment at all. I love you and I know we can make a better go of it. I thought we were going to have a baby but now we aren't and Robert I wish it hadn't all gone wrong . . .* Nancy pulled the paper from the typewriter and crumpled it into a ball smaller than her fist. She felt a perverse satisfaction in the waste of paper.

She threaded a fresh sheet into the typewriter. *Dear Robert, Thank you for your letter. I hope you can appreciate how needed I am here. My grandfather is about the same.*

But Scudder was not the same. She hadn't said this to any-one, in case she was mistaken. He had been eating more and his grip had grown stronger. Several times she thought she felt him squeeze her hand. That afternoon his eyes had opened and rested on her. And then they had widened, ever so slightly. Nancy was sure that he'd known who she was.

Nancy folded the letter and put it in an envelope. It was nearly midnight. She leaned over and gripped her grandfather's knobby shoulder. "Good night," she whispered into his still face. "I'm going upstairs, but don't worry. I'm here."

Roy woke in the dark. For a moment he did not know where he was. A woman's warm, bare hip was pressed against his thigh. It felt so strange he could hardly credit it.

Lying in Judith's bed, he thought of a night in his wild youth when he had gotten drunk with his friend Wes Hart and Wes's brother Garrett. The three of them had made twenty dollars each unloading boxes down by Indian Landing under cover of darkness. No one said anything about the contents, but they all knew there was booze inside. It must have been two in the morning by the time they were through, and the man in charge—they never learned his name—slipped them each a bottle of bad whiskey. They'd gone to a house Garrett knew about over in Moriches. Roy didn't remember the girl he'd gone upstairs with, only that the laces of his boot had snarled and he'd sawed through them with a pocketknife to the sound of her high-pitched laughter. He woke up wet and cold in the bottom of a rowboat, his temples throbbing. A strange, persist-ent barking rang in his brain. Overhead, the dawn sky loomed fresh and pink. He reached for the oarlocks and gingerly pulled himself up till he could peer over the gunwale. White ducks surrounded him as far as he could see; thousands upon thousands of ducks, all of them quacking from their orange bills. He was adrift in a rowboat at Epher Brown's duck farm, on the east side of the river.

Judith Purlowe shifted in her sleep, and Roy felt her hair brush against his shoulder. In the barn, the pheasant chicks would be pressed together under the low brooding lights. He remembered the little bolt he'd convinced himself had gone missing from the engine of his being, that day in the middle of the Great South Bay. It seemed to him now that the problem might just as easily be something different. A little dirt in the carburetor, he thought to himself, and grinned in the dark, like an idiot.

Clayton pulled open the thick curtains, and the yellow morning light streamed into the aviary at Washington Lodge. The birds rustled and squawked in their cages. He was giving the last piece of sliced apple to the gray parrot when the gardener stopped by outside, leaning on the open window. Stooped and wizened, his hands seamed with dirt, he cared for the grounds with a jealous tenderness and waged constant war on crabgrass, beetles, and the moles he killed in steel traps and whose perforated bodies Clayton sometimes found on the compost heap, their gray fur like ripped velvet. The gardener usually kept to the grounds, but today Mr. Washington was away on business and he had felt like chatting. He and his cousin had gone up the Barto River in a rowboat and found a mass of watercress, he told Clayton. "I could grow it in the pond here, but the ducks would foul it." Mr. Washington kept a flock of fulvous tree ducks that had the run of the grounds and roosted at night in the orchard.

Walking home with the sun on his face, Clayton wondered if Roy would take him upriver for watercress. His uncle was different lately, and it seemed to Clayton in his innermost heart that he himself might somehow have effected the change. Roy had confided in him. He noticed him more. When he'd started up the pheasant business, before he even ordered the eggs, he'd asked for Clayton's help. Maybe Roy would take him upriver. He started to run, hoping his uncle was home.

Clayton burst into the kitchen of the house on Salt Hay Road, his chest heaving. Roy sat at the table with the newspaper. "There's watercress upriver!" Clayton cried. Mavis looked up from the sink in surprise, and Roy put down his paper. Embarrassed, Clayton felt his neck flush.

Then Roy said, "Well, don't just sit there, woman!" Winking at Clayton, he stood and drained his coffee with a show of haste. "Organize the provisions." He put his cup in the sink. "There's watercress to hunt."

Roy headed for the boatyard to ask Sam Burnett if they could borrow a boat. Mavis, grumbling, began to pack a picnic lunch. "What have you done to your uncle?" she asked Clayton. "You know he's not a man for the water." Clayton shrugged, grinning, and ran out to the shed for buckets and pails. It wasn't his imagination, he thought; even his aunt had noticed that Roy had changed. Clayton moved quickly, knocking over a can of nails in his haste.

He was in the kitchen helping Mavis with the hamper when Nancy came downstairs looking sleepy. "We're hunting watercress. In the boat," Clayton told her. "Hurry up."

Roy whistled from across the field and waved for them to join him.

"Shouldn't someone stay here?" Nancy nodded toward the living room.

Clayton shook his head. He grabbed at her hand and pulled her, expansive in his happiness. "He's sleeping. Come on. We need you."

They made their way through the boatyard to the dock where Sam's boat was tied, and Clayton jumped in and held out his hand to help his sister. A group of ducks swam over and eyed them meaningfully, hoping for bread. "Shoo," said Mavis, to no effect. She waved her hands at them. The ducks, thinking she was throwing something, swam closer, and Nancy caught Clayton's eye and grinned.

Roy and Clayton took turns rowing while Nancy sat in the bow and shaded her eyes against the sunlight. In the stern, Mavis clutched the hamper that held their lunch. The single glossy feather in her black hat jerked in the air above her head to the motion of the oars. She faced straight ahead; like her brother, she disliked boats.

They passed Big Fish Creek, Runny Nose Creek, an osprey nest high in a dead tree. Roy pulled on the oars, leaning forward, and Clayton watched the water swirl around them, making a pattern on the surface of the river.

The tide was high, and when they came to the narrow railroad bridge, it looked at first to Clayton as if they wouldn't fit under it. "Heads down," Roy called. They bent low in the boat as Roy guided them underneath the trestles. Between the wooden beams Clayton saw the mud nests of barn swallows. As the rowboat floated by, stirring the air, the hatchlings rose in their nests and flung open their yellow beaks like clusters of blooming flowers.

Clayton spotted the watercress past the bridge on the east side, in a stretch of shallow water near the bank. They collected it by hand, filling buckets and wicker baskets with dripping green leaves and stems. Roy and Clayton chewed it while they worked. Mavis stayed in the boat, unwilling to take off her shoes. In less than twenty minutes they had enough for both their house and Washington Lodge, as well as a basket for Sam Burnett and one for Judith Purlowe.

"That's enough," said Mavis. "Unless you want watercress soup for a month."

On the way back downriver they stopped at Indian Landing for lunch. Clayton jumped off first, still barefoot, and pulled the rowboat up onto the sand. Roy helped Mavis off, and she spread the picnic blanket on a grassy spot under the cherry tree, with a view of the river.

Mavis unpacked the hamper while Nancy poured lemonade. It felt to Clayton as though his sister had never really left them, her marriage a brief folly for which they could now forgive her. They ate cold venison with yellow tomato preserves and Spanish pickles, spring salad, cornbread, and molasses cookies. The sun fell through the trees in dappled shades of green. Clayton finished the last of the cookies and sat back, watching a great blue heron on the opposite bank unfold its wings and launch itself into the air. Roy got up and disappeared into the woods. Mavis began to sing, almost under her breath, and Clayton was surprised to hear Nancy join in. It was a song he remembered their mother singing, "My Darling Clementine."

Roy came back and sat beside the hamper on the flattened grass. He put his fist to his mouth and coughed into it, loudly clearing his throat. Mavis and Nancy had finished the song and were packing up the lunch things. Roy coughed again, and Clayton looked up at him, his daydreams pierced by a sudden concern.

"Can you breathe?" asked Mavis sharply. Roy shook his head, red in the face. He gave another long hacking cough, covering his mouth, and the next moment a small brown bird shot out of his hand. Clayton let out a strangled yelp. Mavis dropped the jar of pickles. They stared in astonishment as the bird flew into the bushes.

"There," Roy said. "I *thought* I had something caught in my throat." He collapsed forward onto his elbows, shaking with laughter. A joke, Clayton realized, more amazed by this revelation than by the sight of the bird issuing from Roy's mouth. His uncle had played a joke on them!

"What in the world . . ." said Nancy. Mavis stared at her brother, then at the bushes where the bird had flown, then back at Roy. Tears streamed down his cheeks.

"Marsh wren," Roy said, wiping his eyes. "I found a nest." His cheeks and ears were red from laughing. He doubled over again. "If you could see your faces!"

In the still, hot afternoon, trapped in the living room, Scudder was thinking about clams: the salty flavor of the raw flesh in his mouth, like eating gobbets of the sea itself. Back when his children were young, he'd treaded for clams on the bay on summer afternoons. Waist-deep in water, he felt along the bottom of the bay with his bare feet for the smooth shapes of cherrystones and little necks while his wife fixed lunch and the children played on the deck of the catboat and splashed along the side. Laughing, he held up a rock he'd mistaken for a clam and showed it to Roy, who frowned and turned it over in his little hand.

In his daybed by the cold woodstove, fear started with a ripple, like a cat's-paw on the surface of a bay: What if he never left this bed in the downstairs parlor? He could feel himself settling, a ship on a sandbar, another hulk destined for the breaker's yard. He thought of the motto they'd joked about in the

Life Saver's station house: *You have to go out, but you don't have to come back*. Setting his jaw, he pushed himself out into the fear like a lifeboat into the running surf.

The family ate a late crab dinner in the kitchen that night. The windows were open. Clayton could hear the katydids, the moths bumbling against the screen. Out in the field the fireflies were beginning to appear. The family ate without speaking, cracking the shells between their teeth and picking out the flesh. It was a messy meal, and the table was spread with newspaper. Near Clayton's plate a headline read NOTES FOR A GEOGRAPHY OF MORALS, and he wondered at the strangeness of the phrase. The table was quiet except for the snapping of crab claws and the clattering of discarded shells into the bucket on the floor. When Clayton heard a muffled bumping from the living room, he thought at first that it was one of Roy's dogs trying to get through the side door. He looked up from his plate. There stood his grandfather, gripping the frame of the doorway with his bony hands. The old man braced himself against the wall. His white hair was stiff and uneven, his face tight with effort. His eyes blinked in the soft light of the kitchen. Clayton dropped the crab he had been holding, and it banged against his plate. The others looked up. There was a moment of complete silence before Nancy cried out and Mavis staggered from her seat, upsetting the bucket of discarded crab shells. Roy bent to help her pick them up. Nancy threw her arms around Scudder just as his knees gave out. In that moment of chaos a look passed between Clayton and the old man. He caught the triumph in Scudder's ancient eyes.

That night as he lay in his bed Clayton thought to himself that he had watched his grandfather rise from the dead.

———

Nancy wrote to Robert first thing the next morning. The typewriter seemed too formal, so she used a pen and told him the good news in sloppy haste. Buoyant with happiness, she realized how much her grandfather's coldness about her marriage had weighed on her. Now he was better. She'd stayed in Fire Neck far longer than she'd meant to, but it had been worth it. And maybe Robert had missed her, she thought; maybe the time apart had been good for both of them and everything would seem easy once they saw each other again. She remembered the dark bedroom of their apartment in Boston, and the time she'd shaken Robert awake, convinced she could hear a rooster crowing in the street; he'd taken her in his arms and explained in a sleep-slurred whisper that Boston was plagued by roosters, it was a terrible epidemic, and no one could stop it because the mayor himself was a famous chicken fancier. He began to shake, and she realized he was laughing and hit him with her pillow. They had not gone back to sleep.

Robert's brief reply arrived two days later. Home from the Smithsonian, he offered to come down to Long Island from Boston and escort her back. He wrote that he was happy to hear of her grandfather's *remarkable recovery*. What did he mean by putting it that way? Nancy thought. Flat on the page, the uninflected phrase conjured up a vision of Robert's sardonic face, one eyebrow slightly raised. It seemed to mock not only her former anxiety but also her present relief. She wondered suddenly if he had doubted Scudder's decline in the first place. Did her husband actually suspect her of fabricating it?

From the kitchen came the sound of Roy and Scudder talking. Nancy left the porch, the screen door slapping behind her, and strode blindly across the yard. As a girl she'd once walked into a glass door at a birthday party. Distracted by the balloons on the lawn, she'd turned toward the porch with her paper cup of lemonade and smacked right into it. The lemonade spilled down the front of her red party dress and soaked her white socks. Worse than the pain was the shock of finding glass where she'd expected air. Someone's sympathetic mother patted her with a napkin as the other children stared. Nancy, dazed, felt obscurely wronged. The helpful mother tried to press a cold towel to the bump on her forehead, but Nancy pushed away, humiliated by her mistake and by the lemonade on her socks and the way it looked as if she'd wet herself. In her distress everything around her seemed unjust, from the door to the woman with the cold towel, even the clown out the window on the lawn surrounded by pink and white balloons.

Still holding Robert's letter, she passed the woodpile and skirted the edge of the pond. She was too shocked even to cry. All her shame about her own behavior evaporated in a blaze of indignation. When she most needed his sympathy, her husband had not even believed her. She couldn't imagine telling him now how she'd thought she was pregnant, how she had suffered on the train. He might think she'd made that up as well.

Her feet were wet. Looking around, she realized she'd walked out onto the marsh, following one of the trails made by the deer. She supposed her brother would be familiar with the place, but she herself had never come this way. Around her on all sides stretched the thick marsh grass. It grew lush and coarse, springy under her feet, pushed by the tide and the wind into clumps like cowlicks. Standing on it, Nancy imagined the hide of an enormous animal that had been licking its vivid fur. The warm breeze carried the smell of brine. In the distance the sun flashed on the river. Still and green, the marsh seemed, to Nancy, as far from the apartment in Boston as she could get.

Maybe she wouldn't go back at all, she thought angrily. Maybe she'd stay here on Salt Hay Road.

Just like Mavis, a small voice whispered. At that, Nancy rallied. Of course she had to return. She wouldn't hide any longer. She would go back to Boston and make the best of it. She thought, melodramatically, of soldiers returning to the front after their leave was over. But she would not allow her husband to treat her like a package that needed to be delivered; she could make her own travel arrangements.

Nancy walked back across the marsh and along the pond to the house. Upstairs she typed a quick, stiff note, telling Robert she would return by herself on the following Tuesday. She chose the date at random, wanting the certainty of something specific. *Your assistance*, she wrote, banging on the keys, *is not required.*

She might as well go riding, she reasoned, having given herself so little time left on Salt Hay Road. Going into the barn for Buckshot's saddle, she found Clayton wrestling a long roll of wire down the stairs from the hayloft. He was helping Roy mend a hole in the dog kennel. Looking up, he grinned at her, straw in his hair. Nancy, anxious to get it over with, said quickly, "I'm going back to Boston." She held up the letter she'd just written to her husband. "On Tuesday."

Clayton rested the wire on the cement floor of the barn. His gaze seemed to flatten.

"I can't stay here forever!" Nancy snapped. "Grandfather's better now." She hadn't expected any sympathy from her brother, and yet she wished he would say something. "And I'm married, Clay. Everyone seems to forget that."

Clayton didn't answer. He picked the wire back up and began to drag it toward the corner of the barn, as if she had already gone.

The next day, Clayton decided to show Nancy one of his best-kept secrets, something they didn't have inside a museum. When she asked where they were going, he told her it was a surprise. They walked together across the field with the sun on their faces. The warm air smelled of dry grass and, as they neared the boatyard, hot tar. At the boat shed, Clayton asked Sam for the loan of a rowboat, "to go to Knowles Point." Sam motioned with his chin toward a fish carcass discarded beneath the cleaning table, and Clayton seized it by the tail, disturbing a cloud of flies. Nancy made a face. "What do you want that for?" She would see, he told her, clutching the fish, an ace up his sleeve.

The fish carcass lay in the dirty water on the bottom of the rowboat, its tail moving slightly with the motion of the oars. On the other side of Knowles Point the remains of a sunken boat stuck above the water. Clayton brought the rowboat up alongside the gunwale. It was one of his and Perry's favorite places, and today the tide was just right. The half-submerged boat was slick with green-black algae. It listed forward, the stern protruding. In the dark water of the cockpit, beneath the overhang of the remaining deck, half a dozen snapping turtles craned their thick necks toward them. "There!" Clayton exclaimed. A snapping turtle could bite a broomstick handle clear through, even take a man's hand off at the wrist. "Aren't they beauties?" Black and gleaming, the turtles sat nearly motionless in the bilge of the ruined boat. "Watch this." Clayton picked the fish carcass up from the bottom of the rowboat by the tail and flung it over the side of the wreck. It fell among the snapping turtles, and there was a thrashing of thick limbs as they churned around it. The turtles lashed and snapped, and a shiver ran up Clayton's arms. Nancy stared. In a moment every shred of fish had disappeared. Clayton sat back, his hands on the oars, and glanced at his sister.

She stared back at him, perplexed. The look on her face was one of confusion, touched with distaste. It was clear that the turtles did not interest her. Clayton lifted the oars. In silence he rowed his sister back across the river.

Over the next few days Nancy tried to broach the subject of her departure with Scudder. He grew stronger by the day and would sit on the porch overlooking the marsh for hours, as long as Nancy sat with him. One warm day she helped him outside to a chair she'd set in a shady patch of the lawn and trimmed his still thick white hair. "I felt myself going under," he told her gruffly. "Like a derelict ship. But I knew you'd come home. I couldn't do it."

She laughed nervously. "I think it was all the Kipling."

Now they sat on the porch drinking lemonade. The thick, humid air smelled sweetly of overgrown privet. Neither of them had made any mention of her marriage or the fact that she was expected back in Boston. He'd taught her to play cribbage, and as she won yet again, it dawned on her that he'd been throwing the games in her favor.

"I'd better get back to my husband soon," she told him, trying to make it into a little joke. "Before he forgets all about me!"

"Your turn to shuffle," Scudder said.

Nancy tried again. "I'll write to you from Boston. Will you promise to write back, to tell me how you're doing?"

Scudder picked up his cards and fanned them out. "You don't know how much your brother missed you." He stared at his hand as if disappointed with it. "Poor motherless kid."

On Tuesday the ferry to Drowned Meadow came and went without Nancy. In the house on Salt Hay Road, no one asked about her plans. Mavis set her place at the table as usual, and afterward she and Clayton washed the dishes. Nancy wrote to Robert, explaining that she'd been delayed. He would have to wait a little longer, she told herself. She imagined him coming home from the museum to an empty apartment, whistling as he took off his hat in the hall. He'd fry himself an egg for dinner and eat it standing at the counter, and then he'd sit by the window, because he liked the evening air, and read the *Journal of Field Ornithology*, not thinking about her at all.

Three weeks later a telegram arrived for Nancy. She read it in the kitchen, where Clayton was eating a bowl of Grape-Nuts with cream. "Robert's coming down tomorrow," she said, half to herself. Clayton stopped chewing. He sat still, braced for the inevitable. "Why don't you come back to Boston with me?" Nancy asked brightly, as if the idea had just occurred to her. "You could come for a visit, just a few weeks. You wouldn't be missing any school." She sat down next to Clayton and put her arm around his shoulder. "I'll take you to the park and we can ride the swan boats."

Clayton shook his head. "I have to help with the pheasants. And I'm working for Mr. Greaves and Mr. Washington."

Nancy sighed. She tilted her head until it was just brushing his. "I'll miss you."

Clayton, relieved that she was not going to insist, patted her stiffly on the hand. But a familiar tightness gripped his lungs. He felt the way he had on his first day of school at Fire Neck Elementary, standing by the doorway of the strange classroom as Nancy spoke with a formidable-looking teacher in a black suit that reminded him of the men at their mother's funeral. He'd known she had her own school to go to, and that she would be late herself, but all the time she talked, he kept his eyes fastened on her, ignoring the whispers of the unknown children at their desks, half believing he could will her not to leave him.

It did not take Nancy long to pack. She carried her small suitcase down the stairs and set it on the floor in the living room, where it was visible from Scudder's bed. His eyes lingered on it, but neither of them said anything. After dinner they played cribbage and ate the orange charlotte that Mavis made in honor of Nancy's departure.

That night, asleep in her single bed, Nancy dreamed of carrying her brother in her arms. In the dream he was very small again, a baby as light as a laundry basket.

Clayton was on the roof, smoking a cattail cigar and looking through the Captain's deck of pornographic playing cards, when his brother-in-law arrived. Mavis had left for the lodge already, after saying a tearful goodbye and packing a large picnic lunch for Nancy and Robert to share on the ferry. Clayton ducked his head and shoved the deck of cards into his pocket. In a minute he would come down to say goodbye to Nancy. In the meantime, he didn't want to reveal his hiding place. He heard Robert knock on the side door, the one that led into the kitchen, and then call Nancy's name. No one answered. From where Clayton sat on the roof, he could just see the top of Robert's head. He remembered hearing that soldiers in besieged castles had dumped boiling oil on the enemy from above.

"Hello?" he heard Robert call again. "Nancy?" The silence stretched on. Clayton shifted his elbow. He wondered what was taking his sister so long. There was another, louder knock. "Nancy?" he heard Robert say. "Anyone home?" After a moment Clayton heard the squeak of the kitchen door opening. "Nancy?" came Robert's voice again, sounding hollow. The door slammed shut. Moving quickly, Clayton slipped down the wisteria trellis and into the yard.

Just as he straightened up, Robert came back out of the house. "Clayton!" he cried, his face brightening. "I was getting worried. It's like a ghost town here." He looked smaller than Clayton remembered him, his face young and tired. Since he'd seen him last, at the wedding, Robert had slowly changed in Clayton's mind into a comic-book villain, with heavy brows and a thick neck. Confronted with the real person, Clayton found himself disarmed. Robert had brought him a present. "It's in here somewhere," he said, fumbling in his bag and pulling out a dented cardboard box. Inside was a yellow model airplane with red silk wings. Clayton stared at it in surprise. He had never been particularly interested in model planes, but this one was undeniably beautiful. Framed in wire, it was twice the length of his palm and looked like it could really fly. He pulled it through the air above his head, testing the wings.

"How's your grandfather?" Robert asked Clayton. "I hear he's better?"

"*Now* he is," Clayton said. "You should have seen him a few weeks ago." He felt grown-up, having witnessed his grandfather's brush with death firsthand. Lowering his voice slightly,

Clayton used an expression he'd recently learned. "He almost *bought the farm*." He was gratified to see Robert's eyes widen.

"I didn't realize it was that serious," Robert said, after a moment. He seemed suddenly impatient. "Where's your sister?"

"Inside."

"I didn't see her."

"I'll get her." Clayton ducked into the house, still holding the plane. The kitchen was empty. In the living room Scudder lay on the daybed, sleeping or pretending to sleep. Nancy's suitcase stood at the foot of the stairs. Clayton called for her. There was no answer. Upstairs, her room was empty, the sheets stripped from the bed. Clayton peered into the other rooms, one by one. They were all empty. He felt a prickling on his arms; supposing she had vanished, he thought.

Standing in his own room, Clayton heard a faint movement above him, like the darting of a squirrel. Very quietly, his heart pounding, he climbed the narrow stairs to the attic. Outside the door he stood and listened. There was a rustling sound and a tap, as of a finger resting against a windowpane. Clayton reached forward to open the door. The lock caught, holding it closed. In a moment there was a thud and the door thumped in its frame and he realized that Nancy had thrown herself against it. They stood on either side of the door. Clayton could hear his sister's breathing. "Robert's here," he said. He felt frightened without understanding why. It seemed important to act as if everything was normal.

There was a long pause. "I'll be down in just a minute," Nancy said at last. Clayton felt his lungs empty with relief. "Go tell him that."

Coming downstairs, Clayton could see his brother-in-law in the kitchen, fiddling with the brim of his hat. He looked up at the sound of Clayton's footsteps, his face creased. Clayton hardened his heart. As far as he was concerned, it was Robert's fault that Nancy had left them and moved to Boston. They had been happy until Robert came along, uninvited, and broke the family up. "She's in the attic," he said.

Robert's expression tightened. "What's she doing there?"

Clayton shrugged his shoulders. "She wouldn't tell me." This was not a lie, exactly.

Robert stepped toward the stairs. "Don't go up," Clayton told him quickly. "She's locked herself in. She said she'd come down when she was ready."

Robert hesitated. He looked toward the stairs and moved from one foot to the other. Clayton had the momentary fear that the man might cry, though he felt sure this was ridiculous.

"If you bother her," Clayton added, "it'll just make things worse."

It was lunchtime, and Clayton felt hungry. He wasn't used to playing host. "There's bread in here," he said, "if you want some." Robert stopped toying with his hat and put it on the counter. He stood in the doorway leading into the living room while Clayton got out a plate of cold venison and the pot of mustard and made them each a sandwich. They ate in silence. Every few minutes Robert glanced at his watch.

After they'd eaten, Robert paced around the kitchen, looking toward the stairs. Clayton cleared up the food. He was confused by his sister's behavior. But if she'd locked herself in, it stood to reason that she didn't actually want to leave.

Robert stopped his pacing and turned toward the stairs, where Nancy's suitcase sat like something in a lost and found.

"I'll go see if she needs any help," Clayton offered.

"Tell her . . . tell her I'm sorry," Robert said. "I might have offended her. I didn't mean to. I just want to see her, to explain."

Clayton ran up to the attic. He could hear rustling on the other side of the door. "I'll be there in just a moment," his sister called. Her voice sounded thick, as if she had a cold.

"Take your time," Clayton told her. There was no answer. He turned back toward the stairs, wondering how to get his brother-in-law out of the house before she came down.

In the attic, Nancy listened for the sound of footsteps. She needed a moment of privacy with Robert before she had to brave her grandfather and Clayton. She wanted to be sure of where things stood between them. If Robert would just come up the stairs, she thought, and say her name, she'd open the door and he'd realize how real her suffering had been. She imagined his arms wrapping around her, the things she would then be able to say.

The attic smelled of pears and old, dried paint and the wax Mavis used for canning. Motes of dust hung in the air. Nancy turned her head from the door and glanced out the high, small window. Far below her, she was surprised to see two figures walking away across the field. She would recognize Robert's stride anywhere, the way he tipped his head and swung his arms. The sight of him made her rush forward. She leaned against the dusty glass. Where were they going? Watching Robert turn the corner of the woodpile and disappear, Nancy felt a terrible panic. She wanted to fling herself after them.

But what would she say when she caught up to him? She thought again of the letter he'd written and the reference he'd made to Scudder's *remarkable recovery*. It *had* been remarkable, almost miraculous, she thought. Maybe Robert had meant what he wrote, maybe she'd been wrong to take offense. That was what came of being sarcastic too often, she thought in frustration. How could it be her fault if she couldn't tell what he meant? Would she know when she saw him? Or would they just stand there, stiff and unfriendly, eyeing each other like roosters in the spring? A claustrophobic feeling seized her. It could go wrong in so many ways, she thought in despair.

She would have to go down to the kitchen and wait, she decided. She didn't know which trail they might have taken. They'd come back from the marsh and find her on the porch with her suitcase beside her. But why had Robert left the house at all? Why hadn't he just come upstairs? She remembered his brother suddenly, and the stiff way he'd wished them happiness at their wedding reception, making her feel that he thought them ill suited for each other. Had he sensed an incompatibility she hadn't seen? Maybe she and Robert had simply been mistaken about each other, the way the Carolina parakeet he'd hoped to find at Washington Lodge turned out to be another bird entirely.

A memory came back to her of walking between her father and her grandfather. They must have been in Southease, she thought, on their way to the dock to watch a sailboat race. She'd have been about seven, in a new white dress, with ribbons in her hair, and people had smiled at them on the street and remarked on how pretty she looked. What she remembered most was her awareness of the two men beside her. She was proud to be allowed out with them, not left in the care of her nanny. Flanked by their masculine presence, she'd felt the world spread out like a picnic before her.

———

Clayton and Robert walked in silence. It was hot and bright. They made their way through the far field and along the edge of the pond. Outside the Captain's squat cottage Judith Purlowe was hanging laundry on the line. She stopped to wave at them, smiling with her mouth full of clothespins. From the distance it looked as if she were about to light three cigars at the same time.

Clayton led Robert through the high-tide bush and cattails along a trail he and Perry had made. The falling tide had left the ground wet. Clayton considered his brother-in-law's shoes, which were shiny leather and entirely unsuitable for the marsh. They made a gratifying squelching noise. "We might see a diamondback terrapin," Clayton explained, deviously thinking of a reason to be taking this muddy path. He stopped to point out a red-winged blackbird on a reed. But Robert merely nodded, his eyes unfocused. Clayton glanced down at the inappropriate shoes. They must be getting wet inside. Unfortunately, Robert didn't seem to notice. Clayton led him out onto the yellow-green salt hay. It was wetter here, and his own canvas shoes were soon soaked through.

Down at the bank of the river stood a pole dock where Scudder had once kept his sailboat. Approaching it through the low screen of high-tide bush, Robert tripped on a stump. He went over with a muffled thud. Clayton stared openly, awed by how well his plan was working. Robert's pants were wet from the knees down with marsh water that had also splattered up the front of his shirt and jacket. There was a smear of mud on Robert's cheek. His hands dripped with brown water the color of weak coffee. He straightened up and began to brush ineffectually at his soggy knees.

There was another place to look for turtles at low tide, Clayton told him quickly. But they'd need to borrow a rowboat. "Come on." He turned and sped back over the salt hay before his brother-in-law could complain. Behind him came the squelching sound of Robert's unsuitable shoes.

At the dock, Clayton told Robert to sit in the stern of the borrowed boat. He would wait until they were out in the river, he decided, and then capsize in a way that would look like an accident. He imagined Robert swimming back to the bank in a drenched suit, returning to Boston alone.

Clayton shoved off from the dock and jumped in, taking the seat in the middle and hurriedly extending the oars. To row he had to sit directly in front of Robert, facing him in the small boat. Robert's face was pale. He looked seasick, and so harmless that Clayton felt his resolve weakening. He thought of the beautiful little airplane that Robert had surprised him with. But then he remembered how empty the house felt with his sister gone. A dunking in the river wouldn't hurt anyone, he thought, steeling himself for the moment when it would be time to capsize. The wind had picked up. As they came out of the canal into the river, Clayton felt the spray on his face.

He rowed along the east side of the river. Robert gazed off in the direction of the marsh. Clayton wanted to wait until the boat would be shielded from sight by the riverbank before he made his move. "I bet she's ready now," Robert said suddenly. Clayton, his eyes on the shoreline, wondered at first if he was talking about the boat. "Let's get back," Robert urged. "She'll wonder where we are."

Clayton was trying to judge how much force he'd need to apply to the gunwale in order to tip the boat when he remembered the playing cards. He'd been admiring them on the roof when Robert knocked, and they were still in his pocket. Distracted by the plane and by Nancy's refusal to come downstairs, he'd forgotten to hide them back in his room. Clayton couldn't bear to think of the cards exposed to the brackish water; the colors might run. Angry at himself for planning this so badly, he nodded to Robert and brought the boat around.

Halfway to the mouth of the canal, they heard a clap of thunder. A moment later it began to rain, big, pelting drops that dimpled the surface of the river. Clayton hunched his shoulders and kept rowing. In the stern, Robert seemed indifferent to the rain, so lost in thought that a dunking in the river would have been wasted on him anyway. The sun shone through the rain and each splash glistened. Just as they reached the boatyard it stopped. Sam Burnett poked his head out from the boat shed as first Robert and then Clayton stepped onto the dock, the water coursing from their clothes and hair. Around them in the cattails the perching swallows preened their wet feathers.

Up at the house, Clayton glimpsed his aunt through the screen door. She was unloading the shopping onto the kitchen counter. He put a warning hand on Robert's arm. "Nancy?" Robert called, oblivious. He had opened the door and was making the grave mistake of stepping inside.

"Out of those clothes!" Mavis looked scandalized. She rushed to the closet. "You're dripping onto my clean floor."

She came back to the door and passed them each a flannel rag. "I thought she'd be with you." She gave Robert a pointed look, as if to suggest he had been out on the marsh in the rain on some sort of boyish lark.

"I suppose you'd better dry off in the parlor." Slowly, as if with reluctance, Mavis stepped aside. "Don't put your wet things on the table. That's mahogany." She turned back to the counter and picked up a bag of onions.

Clayton had wriggled out of his sodden pants with the strip of flannel wrapped around his waist. "I'll run up to the attic," he said. He darted toward the stairs with his wet shirt and pants jumbled in his arms.

Behind him, he heard his aunt demand, "The attic? What would she be doing there?" Clayton glanced back, one hand on the newel post. Robert stood hunched and shivering with a rag around his waist and his socks and pants in his arms. He tried to shrug, but in his wet clothes the movement became an awkward hunching, and it looked to Clayton more as if he were fending off a blow. His shirt, dark with water, was plastered to his back; his legs were white and bare under the skirtlike flannel.

Then Clayton heard a cluck of displeasure from his aunt. She was swooping down toward something on the floor. With a feeling of horror, he recognized the blue-patterned back of one of the Captain's playing cards. Without waiting, he ran up the stairs. At the top he paused, his heart pounding. It was utterly silent below, the silence of two people staring at each other. Moving very slowly, Clayton ducked his head just enough to peer down into the room. His aunt must have seen the picture on the card. She was holding it out to Robert, with a look of condemnation and disgust. Clayton shrank farther into the shadows.

From where he sat he couldn't see Robert's face, only the shaking of his head. Mavis looked him over with utter scorn. Holding the card like a dead mouse, she turned and flicked it neatly into the cookstove. Clayton saw Robert glance helplessly toward the stairs, as if in the hope that either he or Nancy might appear. Moving stealthily, Clayton pulled his head back out of the line of sight. He tiptoed to his room.

Later, he heard the sound of the front door slamming.

That night Clayton overheard his aunt tell his uncle that Nancy would be staying on Salt Hay Road.

"What about her husband?" Roy asked.

Mavis made a clucking sound. "That awful man . . ." His aunt's voice dropped, and Clayton didn't hear any more.

The next morning Clayton was in the kitchen making scrambled eggs when Nancy came downstairs. Her eyes were puffy and swollen. "Where's Robert?" she asked.

Clayton stared at her. "He left. Last night."

"Yes, I know," Nancy snapped. "*Where* did he go?"

Clayton shrugged. "I guess he went back to Boston."

"Just like that?"

Clayton paused before answering. He wondered if she could suspect him of trying to make Robert leave. "You were in the attic," he pointed out, defensive.

"So he just went? Didn't he leave a letter or a message?"

Clayton shook his head. He picked his plate off the table and carried it to the sink, worried she would ask him more questions. But Nancy was silent. She sat at the table with her chin thrust out. Her eyes shone with fresh tears.

Clayton left for school before he had to and waited at the Gilpins' house while Perry finished his Cream of Wheat. His brother-in-law had been driven away, just as Clayton had intended, but instead of feeling happy, he was ill at ease. Had Robert told Mavis the playing card wasn't his? If he had, would she have believed him? Clayton almost wished that Robert had stormed and yelled, proclaiming his innocence. The thought of him guessing the truth and keeping silent about it made Clayton squirm.

He would bury the cards by the pond, Clayton decided.

That way they could never be traced to him. This conviction soothed him a little.

In the wake of Robert's departure, a charged silence fell over the house on Salt Hay Road and the subject of Nancy's continued presence within it. Only Scudder seemed to treat the matter as permanently settled, dismissing her lapse in judgment now that she was back among them. For the others, it was a relief to have a straightforward problem to talk about when, nearly a week later, Clayton first noticed the bees.

He'd found one crawling across the window at the top of the stairs and trapped it in a specimen jar so that he could sketch it before releasing it outside. On the floor below the window lay the dry bodies of several more. Later in the day he was up in Scudder's unused bedroom looking for a clean shirt for the old man. Checking the bottom drawer of the dresser, he happened to put his hand on the wall. The plaster felt strangely warm against his palm. He touched the wall by the door for comparison; it was cool as wood. At the same moment he became aware for the first time of a low background humming, a sound he could almost feel. The hair stood up on the back of his neck. He thought of the ghosts that Mavis and Captain Kelley had tried to contact by Ouija board. Then his rational mind reasserted itself; he remembered the bee at the window and realized there must be a hive inside the wall. Clayton ran downstairs and out the door, forgetting the clean shirt he'd been sent for. Standing in the grass, he stared up at the east side of the house. He watched for some time before a bee drew near, bumbled onto the white clapboard beneath the window frame, and disappeared.

He remembered his sister taking a yellow jacket out of his

hair. They'd been somewhere he could envision only dimly, a party at the neighbor's house perhaps, one late summer afternoon. He'd been four or five years old, and had wandered off behind the fence to look for a tree to climb. The nest must have been under a log he tripped on. The yellow jackets flew up at him like embers stirred in a fire. He ran toward the house, screaming and swatting the air. On the lawn the grown-ups in their linen suits and summer dresses rose and turned, their conversations broken off. "What is it, darling?" His mother stretched out her arms. But Clayton ran past her, swinging his head from side to side like a bull, toward his sister. He could feel the buzzing just above his ear.

Somehow Nancy understood. "Keep still," she told him. "I'll get it." She worked through his thick curls while he blubbered with relief. She held his head with one hand and used the other to slip off her shoe. One moment the buzzing seemed nearly deafening. Then he heard a faint crunching sound just above his ear. "There," she said, with a mix of satisfaction and disgust. Their mother came over and led him into the house to wash his face and smear the stings with a paste of baking soda and water. Over his shoulder he'd seen Nancy wipe the heel of her party shoe briskly on the grass.

Clayton announced his discovery to the others at dinner. Roy suggested leaving the bees alone. They hadn't stung anyone, and it would be difficult to remove them. Mavis put down her knife and fork. "I don't intend to live in a beehive, Roy. I can't stand the thought of them crawling inside the walls." She shuddered and rolled her heavy shoulders. "Let's get rid of them before they spread." Clayton imagined what the house would look like filled with bees. Not content with the hive they'd built, they'd crawl on the walls and ceilings, clog the kitchen sink with honey. He looked over at Nancy, trying to catch her eye. But she was staring out the window as if the bee-hive in the wall didn't interest her at all.

The next day Roy examined the wall in Scudder's upstairs room, shadowed by Clayton. Then he set up the ladder and studied the outside wall. Nancy helped Scudder to a chair on the lawn, and the two of them played cribbage and watched. Roy sent Clayton and Perry down to the pond for cattails. While they were gone, he wound a piece of wire around his ankles, bunching his trousers against the skin and then around his sleeves at the wrist. The boys came back, and he took out two smokers, like tin lanterns, filled the bases with the cattail punk, and lit them. Clayton and Perry each held a smoker, reverently, as if in church, while Roy rigged himself into a brimmed hat that he'd covered in mosquito netting. Veiled like a bride, he climbed the ladder with one gloved hand, clutching a smoker in the other. At the top of the ladder he took a ham-mer and nail from his belt and made a hook on which to hang the smoker. He felt along the clapboards with his hands, occa-sionally pressing his ear against the wood. When he'd mapped the contours of the hive by feel, he braced himself against the wall and cut a hole into one of the white clapboards with a small saw. From below, Clayton could see bees emerging, slug-gish from the smoke. Roy worked quickly and deliberately. With a pry bar he pulled up first one board and then another. Underneath, the comb showed dirty white with the black bod-ies of bees crawling over it. Roy took the smoker off the nail and waved it over the exposed hive like a censer. Clayton smelled the rich sweetness of honey mixed with the scent of burning cattail. Above him, Roy pulled up another board. The nails squealed against the wood.

Roy managed to trap the queen and most of the drones using half a cardboard cereal box like a scoop. The air around the swarm as he lowered it into the bucket, following the queen, felt heavy with electricity, like the humid pressure that comes before a storm. The bees flowed into the bucket in a liquid swarm. Roy clapped a glass pie dish over the top. Clayton and Perry stared through it as if it were a window, hypnotized by the dark, crawling mass. More bees buzzed around their heads, and Clayton brushed a few from Perry's back with the sleeve of his shirt.

The comb broke apart in jagged, dripping clumps. Clay and Perry chewed on the broken fragments, and the bits of wax crumbled in their mouths and stuck in flecks to their teeth. Roy collected the comb in a second bucket, using the smoker to fend off the bees and setting a piece of oilcloth over it to keep them out. When Judith Purlowe came from across the field to watch, she stood beside Roy while the others gazed up at the rough hole in the wall of the house and the confusion of bees around it. Out of the corner of his eye, Clayton glimpsed Roy handing her a clump of honeycomb; the widow took it from his fingers with her lips, like a horse accepting a lump of sugar.

When the last of the hive had been fished from between the walls, Roy went to his car and unloaded the extractor he'd borrowed from George Rowley's brother. This was a metal drum with a spigot at the bottom, fitted inside with chicken wire and turned with a crank. He carried it into the cool barn, away from the agitated bees, while the others followed, Clayton carrying the second bucket. The boys watched him shear off the outer layer of wax from a piece of honeycomb using a knife warmed first in boiling water. Then he placed the comb inside the wire and turned the crank; the honey spun out of its wax pockets and collected on the bottom of the drum. It took the rest of the afternoon for Clayton and Perry to extract the honey while Roy mended the hole in the wall. They weighed the honey, jar by jar, on Mavis's kitchen scale. There was over seventy pounds of it.

PART THREE

Falling Houses

Clayton walked down Salt Hay Road with his schoolbag over his shoulder, wishing he were on the beach at Fire Island. The day before, in the aviary at Washington Lodge, Mr. Washington mentioned that a whale had washed up near Old Inlet, about three miles away across the bay. Clayton badly wanted to see it. Mr. Washington hadn't been able to tell him what kind of whale it was, only that a hobby pilot he knew had spotted the carcass while flying over the dunes. At the end of Salt Hay Road, Clayton paused. Perry wouldn't be ready for another few minutes, he told himself. Maybe he'd just dash to the boatyard to see if Sam Burnett knew anything about it.

By this time of year, most of the summer people had gone back to New York City. Beside the long shed at Starke's Boatyard, vessels hauled out for the season lay upside down, exposing the wear on their black-and-red hulls. Sam Burnett sat on his high stool by the boat shed, mending an eel pot and smoking his pipe. He hadn't heard anything about a whale on the beach. "It's getting ready to blow, though," he told Clayton.

Clayton wondered what a storm would do to the whale. It was only Wednesday, he thought desperately. The whale might be washed away before the weekend dragged around, or covered in sand. Clayton ran down to the canal and scanned the docks on the off chance a boat might be headed across the bay. After Labor Day, the ferries ran only on weekends.

The promise he'd made to his sister not to skip school came back to him, but he pushed the thought away. The morning was hot and humid, and now it began to drizzle. The canal that led out to the river looked gray and choppy. Clayton wondered if the whale had teeth or baleen plates; could it be a humpback? A fin? Mr. Washington knew only that it was bigger than a pilot whale.

The honk of a horn made him turn. Back near the boat shed a blue truck idled by the door. Sam Burnett waved Clayton over. Did he want a ride across the bridge? The plumber who owned the truck was on his way to Taffy Point.

He had made a promise to his sister, a small voice insisted. But she had never understood, Clayton thought. She didn't love it here the way he did. He remembered the day he'd shown her the snapping turtles at Knowles Point, his stupidity in thinking she'd be impressed by them. He was skipping school today as a point of honor, he thought hotly. Not because of the whale at all, but because he loved Fire Neck. *He* loved it, and he would go to the beach in spite of the weather, and in spite of the assurance that had been forced out of him.

Clayton hauled on the door and hopped up into the cab. "Thanks, mister," he told the driver.

"Regards to Moby Dick," said Sam.

———

As the truck crossed the bridge, Clayton noticed whitecaps in the bay. To the east of the Gilpins' cottage, two more beach houses were going up. The scaffolding jutted above the sand like the hollow husks of giant insects. At the construction site, he jumped down and thanked the plumber, who waved and wished him luck. Clayton put his shoes in his schoolbag and wound his way through the sandy hillocks of beach grass and the hollows where the beach plums and rugosa roses grew. He climbed over the dunes. At the crest he stopped and looked down with the thrill he always felt gazing out on the Atlantic. Along the beach, breakers hurled against the sand. Mixed with the salt spray flew orange-and-black butterflies; the monarchs were migrating south along the coast. Clayton walked down toward the surf, breathing in the smell of the sea. He could hardly believe he had almost gone to school, and he spared a thought for Perry, stuck indoors. Tumbling over the sand were bright scraps of butterflies that had been ripped apart in the wind. Others struggled through the spray and the drizzle. The air felt warm and heavy, in spite of the breeze and the pounding surf. Clayton strained his eyes, looking for a shape on the expanse of sand. But on either side the distant beach dissolved into fog. He felt gloriously alone as he started west toward Old Inlet, an explorer on an unmapped shore.

Clayton smelled the whale before he saw it. The warm air carried the oily, rotten stench, and then the whale itself came into view, dark against the pale beach, a mound that seemed to expand as he trudged toward it across the damp sand. It lay on its side. A black-backed gull stood on its huge cheek like a child playing king of the castle and hammered its yellow beak at the whale's sunken eye. Clayton had hoped to see it while it was still impressive, still whalelike. But the carcass was already a

ruin. The enormous hulk lay before him like a collapsed diri-
gible. He guessed it was over fifty feet in length. Its arched
mouth gaped open, and he could see the baleen plates, longer
than Roy was tall, and the bristly gray baleen. Maybe a right
whale, he thought. The gull had savaged the paler flesh of the
enormous tongue. He stepped closer and waved his arms, and
the bird lifted itself and flew a few feet off to wait him out.
Clayton ran his hand along the cold, colossal face; the whale's
skin felt like a massive punctured tire. There were thick black
hairs on the tip of its lower jaw. He concentrated on breathing
through his mouth. The water had scooped out the sand beneath the whale's weight, so that it was half buried already.

Around the other side Clayton counted two blowholes.
Mysticete, he scribbled in the back of his math notebook; *two
blowholes and baleen plates*. He began to sketch the whale's head,
struggling to capture the wartlike patches on its face and snout;
in his drawing they bore a frustrating resemblance to mush-
rooms. Crouched on the wet sand, the book balanced on his
knee, he tried to shelter the paper from the drops of rain as best
he could. He went through a handful of pages, growing more
and more dissatisfied. Every sketch he made looked flat and
lifeless.

The tide was rising. With each wave the water hurtled
farther up the sand, frothing around the massive tail, beating
against the limp black form. The dull sunken eye of the whale
appeared through the foam and disappeared, as if winking. The
rain had picked up. Reluctantly, Clayton closed his book and
tucked it into his schoolbag. For the first time, he considered
the problem of getting back to Fire Neck. He chased the gull
off again, in a token gesture, and then turned from the forlorn
and monumental body. Trudging east along the beach into the
wind, he wondered where he was in relation to the mainland.

He wanted to come back with Perry this weekend to see what would be left of the whale. One day, after the flesh rotted, they might be able to salvage some of the bones. He imagined an arch made of massive ribs in front of the house on Salt Hay Road.

The waves grew wilder and it became hard to walk on the shifting edge of the sand. Clayton climbed over the dunes. The wind was quieter in the hollow of land between the ocean and the bay. From the lee of the dunes he could look across Fire Island at the whitecapped bay and Fire Neck in the distance. He picked his way slowly through the beach plum and stands of bayberry. The leaves of the poison ivy had begun to turn, brilliant smears of red and orange among the yellow of the goldenrod. Clayton tried to gauge how far he still had to go. He hoped there'd be someone at the construction site where the plumber had dropped him off. Otherwise he would have to walk the seven or eight miles home. Ahead of him a bright flash of spray rose above the top of a dune.

At the house on Salt Hay Road, Nancy glanced up from her cards. Rain was pelting the windows. A large, pale leaf, carried by the wind, flattened itself against the glass like a hand. She went into the kitchen and found the floor wet where the wind had forced rainwater under the doorsill. Scudder sat over his cards with the expression of muted disgust with which he tried to hide his satisfaction in a good hand. Nancy hadn't noticed. She found it hard to concentrate on the game and was playing haphazardly. She tried not to think about Robert, who had written a week before to say he wanted to see her. "We need to come to an understanding," he'd said.

"It's getting worse out there," she remarked.

Scudder nodded. "A line storm. It'll take a while to blow itself out. Where's your brother?"

"It's Wednesday," Nancy reminded him. "He's at school."

Behind the dunes, Clayton strained his eyes. His clothes were damp and thickly caked with sand. They pulled at him, slowing him down. The heavy, salty air made him thirsty, and he realized how stupid he'd been to come without an apple or a canteen of water. He felt sure he'd walked for over a mile already and was wondering if he had somehow missed Taffy Point completely when he saw the shape of a house ahead and to his left. He trudged toward it. It was the Everitts' cottage, the westernmost of those on the bay, still a mile from the point. The Gilpins' beach house was only a few yards farther. Clayton pushed on through the beach plum bushes and the sand. His fingers were puckered, as if he'd been in the bath too long. The sight of the Gilpins' blue door and the listing porch cheered him. He imagined drinking a glass of water, borrowing dry clothes from Perry's upstairs room. He found the key on the little hook under the steps and let himself in.

Inside, it was dark and unfamiliar. The walls creaked in the wind. With a sharp sense of disappointment, Clayton saw that the house had already been packed up for the winter, probably when school had started again. The chairs were stacked along the wall, the rugs rolled up. At the kitchen sink he turned the tap, but nothing happened. The pipes had all been drained, of course, and there was nothing for him to drink. At least he was sheltered, he thought. Clayton found rags in the hall closet. He stripped down and dried himself off, hanging his wet clothes over a chair in the kitchen, where they dripped onto the or-

ange linoleum. Wrapped in an old towel, he made his way upstairs to look in the boys' room for a change of clothes. The
dresser was bare, its drawers stacked upside down on the floor.
The stripped mattresses rested on their sides. Back downstairs,
Clayton pulled his wet and sandy clothes back on. The cloth
caught on his skin. Outside, the wind seemed to be rising.
Clayton realized that anyone working at the construction site
to the east would have left the beach already. He thought of
Perry, warm and dry at school, and decided stubbornly that he
was still glad he'd come.

Roy came into the kitchen on Salt Hay Road in a rainy gust of
wind that rattled the cupboard doors. His hat dripped water
onto the floor. "Nasty out," he said. He'd been on the marsh
with his dogs when he noticed the sky turn the dirty yellow of
an old bruise. Nancy started a pot of coffee while her uncle
went upstairs to change his clothes. When he came down, he
drank his coffee hurriedly, pacing back and forth in the
kitchen. He should have stopped at Judith's first, he thought.
She wasn't used to this kind of weather, and he remembered
that the Captain had complained just before he died about a
leak above the kitchen window. He put his cup in the sink.
Nancy was writing what looked like a letter, and Scudder had
fallen asleep in his chair. "I'd better go down to the boatyard,"
Roy told his niece. "See if Sam needs help doubling lines." He
took a slice of bread smeared with butter and glanced out the
window. Squalls swept over the field and flattened the grass.
The thorny branches of the rosebush on the fence whipped
in the wind. "I'll stop in across the field," he added, heading
for the door. "See how the roof is holding up."

At the cottage Judith had buckets and pans arranged across the kitchen floor to catch the drips. "I don't like the sound the wind's making," she told him.

"We get these storms every fall," Roy said, "when the sun goes over the equator. Wait and see. It'll blow for three days and then clear." Judith was crouched at the kitchen door, mopping up rainwater with an old bedspread. Her hair stuck to her forehead. If he married her, Roy thought, where would they live? Not in the house on Salt Hay Road with Mavis; his sister would never take to that arrangement. The Captain's cottage was simply too small. His head practically scraped the ceilings. He wondered what Gus Hart wanted for the house on Carman Street his mother had lived in. It would need to be fixed up, of course. The prospect excited him. It was on a nice stretch of land, with a path down to Scheibel's Creek.

"I'm making soup for lunch," Judith said, startling him from a vision of her on the porch of a house that was not yet theirs. "Can you stay?"

He shook his head and told her he was going down to the boatyard.

"Come back soon, before I'm swimming in my own kitchen."

Safe inside the Gilpins' house, Clayton quickly grew bored. Outside, the wind howled. Rain and flinging sand stuck to the windows. Clayton wished the house faced the beach, so that he could watch the ocean. From the upstairs window all he could see was the spray off the waves.

As he stared out toward the dunes, hoping for a glimpse of the ocean, he was startled to see a hunched figure moving slowly across the inner meadow. He noted it with a twinge of disappointment; he had been sure he was the only one left on the beach. Then the figure broke apart and he saw it was a woman carrying a child. The child slid to the ground, holding on to her dress, and the woman rested a moment and then lifted it up again. He wondered what they were doing out in the rain. Maybe, he thought, she needed to use the telephone. He went downstairs and unlatched the back door. It jerked out of his hands and flew open, thumping against the wall. Sand stung his face. He waved his arms and shouted uselessly into the wind. Seeing him, the woman moved with renewed purpose in his direction. Clayton saw that she wore a loose pink dress and a pair of incongruous rubber boots. Summer people, he thought.

The woman struggled in and sat abruptly on the linoleum as Clayton fought to close the door. She was pretty in the brittle way city women often were, her glossy brown hair disheveled by the wind. The child clung to her without speaking, a boy of three or four who watched him with wide-set eyes. ". . . *hours* ago . . ." the woman was saying. Clayton handed her a towel, and as she reached out, he saw her hands were shaking. She took it and patted the boy's wet hair. "He told me he'd be back soon . . ."

"Who are you talking about?" Clayton asked. He was not entirely sure she was right in the head.

"Our handyman. We're packing up the house for the season. I sent him into town for boxes. Late this morning. I kept waiting for him to come back with the car. Then the water started coming in. We managed to crawl over the dune. I looked back, and I saw the bathhouse blow away."

Clayton stared out the window again. Salt spray blurred the glass. The sky was darker and the wind seemed to be shifting to the east. "Where's your house?"

She pointed. "On the dunes. It's the white one called Sea-crest. There was a bathhouse, like I said. It's gone now." She be-gan to shake again, harder this time, like a dog getting out of the water. "We'd just passed it. If we'd been a moment later, when the gust came . . ." She pulled the little boy against her and he buried his head in her neck.

"We're safe here," Clayton said. "We'll call someone in town to come pick you up."

The woman stared at him. "The phones aren't working."

Clayton picked up the Gilpins' phone. The line was dead.

"We're on the bay side," Clayton reassured her. "We can wait it out." At that moment there was a popping noise and then a crash. In the living room the east window had blown in and the storm entered the house with a roar of noise. Wind rat-tled the windows. The sashes pinged against the wall. Shards of glass glittered on the floor. Clayton grabbed the broom from the kitchen to sweep up the glass and sand. But rain and wind were howling through the screen. Even moving, the air was strangely warm and heavy. The wind seemed almost due east now. He realized he would have to patch the hole with some-thing and was wondering how he could hold anything big enough in place when beyond the window a flash of white caught his eye. A wave crashed high above the dune in a froth of white water. As it fell, the sand beneath it dissolved like sugar.

Clayton did not own a watch and the woman wasn't wear-ing one. The clock in the Gilpins' kitchen had stopped at ten to twelve on an unknown day in the past. Clayton generally had a good sense of time, but now, with his long walk to see the whale and the strange darkness of the sky, he was unsure if it was one in the afternoon or as late as three. Either way, he knew high tide was scheduled for somewhere around six; it would keep rising for several more hours.

They stood and watched, with spellbound horror, as the waves battered the dunes. It was like seeing a sand castle give way. One moment the line of dunes stood between them and the ocean, and then the line was gone. White water surged through the break, churning with debris. Before their eyes, the break widened, like a sheet of cloth ripping apart. The Gilpins' house stood on a slight rise about two hundred yards from the newly formed inlet. Below them, to the west, the ocean surged around the Everitts' house, sweeping flowerpots and driftwood off the porch, foaming up the windows. Clayton saw how wrong he'd been to think that they could wait it out. Fire Island itself was washing away.

He thought of the bridge, a mile to the east. "Do you think you could make it to the point?" He had to yell to make himself heard, even inside the house.

She gripped the back of the chair. Her knuckles whitened. "We barely made it here." Even if they reached the bridge, Clayton realized, it might already be impassable. He imagined looking down at Fire Island from above, the bay, the thin spit of sand, and then the ravenous ocean.

At the boatyard Roy took care of George Rowley's sailboat first, doubling the spring line and the painter and putting an extra fender on the port side. Sam Burnett came out of the boathouse, his arms full of rope and his pipe clenched tight in his mouth. They started along the edge of the river, where the larger sailboats were, adding lines and checking knots. The halyards slapped in the wind above them, a frenzied twanging. For the most part they worked without speaking. About half the slips were empty, where boats had already been hauled out for the season. Roy noticed that Theron Greaves's boat, the *Leda*, was gone. "Theron's not crabbing in this dirty weather?"

Sam shook his head. "He's out at John Boyle's Island with George. Seining for shiners." The little silver shiners were good bait for snapper fishing. Sam glanced toward the mouth of the river. "They'll be headed in now, at any rate. Probably reefing the main." He paused, remembering something. "Your nephew back?"

"Clayton?" Roy looked at him in surprise. "He's at school."

Sam straightened up. He took the pipe out of his mouth. "He went over to the beach, Roy. Looking for a whale. About nine this morning."

Roy stared out toward the marsh in the direction of Fire Island. Even as he and Sam had been working, the wind had gotten stronger. What would the boy do now? he wondered. How would he get home? "Pigs," he said.

"I suppose he could be anywhere now," Sam said quickly. "He probably left the beach hours ago."

Roy understood that he was being dissuaded. Clayton would have stayed to watch the surf, he was sure of that. He thought of his father and all the times he had ventured into the ocean, risking his life for strangers. When he was six or seven years old, Scudder had taught him how to swim at the end of the pole dock on the river by tossing him in over his head and expecting him to make it back. Panic overtook him as he'd flailed his arms, gulping and choking. His eyes stung and he squeezed them closed. He had been sure he was going to die. When he finally touched the bottom, the mud sucked at his feet, as if trying to pull him under. "That wasn't so bad, was it?" his father demanded when Roy struggled out at last and stood on the bank, shaking in his wet cotton underwear, his teeth chattering in spite of the sun. Roy hadn't answered. Though they never spoke of it, his father had gradually stopped trying to interest him in boats and the water. He'd concentrated on Helen instead, and Roy had been relieved, in spite of a vague but persistent sense of shame.

Roy glanced once in the direction of the cottage. Judith would wonder what was taking him so long, but it couldn't be helped. "Sam," he said, "I'm going to need a boat."

Clayton stood at the upstairs window and watched the Everitts' house wobble on its foundation. It came loose with a popping motion, like a limpet pried from a rock. The waves lifted it for a moment as if it were nearly weightless. Then the walls seemed to stagger and roll, and the water swallowed it. Clayton saw the roof heading toward the bay like a flat-bottomed scow. He turned to where the woman and the boy clung to each other on the bedroom floor. The child's eyes were squeezed closed, and his grubby hands gripped the fabric of his mother's pink dress. They'd come upstairs when the first floor flooded and the surf began running through the kitchen. "We have to go," he said.

"Can't we stay here?" the woman pleaded. "Eddie's scared."

"The house next door just broke up. It's floating away. This one might be next."

The woman began to shake again. Tears welled in her eyes. "Eddie can't swim," she said. The boy opened his eyes at the sound of his name.

"I want Bunny," he cried. "I don't like it here! I want to go home."

Clayton turned away from them and went down the stairs.

Water surged across the kitchen floor and splashed up the sides of the stacked chairs. He could feel the floorboards undulate beneath his feet, a movement that traveled up his legs to his stomach. The straps of his schoolbag flapped on the counter as if attempting to fly. He thought of stowing it upstairs, perhaps under a mattress, but the sight of the Everitts' house had shaken him. The door facing the bay had been forced open. Gripping the door frame, Clayton stepped out into the storm. The sound of the wind vibrated through him; it was as if the power of the wind lay not in its velocity but in that insistent, penetrating sound. Sand cut into his face like slivers of glass. Looking toward the bay, he saw white water. Swirling in it, like twigs in a puddle, were enormous pieces of broken boats and scaffolding. Around the side of the house was the boat locker; he pried open the hinged door and found the life jackets in a tangle of paddles and ropes. Clayton grabbed three cork jackets and a length of line and made his way back upstairs.

He knew very well that it would only get worse as the tide continued to rise. They had to make it to Taffy Point, he thought, and hope the bridge was passable. If not, the mainland was closest there, and they'd have a shorter distance to cross if they had to swim for it. He ran up the stairs, relieved to be moving, to have a plan. In the bedroom the woman was huddled on the floor with her mouth moving in a whisper over her son's hair. She looked up at Clayton in astonishment, as if at a ghost. He thrust two of the life jackets at her. "Get these on," he yelled. "Hurry!"

The woman scrambled up, wiping her eyes with the sleeve of her pink dress. "I thought you'd left without us."

They stepped outside, and the wind howled around them with a sound like that of a train going past. Off the porch, to the west, the surf ran in a wide torrent, awash with wreckage from the houses on the dunes. Crouching low to the sand, they set off east, away from the new inlet. Clayton walked in the lead. The woman followed haltingly, carrying the boy on her back. As they scrambled over the hillocks of sand, Clayton saw a flock of small birds, chipping sparrows, he thought, huddled in the lee. The birds squatted close to the ground in a wedge-shaped formation, their beaks facing into the wind. As Clayton and the woman drew near, the birds rose in alarm, and the wind whisked them away like specks of dust.

The woman, burdened with the boy, began to lag behind. Clayton forced himself to wait. He was anxious to get to the bay's edge and angry with himself for not insisting they leave the house earlier. The woman was struggling through the beach plum, which caught at her boots. Clayton went back and signaled that he could take the boy. But the child clung to his mother, his arms clamped around her neck. "Just for a minute, Eddie," the woman pleaded, raising her voice. "So Mama can rest." The child closed his eyes and held on with a death grip, shaking his head so violently it looked as if he were having convulsions. The woman lowered her head and struggled on with the boy on her back.

As they neared the bay, the bridge came fully into view. It was standing, Clayton saw with relief, though the span seemed to sway in the wind. But it looked farther away than he'd imagined. Beside him, the woman had collapsed on her knees and was holding the boy in her arms now, sheltering him from the wind. Clayton looked back along the bay toward the Gilpins' house. It was still there, though part of the porch had disappeared. Behind it, where the Everitts' house had been, the ocean was running headlong into the bay. Between the inlet and where they stood, Clayton saw the Pastorizas' dock. The Pastorizas had a big house on the dunes and kept their cabin cruiser on the bay, along with several other vessels. These had all ripped free in the wind, except for a small white rowboat tied on the leeward side. It would just fit the three of them, Clayton thought. He pulled at the woman's shoulder and shouted, "This way."

As they approached the dock, Clayton saw it shudder. The rowboat was tied fore and aft, stretched out like a man on the rack. Clayton strained to pull the boat in by the painter and cleat it closer to the dock. "Get in," he yelled to the woman. He helped her free herself from her son's arms. The boy screamed and writhed. "Hold on," Clayton shouted uselessly. "Just a minute." The woman jumped down into the boat. The instant her feet touched the seat, the painter snapped like a guitar string. The boat whipped around in the wind, pivoting on the stern line. With a scream that Clayton felt against his arms, the boy catapulted out of his grasp and flung himself after his mother. He hit the water with a noiseless splash. Buoyed by the life jacket, the child swept toward the rowboat like a bit of flotsam. The woman lunged out, nearly capsizing the boat, and grabbed him by the strap of his cork jacket. She hauled him over the side and into her lap. At the same moment the stern line parted. The boat with its two passengers shot into the bay like a horse from the starting gate at a racetrack. Standing on the dock, Clayton stared after it. It moved as fast as a car on Old Purchase Road. He was utterly alone. The boat dwindled before his eyes. Already he could hardly see their faces.

Beneath his feet the planks began to ripple. Clayton moved to the locust pole that secured the dock to the shore. Boards and logs swept past him, pulled from the dunes through the new inlet to the bay. An icebox floated past, and then a bathtub, carried upright at a jaunty angle. Above him, high in the air, sailed a green door with a brightly polished handle. Every few seconds another wave hit, and white water and debris surged around the dock. Turning toward the inlet, Clayton saw the bulky shape of a house moving in silent slow motion through the shallow chop like a clamshell tumbled in the surf. As he watched, the front crumpled inward like a wad of paper. The gabled roof peeled off and sailed into the air toward the bay. It landed on top of the water with a bounce and spun toward him. Clayton threw his arms around the pole. With a crunch he could feel but not hear, the roof lodged itself against the Pastorizas' dock. Clayton jumped onto it and scrambled over the wet shingles to the peak. In the next instant the dock gave way beneath its weight, and the unmoored roof set sail.

In the kitchen at Washington Lodge Mavis was having trouble with the pilot light. The huge house seemed oddly still, though outside, the branches of the copper beeches flailed. It had grown darker. She walked to the kitchen door and opened it. The wind made a sound she'd never heard, a keening cry. Mavis felt a creeping sensation travel up her back. The yard was deserted, the gardener's bicycle gone. She stepped back into the house. Mr. Washington was due back that afternoon from his factory in New Jersey. She had to cook the chicken for the salad mold she'd planned. She knelt on the kitchen floor and fumbled in the dark interior of the stove. Standing up heavily, she bumped a round metal tray off the table. It hit the floor and rolled into a cabinet with a thunderous clang. The sound echoed off the walls. Mavis picked up the tray. Still holding it, she stepped out into the hall with the superstitious fear that the noise had summoned something. The house was quiet. Mavis walked softly down the hall. Outside the aviary she realized why it seemed so still: the room full of birds was eerily silent.

She clutched the tray and rushed back down the hall, mumbling a prayer under her breath. In the kitchen she felt safer. She sat beside the cold stove and listened to the wind become a deep thrumming, like a low note played on a cello. The sound seemed to leach into her spine.

At the house on Salt Hay Road the rain leaked in even through the tightly closed windows. The drops hit the double-hung sashes so hard the water was forced up between them, until a moving sheet of water obscured the lower half of the glass. Rainwater coursed down the pane on the inside and streamed onto the floor. Nancy ran between the windows and the kitchen door, mopping the floor with rags and towels and wringing out the water into a bucket. "They've never leaked," Scudder began to say, then stopped himself. He didn't want to frighten her further. But he could tell that the wind was still rising, and he'd seen, while she was busy with the streaming windows, a cherry tree in the field below them lurch over onto its side and tumble along the ground. The pond had overflown its banks and now lapped against the woodpile.

"Clayton should have been home already," Nancy was saying anxiously. "Maybe they're keeping them at school." As she spoke, there was a sharp bursting smash against the outside wall. She and Scudder stood perfectly still. The sound repeated itself. They peered out the rain-smeared window. The wind was whipping panes of glass from Roy's greenhouse against the wall of the house like a boy pitching pennies.

Scudder hobbled to the opposite side of the room and began to open the windows. "What are you doing?" Nancy cried.

"It stops the pressure building inside." With the windows on the leeward side of the house open, Nancy and Scudder looked out toward the driveway. The telephone pole bent at a thirty-degree angle. Nancy glanced back toward the green-house and saw the shingles on the roof of the barn ruffle like the feathers of a hen in a dust bath. Then the shingles began to lift off and spiral upward.

Nancy picked up the phone; there was only silence. Angrily she hit the receiver. It was probable, she thought, that Clayton had taken shelter with the Gilpins on Carman Street. Walking into the kitchen, she found water pushing under the door around the sodden bathmats and towels. She got out the mop and moved what she could off the floor, but the water surged in again a moment later. Back in the living room, she tugged Scudder gently by the elbow. "We'd better get to higher ground. The kitchen's flooding." He nodded, unprotesting, and she thought of how much he had already lived through.

Upstairs, the windows were clearer and they saw that the pond had risen until it surrounded the house. Logs from the woodpile drifted by in water thick with leaves and branches. "I'll be damned," Scudder said softly. It looked as if the house were floating once again.

Nancy settled Scudder into his old room. Then she sat at the top of the stairs and stared down at the water rising below her. At the foot of the stairs, a saucepan set loose from one of the kitchen cupboards bumped against the wall. She felt marooned. If only Roy or Clayton would come back, she thought. Even Mavis. Lonely, she missed her husband. She imagined describing the scene to Robert in one of the letters she typed meticulously but did not mail.

A splashing noise came from downstairs. Clayton! "Hello?" called a woman's voice. Judith Purlowe appeared in the living room, dressed in her ancient overcoat and a fisherman's sloped rain hat. The water foamed around her legs.

"Up here," Nancy called, trying to hide her disappointment. She had so badly wanted it to be her brother.

Judith looked up. Her eyes under the rain hat were wide with fear. "Is your uncle here?"

"I think he's waiting it out at the boatyard," Nancy said. "Come join us."

Judith looked as if she might burst into tears. She sloshed toward the stairs and gripped the banister. "What's happening?" she cried. "The field's completely flooded. There's water at my windowsills."

Judith began to climb the stairs, and Nancy saw with surprise that she was barefoot. "My boots filled with water. I had to take them off," Judith explained. Nancy thought of the horses. They would be huddled at the far edge of the field where the land was highest. The biggest danger for them would be falling trees.

"I'll get you some dry clothes," she told Judith. Mavis might be stranded at the lodge, Nancy realized; Roy and Clayton would come in hungry, and she had no idea what to make for dinner.

At Washington Lodge Mavis returned to the relative safety of the kitchen. From time to time she ventured out into the hall and tried to reach Roy on the telephone, but the line wasn't working. After nearly twenty minutes, she managed to relight the pilot by herself, and this small accomplishment reassured her. Everyone else had disappeared, but she'd bravely stayed on, in spite of the storm, and done her job as Mr. Washington would have expected. Mavis boiled the chicken, and then she shredded the meat and placed it in the mold. She garnished it with celery tips, making sure each one was the same size.

Looking up as she finished, she was surprised by how much lighter the kitchen had become. The terrible noise of the wind was gone and a hush like that of an empty church hung over the rooms. She opened the kitchen door. Outside, the sky was clear and blue and the sun shone on a lawn strewn with wet leaves and branches. Furrows of dirt had been gouged by the rain and the air smelled heavily of damp soil. Several trees were down and a telephone pole listed by the road, wires dangling like vines. Mavis went inside and put the plate of chicken on the lacquered tray and covered it with a sheet of waxed paper. Mr. Washington would be delayed by the storm; there was no point in her staying, now that his dinner had been prepared. She put her hat on in front of the little mirror by the kitchen door.

Outside, the ground was soft and muddy. Mavis picked her way down the long white pebble drive, realizing sadly that the walk home would ruin her shoes. At the end of the drive she turned onto Old Purchase Road. There was not a human figure in sight. Mavis had the uncanny feeling that everyone else in the world was gone; she knew it was absurd, and yet she couldn't shake it. She thought of the Rapture that Captain Kelley had spoken of, how everyone was supposed to ascend to Heaven. It would be just her luck, Mavis felt, to be left behind.

She walked down Old Purchase Road toward Fire Neck, stepping carefully around the fallen limbs and tangled wires. At the foot of the hill a huge puddle had formed like a muddy lake. On either side the water gave way to washed-out earth and sodden grass. Mavis was trying to decide between skirting along the edge and walking through it with her shoes off when the sky darkened. It seemed to happen in an instant. The sun disappeared and the wind picked up again, blowing even harder than before. The surface of the puddle broke into chop. Mavis grabbed at her hat and held it down. She was only a fraction of the way home. As she stood staring across the puddle, a tree lurched over on the far side of the road. She turned, fighting against the strengthening wind, and struggled up the hill down which she had just come.

Back in the lodge, Mavis paced the length of hall. It was hard to see out of the ground-floor windows, and she didn't dare go inside the aviary, where the birds, unnaturally quiet, would fix her with their small, bright eyes from inside the hundred cages. At the end loomed the wide stairs that led to the second floor. Mavis hesitated. Her heart thudded in her chest as if she were about to break the law. But she forced herself to ascend the stairs to the landing, so that she could get a better view of what was happening outside. Below her, the copper beeches whipped in the wind. A flock of pigeons flew past in a gray blur. Mavis stood and stared as the small gazebo by the pond backed itself across the grass and lodged with a shudder in a stand of white pine. More shapes flew by the window, and Mavis saw that what she'd thought were pigeons were actually shingles. The wind flung them off the mansard roof like a pack of playing cards. Mavis crossed herself. It seemed to her that God intended to peel the earth back like a scab. As if, beneath its hardness, something tender and new had been forming all this time.

Roy headed out the mouth of the Barto River in a borrowed powerboat. The wind came straight at him. The bow of the boat rose and fell into every wave with a motion like a bucking horse. Roy wished he were riding one. Anything but this, he thought. He gripped the throttle in one hand and shielded his face as best he could with the other. The rain drove into his skin like needles. Sam had insisted he borrow an oilskin, and he was grateful for it now.

At the mouth of the river the waves became steeper. Roy held the throttle with two hands, fighting to keep the boat faced into the wind. The bay was unrecognizable. Squinting into the rain, Roy couldn't see anything beyond the whitecaps, no glimpse of the familiar shoreline or houses or trees. The sky was a greenish black. It was as if he had somehow found his way onto the open ocean. He knew that John Boyle's Island should be to one side and the tip of Long Point to the other. But he couldn't find a single landmark. He felt lost in a hostile, foreign landscape.

Roy couldn't tell how far he'd gotten when he first felt the motor skip. It would be the ignition wires, he thought. Water must have leaked in with the spray. There was no escape from the water. Even worse than the pelting rain was the air itself, full of spray so fine it seemed to smother him. The motor sputtered, and Roy hit it hard with the flat of his hand. "Pigs," he said out loud.

In the moments before the motor failed completely, Roy understood that he would not make it to Fire Island. He would not save his nephew. He saw the stupidity of coming out on the water, a novice like himself. He hoped the boy had had the sense to make for the bridge in time. He thought of Judith, stirring soup while the rain leaked into pots on the floor. And he remembered, with a sense of incredulousness, how he'd wanted to drown himself nearly twenty years before.

Without the engine to hold it into the wind, the boat swung like a wide door opening. In the next instant a wave hit it broadside, swamping the boat with swirling water. Roy felt his feet slip out from under him. He managed to grab the gunwale. Then the boat was hit again and he found himself pitched overboard. The water exploded into his mouth and eyes. He fought against it like a cat in a bag.

Clinging to the floating roof, Clayton felt a wild exhilaration. He was glad to be alone, unencumbered by the woman and her clinging child. The rest of the world fell away, like meat from a bone; there was only the storm, and he and the storm merged together, so that the wind throbbed through him, pounding in his blood. His body moved without hesitation, independent of conscious thought. One minute the roof had crashed against the dock, and in the next he felt the grooved shingles, rimed with salt, under his scrabbling hands. Each instant was charged with a shimmering physicality. He felt entirely sure of what he needed, moment by moment, to do. The possibility of death did not occur to him.

Looking up from his makeshift raft, he saw the Taffy Point bridge in the distance. As he watched, it broke apart, silently, as in a Buster Keaton movie. It seemed to be happening in the past, as if he already knew that the bridge was gone. The minutes were both condensing and expanding. It might have taken a second for the bridge to break apart, or half an hour, or four hours, a lifetime. He looked for the woman and her little boy without really expecting to see them, remembering them only vaguely, as if they were people he had met a long time ago or had heard about in one of his grandfather's stories. Sheets of water blocked his view. Clayton clutched the peak of the roof and wondered for the first time what it had been like to be born. He felt thrust into the headlong fury of the world, and at the same time it seemed clear that the world was ending, that it was coming apart before his eyes. The storm was like time intensified, exposing the inevitable ruin of every earthly thing: houses, trees, people, the land itself, which broke apart, ripped like old fabric, and was crumpled and tossed aside.

The sky cleared a little, and Clayton tried to get his bearings. He saw that he was still on the Great South Bay, though it was nothing like the bay he had known. A massive migration was under way; every stick of wood, every plank of lumber, every broken piece of flotsam seemed to struggle in the same direction. With each blast of wind, bits of debris lifted off the surface of the water like flocks of misshapen birds. A black dog passed close by, riding on the red hull of an overturned boat. When it saw Clayton, it raised its black hackles and barked without sound.

A shoreline appeared, flattened in the wind. Beyond the grasses, trees were writhing. The roof grounded with a shudder on a sandbar near what Clayton guessed must be the mouth of the river. Stretching his cramped legs, he crawled to the edge. He dropped into the water and found that it reached only to his knees. The bay felt warm as a bath. Clayton picked his way carefully to shore. The wind still howled like a train. Doors and chunks of flooring flew by. He crept to a rise in the grasses near where the trees started. The trees themselves bent and flailed in the wind. Clayton fell exhausted in the marsh grass, his face pressed against the rough spartina. His mouth was parched with salt. From where he lay he could look out at the Great South Bay, and he watched as the wind scooped the water out of the basin like a child cupping sand to make drip castles. The water rose into the air. Revealed beneath it were dark patches of seaweed, gullies and troughs, and the black, straight lines of ancient shipyards. The air smelled of the ocean and the bay together and, mixed with the two, a charge like the one he had felt in the air around the swarm of bees.

It was dark at Washington Lodge when Mavis heard the sound of a car on the drive. Roy, she thought, coming to take her home. For hours she had been sitting in the kitchen, trying to read her pocket Bible by the light of the candles. She ran to the door. The car's headlights sliced through the dark. They stopped at the front entrance and Mavis hesitated. It was not Roy's Ford. And Roy would come to the kitchen, never to the front. A moment later the lights were cut and the engine coughed and went silent. The car door swung open and a figure stepped out. Mavis darted back inside the kitchen and hurried down the hall just as Mr. Washington came through the front door. He had left his factory in New Jersey that morning as planned and had driven through a labyrinth of impassable roads and scenes of increasing devastation. Now he stood in the hall before Mavis, his eyes glassy, his dark hair plastered to his skull. His silk scarf clung to his neck like a limp rag. Staring at him, Mavis was overcome by a deep uneasiness. The sight of Mr. Washington so disheveled disturbed her more than all the uprooted trees on Old Purchase Road.

Mavis turned to the sideboard and poured him a glass of brandy. He drank it down, and spots of color appeared on his cheeks. "How are my birds?" His voice was thick. Mavis assured him they were safe. "I'll change for dinner," he announced. He seemed unsteady on his feet, and Mavis wondered if she should follow him. But she didn't want to overstep her place. She went back to the kitchen and took his dinner out of the refrigerator. She removed the wax paper and set the plate on the black lacquer tray. The celery garnish had wilted somewhat. Mavis pulled at the limp tips of the leaves. She found more candles and set them on the dining-room table. They shone in the long gilt-edged mirror. The sight of the chicken salad, so pretty in its mold, pleased her. After a moment's hesitation, she poured Mr. Washington a second glass of brandy and set it by his plate. Then she stood in the doorway and waited for him to reappear.

He never did. She found him in the bathroom twenty minutes later, dressed in a dinner jacket, his hair neatly combed. He had collapsed with a bottle of cologne in his hand; heart failure, the doctor would determine later. The cologne had emptied out onto the white tile floor and shrouded his body with a smell of musk and cloves.

Theron Greaves and George Rowley made it back up the river on a reefed jib, in a feat of seamanship the men of the boatyard would speak of for years afterward. At times, the strength of the wind pushed the bow completely underwater; "more like plowing than sailing," Theron said later, rendered almost loquacious by the memory. George had bailed without stopping while Theron steered and the dog with the spotted face whimpered in the bow. Sam Burnett saw the *Leda*'s sail and watched them approach, waves breaking over the gunwale and the wind forcing them nearly sideways. He helped them ashore, and they fought to secure the *Leda* to the dock. "We saw a fellow go over," George told him. "Not far from Rose's Point. It looked like the Marchands' boat."

Sam, a lapsed Catholic, crossed himself. "Roy. His nephew's on the beach," he said. "Any chance he made it to the point?" Theron and George glanced at each other. They shook their heads. The three men stood for a moment and stared toward the mouth of the river, where water rose off the surface in twisting sheets of vapor.

"Someone should go up to the house," Sam said finally. He gestured across the field toward the house on Salt Hay Road.

From the top of the stairs, Nancy and Judith watched the lapping water recede. The wind had shifted direction, and the water that had been blown out of the pond and over the field was now being swept back and forced into the river. From where they sat they could see the high-water mark, just past the third step, grow dark against the lighter wood. The cooking pot had long since capsized and sunk. After a time the tread below the high-water mark emerged. Then the next. They were standing on the stairs, curious to see the state of the kitchen, when they heard a hammering from outside. Nancy sloshed across the floor. She opened the door and saw George Rowley standing with his hat in his hands.

It was nearly ten o'clock when Mavis made it back to Salt Hay Road in Dr. Thayer's car. The house glowed with the lights of kerosene lamps. As she stepped into the kitchen, a terrible stink assaulted her. The floor was thick with mud and silt. Junk lay jumbled in the corners and along the edges of the room. At the kitchen table her niece and Judith Purlowe sat motionless in front of a pot of coffee. Nancy rose without speaking and came forward. It seemed to Mavis that the girl had a shifty look on her face. Nancy put her arms around her shoulders, pressing a cheek against her neck. In the back of Mavis's mind an uneasiness grew. She looked at Judith, whose eyes were red and swollen. Even as she watched, the widow's face crumpled. Mavis pushed Nancy away. "What happened? Where is everyone?"

"We don't know," said Nancy. "We're worried about two things." She spoke slowly and quietly, as if to a child. "One is Roy, Mavis. His boat went over."

"Don't be stupid," Mavis snapped. She had sat alone for hours in a dead man's house and her nerves were frayed to the breaking point. "Roy doesn't have a boat." Nancy had guided her to a chair and pressed her into it.

"He borrowed one from Sam." Nancy's face twisted, and her dark eyes teared. "He was trying . . . He wanted to get Clayton off the beach."

Mavis stared at her. "Clayton . . . ?"

Nancy nodded, and Mavis recognized the raw fear in her face. "He was on the beach. We don't know any more. Whole houses got swept out to sea . . ." She paused, and Mavis saw her swallow. "George Rowley came by to tell us. He saw Roy's boat go over."

"That doesn't mean anything," Mavis cried. Already her mind bloomed with possibilities: Her brother had clung to a piece of wreckage; he had made it to the beach but had been knocked unconscious; he was safe in a house across the river, suffering from amnesia.

A snuffling sound intruded on her thinking. At the table, the widow's hair hung messily over her shaking shoulders. Through her shock and disbelief, Mavis felt a bracing flare of anger. "Stop that!" she yelled at the other woman. "Pull yourself together!"

Nancy had gripped her by the shoulders and was repeating something into Mavis's face. Mavis heard the words "high school." What was the girl talking about? Nothing made sense. In a swift motion, Mavis shoved her hard. The girl staggered back, catching herself from falling. She stood on the other side of the table, and Mavis watched impassively as her eyes closed for a moment before reopening.

"Someone needs to go to the high school," Nancy repeated slowly. "To look for them."

"The high school? Clayton goes to the elementary . . ."

Nancy stood very still. "That's where they're taking the bodies."

Mavis glanced away from her, down toward her feet. A layer of green-black mud was spread over the kitchen floor like badly applied icing. There was something in the dark corner that looked like a sodden loaf of bread. She had a sudden memory of coming home to Fire Neck from Ohio after Ramsay left her and how filthy the kitchen had been. This was a hundred times, a thousand times worse. Nothing would bring the room back to rights. The smell in the air was thick and oppressive, the stench of marsh dredge and manure. Unbearable. She stood up too quickly and bumped against the door frame on her way into the other room.

Her father sat on the daybed in the living room. The light of the kerosene lamp made his skin look sallow; his eyelids drooped, too heavy for his eyes. He seemed ancient, mummified. "What was he doing out on the water?" he asked, looking up at her. His voice, often so stern, sounded weak and querulous. "I don't understand it. It isn't like Roy at all."

Roy. Mavis dropped into the chair beside the daybed. Her head pounded, as though the storm that had blown itself out had found its way inside her skull. What did it all mean? What did Roy have to do with bodies at the high school? She remembered the fist-shaped cloud that had appeared in the sky the day the fireworks factory exploded, bringing with it the smell of destruction, the ring with the curse inside its opal setting. She'd tried to understand these things, but she'd misread the warnings. All this time, she'd feared her husband, imagining him coming after her when he was really two thousand miles away, remarried. She'd been so sure that she was the one in danger. Now Mr. Washington was dead in his own house and Roy was out on the water, unguarded, unprotected.

A blasphemous frustration seized her: Why couldn't God make Himself clearer? Would it be so hard for Him to tell her plainly what He meant?

In the kitchen, Nancy pulled on a pair of boots that Clayton had outgrown. They were too big for her; she felt her mind catch on this fact, unable to go any farther, as she tightened the laces until the leather buckled. "I'll come with you," Judith said suddenly, and Nancy jumped. Thinking about Clayton, she'd forgotten for a moment where she needed to go.

She glanced up at Judith, grateful.

Nancy found a jacket of Roy's for Judith and grabbed Scudder's brown wool coat for herself. The familiar smell of hair oil and tobacco did something to comfort her. She found the big flashlight Roy kept in a drawer for checking on the dogs at night. Before leaving, she peered into the living room. Scudder lay on the daybed with his eyes closed, the red-and-black-checked blanket over his legs. Mavis sat on the sofa as if carved from rock. "We're going now," Nancy told her quietly. Her aunt did not look up.

It was nearly a mile to the high school. The night was clear and the stars shone bright and cold. Nancy and Judith walked without talking. It was very dark. Nancy carried the flashlight, and its faltering beam made the surrounding night seem vast, their passage through it temporary and uncertain. The only other lights were the soft circles of yellow thrown by kerosene lanterns through the windows of houses and then, as they drew nearer to the crossroad, the headlights of a turning car.

A group of lanterns had been set at the front entrance. As they came closer, Nancy saw a flashlight click on as a huddled group stepped off the sidewalk and passed them. Someone sobbed while another voice murmured something kind and ineffectual.

The squat brick high school seemed to Nancy to crouch against the ground. Inside, it was dark, the air close and infused with that smell of frustrated youth peculiar to buildings of public education. She and Judith followed the ray of light to the gym, where Nancy had only a few years ago played basketball with Enid Snow and danced at school dances. Lit by kerosene lamps, the room looked dark and cavernous. On the polished hardwood floor, half a dozen dark shapes lay awkward and unmoving. Nancy averted her eyes. A balding man with a short grizzled beard sat at a small desk by the door with a pad of paper. He looked like a bayman, weathered and capable.

"We're looking for my little brother and my uncle." Nancy kept her eyes on the man's lined face, blocking out the half-lit room around her, and spoke softly, as if the still figures on the floor were sleeping and shouldn't be disturbed. "He's thirteen. He should have been at school."

"And Roy," Judith prompted, beside her. "In a green canvas shirt . . ."

"And my uncle too. Dark hair . . ." Nancy stopped, because the man with the pad of paper was nodding gravely, without surprise, as if he'd been expecting them.

"They brought a boy in less than an hour ago," he said. "I'm sorry. A terrible business." Nancy was aware of Judith reaching for her hand and gripping it hard. The man stood up, flashlight in hand, and led them toward the middle of the room. The few bodies rested against the backs of upturned chairs taken from the school cafeteria. They were tilted upright, each in the posture of someone reading the paper in bed. Nancy saw that some of the chairs were empty; they seemed to wait in mute anticipation. She looked quickly away.

"Here." The man shone his light on a small figure. It was a boy of seven or eight, with a pale, puffy face that was nothing like her brother's. There were freckles on the dead boy's nose. His mouth was open slightly, the way Clayton's sometimes was when she checked on him before she went to bed. A savage joy tore through Nancy, as if the death of this unknown child meant somehow that Clayton had been spared. Tears flooded her eyes. "He's not ours," she said hoarsely, turning away, ashamed of her relief. The beam of her flashlight fell on a woman's white legs and then on a bare elbow. Her hand began to shake and the light bounced, creating a ghoulish effect; a face appeared in the beam and seemed to move. Nancy dropped her hand, and the light burned into the shiny floor. She thought of her mother in her coffin in a blue satin dress, her forehead smooth, and Clayton gripping her hand as he repeated stubbornly and with complete assurance, "*That* isn't her. *That* isn't Mama."

"Over here, miss," the man directed them. "There's more." Nancy switched her flashlight off and allowed their guide to light, one by one, the faces of the assembled dead.

After Nancy and Judith left, Scudder fell into a heavy sleep and Mavis returned to the kitchen. Even filled with muck, it was the room in which she felt most at home. She sat at the table and rested her head on her arms. The house was utterly silent, as if the normal noises drowned by the roar of the hurricane had been obliterated and would never come back.

Mavis felt her eyelids drooping. At the sound of the kitchen door, she raised her head. A man stood in the doorway. She could hear him breathing, a raspy, labored sound. The man stepped forward, and the light of the lamp shone on his face; haggard and broken, it was still the face in all the world that she most wished to see. He was barefoot and his clothes were torn, and a dark bruise showed like stubble along his chin. She understood what had happened without his speaking a word. He'd washed ashore by Taffy Point, clinging to a piece of wreckage. He'd twisted his ankle. All night he had struggled home.

"Roy!" she cried, relief choking her throat. He reached out his arms.

She lurched toward him, and her chair tipped over onto the floor with a crash. It was this sound that woke her from the dream. Standing, shaken, Mavis looked around. The kitchen was empty. The door was closed.

Walking home on the east shore of the river, Clayton counted more than twenty boats stranded on the marsh or caught in the trees. He took the shortcut over the railroad bridge. The track was strewn with branches. Once, he had to clamber around a large, waterlogged sofa. Seaweed hung from the limbs of the pitch pines. It was very quiet. It got darker as he left the track for a path through the woods. After a while he sat down to rest and felt himself falling asleep, lowered abruptly into it as if on a bosun's chair. He woke up stiff and so thirsty he could hardly swallow. The air had turned colder, all the strange warmth gone. Shivering, he stood and tried to find the path again. His hands ached where he had scraped them on the roof, and his legs were sore. It was completely dark. After a long time, he emerged from the trees.

He found the split-rail fence and followed it down the length of the field, past the dark silhouette of the Captain's cottage. In the house on Salt Hay Road, a yellow light gleamed through the kitchen windows. He stepped inside and saw his aunt at the table. "I'm back!" Clayton cried. "I walked the whole way home!"

Mavis stared at him. The light from the lantern etched her face severely. There were shadows under her eyes, and he had the odd sense that she was older than he'd thought, her bones fragile under the mass of her flesh, her hair on the brink of turning gray. Clayton faltered. It seemed, in the dim light, that there were tears in her eyes.

"Your sister's looking for you," Mavis said after a moment. There was a catch in her voice.

His first thought was how angry Nancy would be at him for skipping school. He had forgotten everything but the storm and his own heroic progress through it. "Looking for me where? Did she go to the beach?"

"The beach? They said that washed away. No, she's up at the morgue. Looking for you and your uncle."

Exhausted, he did not fully understand what she meant. And yet something began to shake inside him. His sense of exhilaration, of triumph, shifted to uncertainty. He stared around the kitchen for reassurance. It smelled of low tide and the mud that covered the floor, but there was the stippled lampshade, dark now, the poster of the horses. There was the same table where, years before, his aunt had said in her voice so like his mother's that this would always be his home. He thought of the houses he'd just seen caving in upon themselves, collapsing soundlessly before his eyes, and the dark, familiar kitchen seemed to tremble around him. He didn't know how he could keep it from falling.

"For Roy?" he faltered. The dread hardened into a tight ball and lodged itself deep in his throat.

She nodded, still watching him with her strangely shining eyes. "He went out on the bay." Clayton was aware of a shuddering that seemed to be coming from outside him.

"But why?" he said. "He doesn't like the bay." He still didn't understand.

"Sam told him you were on the beach." His aunt's face glistened in the yellow lantern light. "He went to bring you home."

Roy's body was found by a search party two days later. He had washed up among the wreckage on the east side of the Barto River, among the planks of lumber, the disjecta membra of walls and roofs, the odd appliances, screen doors, masts and booms, wire crab traps, buoys, dead gulls and terns. One of the search party, a girl Nancy's age, stepped on something yielding as she climbed around a baby carriage with its wheels in the air. Looking down, she saw a pale, protruding hand. The body was battered but identifiable. Along the same shore many of the boats from Starke's Boatyard had stranded, and strewn among them were the carcasses of hundreds upon hundreds of white Peking ducks. They'd been washed out of Brown's Duck Farm in the storm and swept in again on the next day's tide. The white feathers shone in the bright sun against the brilliant green spartina and the brown drifts of mud and debris.

————

Nancy was carrying a basket of wet towels to the clothesline when she saw a figure in the driveway. She and Judith had spent the morning scraping sour mud off the downstairs floors. A thick crust of salt still covered everything, like an early frost. She'd taken a break to hang out the washing. The lawn was littered with detritus: an icebox, an armchair, the front half of a sailboat, scraps of wood that bristled with nails, and dozens of pale, bloated fish. The man in the driveway stood with his back to the house, staring at Roy's car, apparently arrested by the sight of the maple limb that had pierced the windshield like a javelin. He held his head tipped slightly to the side in a way Nancy knew. Her hand went involuntarily to her hair, covered with a red bandanna. She had on a faded blue skirt and a pair of oversized rubber boots to protect her feet from all the broken greenhouse glass. Her arms were flecked with soap. "Robert?" she said.

He turned. She saw her husband's familiar face. His mouth, tight with worry, fell open. He stretched out his arms. The clean, damp towels tumbled behind her as she dropped the basket and flung herself toward him.

Behind the barn, Clayton pulled at the fallen branch that had ripped a hole in the wire pheasant pens and allowed the whole flock to escape during the storm. He heard his sister's voice from the other side of the house as it rose with breathless, unexpected happiness. Without thinking, he dashed around the corner, and for a sliver of an instant the figure beside her looked like his uncle. The man glanced up, and Clayton stopped short.

"Look, Clay!" Nancy cried. "Robert's here!"

———

Inside the house, Mavis was cutting large rectangles from a piece of Scudder's old sailcloth. Two windows needed to be patched, as well as one at Judith's cottage, and there was no glass to be bought in Southease or anywhere else. When Nancy came in with Robert Landgraf, he looked at Mavis questioningly, unsure of his reception. Mavis nodded flatly and went back to cutting sailcloth.

She could hear them talking about a telegraph office, a train that had been derailed, a ferry that lost power on the Sound and floated aimlessly for a day and a half. She gathered he had walked a long way. It was not knowing what he would find here that had been the hardest, he was saying, his voice husky.

"We'll stay as long as you need, Mavis," Nancy said. "Help get the house in order, things working again." She raised her voice slightly. "Clayton, you'll come to Boston. I want you there with me." Nancy said this calmly and firmly. Mavis glanced up, surprised out of her grief for a moment. She searched for the flighty girl who had teased her about partridges and wept into a bowl of pudding. Already, her niece looked years older.

By the door, Clayton made no sound. Mavis was aware, without looking at him, that he was standing very still, with one hand on the latch. She felt the mute appeal of his bright, anguished eyes. Nancy and Robert had stopped talking. They watched him also, waiting.

In her mind, Mavis saw the dark empty kitchen lit by the kerosene lamp, the sodden loaf of bread in the corner. She told herself again that it was not the boy's fault. It wasn't his fault, and she must forgive him. And yet, she thought, if he'd been at school where he was supposed to be, Roy would have come

home from the boatyard instead of going out into the storm—
she could feel the litany spooling out inside her like thread
from a bobbin, tangling in its hurry—and Roy would be home
right now, he would be standing in this kitchen pretending not
to notice that she was blinking back tears. He would still be
alive, if only the boy hadn't gone.

Mechanically, Mavis raised the sailcloth. The opal ring that
she had ground to powder on the flagstone all those months
before had not been the cause of her unhappiness, nor had it
killed the Captain. She'd imagined a curse, needing a reason,
wanting to put the blame on something she could touch. The
scissors flashed in her hand. The only sound in the room was
the snip of the blades through the cloth. The boy would go
with his sister, as he should. But she couldn't bring herself to
look at him, and she kept her eyes on the line she was cutting
and the cloth that fell on either side in stiff, uneven folds.

After a moment, Clayton turned his gaze from her and
darted out the door like a swallow. Nancy and Robert left a
moment later, murmuring together and holding hands. It was a
relief to Mavis to have them gone, out of her kitchen, her
house. She felt betrayed by the disorder of the world. All she
could imagine wanting now was silence.

When Mavis, going through the mail a week later, saw the
word *Esquire* on the heavy vellum envelope, she opened her
mouth to call for Roy, then shut it again. For the first time since
the hurricane she remembered the letter from the man to
whom she was still legally married. Her bitterness toward him
had broken, like a fever. The papers from Canada sat upstairs
in her room, unsigned. Without stopping to reconsider, she
hurried up the stairs and pulled the brown envelope from the

drawer. She took it back to the kitchen and signed the documents on the lines indicated. Not even the photograph of the baby disturbed her. They were people she didn't know, and now they were out of her life for good. She picked up the fresh letter, the one from the lawyer in New Jersey, with a feeling of being put-upon, as if now that she had washed her hands of this business it was inconsiderate of them to keep harassing her. But the letter had nothing to do with Ramsay White. It was a notice concerning George B. Washington's estate.

It was a warm morning in early October when they gathered at Washington Lodge for the reading of the will. Clayton arrived early and sat waiting on the kitchen steps. Since Mr. Washington's death, he had taken it upon himself to feed and water the birds. Along the white pebble drive, copper beeches lay where they had fallen in the hurricane, leaving gaps in the row like missing teeth. There were bare patches among the shingles on the mansard roof, and the grass had grown in the pathways and around the kitchen door.

The housekeeper and the gardener arrived, nodding to Clayton, and stood talking in low tones. Mavis came last, puffing up the long driveway in her worn black shoes. At five minutes past nine, a sleek DeSoto pulled up. They watched as a man in a dark suit stepped out. He walked around to the other side of the car and opened the door with a stiff little bow. A girl emerged, her skin the color of milky coffee. She wore a simple green dress, and her straight black hair hung nearly to her waist. Clayton thought her the most beautiful girl he'd ever seen; she made the women on the playing cards look coarse in comparison. The lawyer gave her his arm, and they went in through the front hall, followed by Clayton and Mavis and the others. In the dining room, the lawyer took a long time reading the will and even longer explaining it in terms no one could understand.

Mavis received five hundred dollars; Clayton received one hundred. He did not know how he would spend it, now that he was moving to Boston and had no use for either a boat or a hunting rifle.

After the will had been read, Washington's niece indicated that she would like to see the house. She admired the kitchen, with its wide windows and shining tile floor, and nodded to Mavis when it was explained that she had been the cook.

The lawyer motioned toward the door, and they walked down the hallway and turned into the aviary. The air inside smelled of droppings and old apples and damp newspaper. The curtains over the floor-length windows were closed, and the group stood still for a moment, blinking in the darkness. Clayton slipped through the crowd and pulled aside the curtains, as he had done for Mr. Washington countless times before. The morning light streamed into the room in honeyed shafts. Clayton heard the girl catch her breath, and he felt a rush of pride, as if the aviary were his to give her. Around them the waking birds seemed to come to life, stretching and hopping. They began to call, hesitantly at first, then loudly, a ringing cacophony. The girl darted toward one of the enormous windows. Clayton, standing nearby, saw that she was trying to open it and hurried to help her. She gave him a grateful smile. Then she turned toward the cages and began to fumble with the latch of the biggest, an ornate white one that housed a flock of striped finches. Agitated, they hammered themselves against the bars. The girl flung the door open with a metallic clang. There was a moment of stillness. And then the first finch shot out of the cage. The girl laughed. Moving quickly, she pulled open the door to a cage of conures, then of lorikeets. Loose in the room, the birds flew tentatively, testing the air with their unaccustomed wings. A white cockatoo landed heavily on the floor, panting in alarm. A parrot beat its green wings against the windowpane. The lawyer retreated toward the doorway. The housekeeper flapped her hands. A parakeet brushed the gardener's shoulder and swooped through the open window and out of sight. There were over a hundred cages in the room, and the girl opened them one by one, shooing the birds toward freedom.

Clayton stood helplessly in the corner. Tears of frustration welled in his eyes. He knew the birds belonged to the foreign girl. Even if he could speak her language, he had no right to stop her.

Walking into Southease along Old Purchase Road, Nancy and Robert were surprised to see three green birds burst out of the trees ahead of them. "Honeycreepers?" Robert exclaimed. A moment later an antshrike and a trogon flew across the road. "From the lodge," said Robert. They stopped to stare. Lovebirds, motmots, jacamars, manakins, jays; the trees rustled with bright, exotic wings. Robert put his arms around Nancy's waist. "I never know what to expect with you around." In a shrub by the side of the road a green bird with a brilliant blue tail perched like a Christmas ornament. A pair of yellow-headed parrots chased each other above the maples, screeching. Pressed against each other, Nancy and Robert craned their necks toward the sky as birds exploded from the branches around them. A white cockatoo landed in the road and looked around, confused, before taking off again in the direction of the Great South Bay. Watching it dip from sight, Nancy shivered with a sudden realization, and Robert pulled her closer. It was October. The birds were tropical, gathered from rain forests and sunny islands close to the equator. Even if the winter was exceptionally mild, the birds could never survive here. She glanced at her husband and saw from his eyes that he had understood this from the start. Above the trees rose a macaw with a head the color of fire, beating its blue-green wings. They watched without speaking as the last of the birds disappeared and the screeching and the chatter died away.

In their last days in Fire Neck, Nancy pleaded with Mavis to keep Roy's horses. "They need too much care," her aunt said flatly. "What would I want them for now?"

Nancy felt a thickening in her throat. "Just Buckshot, then?" Mavis shook her head. Nancy opened her mouth in the stubborn hope that she could wear her aunt down. But then she saw how petty her concern for a horse must seem to Mavis. Two days later, heavyhearted, she took them to a riding stable in Manorville owned by a friend of Sam Burnett's. Judith Purlowe took Roy's hunting dogs, to keep her company, she said.

Scudder sat in the living room with a book on his lap and listlessly turned the pages. He was entirely lucid. But something about him now filled Clayton with a superstitious fear. Clayton didn't like to be alone in the same room with him. There was an absence, a vacancy, that he could feel, like a cold spot in an otherwise warm room. The force of his grandfather's tremendous will had finally gone. A replica seemed to have been substituted for the man Clayton had known, the way goblins were said to replace human babies with their own.

Nancy had dreaded speaking to her grandfather about their departure. She hadn't even told him she was taking Clayton with her. The night before they left, she brought Scudder a cup of tea. She sat beside him on the daybed and put her head gently on his shoulder. "We leave for Boston tomorrow," she said, as if making conversation. "Clayton's going with me. We're taking the ferry, and then the train." There was no answer. She pulled her head back so she could see Scudder and make sure he wasn't feigning sleep. His eyes were open, though they seemed to be looking at something far away from her. He reached out and patted her hand. Nancy's throat tightened. "I love you very much," she said. "I promise I'll write, and visit when I can. I miss you when I'm away."

Scudder patted her again. He didn't speak. But he rested his hand on hers for a long moment, dry and warm, his fingers stained with tobacco.

Clayton stood at the railing in the stern as the ferry pulled away from the pilings with a grinding shudder. The dock receded, slowly at first, then gathering speed. The crowd grew smaller and less distinct, and he lost sight of Mr. Gilpin, who'd given them a ride, and then of Perry in his red shirt. It felt to Clayton as if he himself were being pulled, stretched thinner and thinner, like saltwater taffy. Now the throng had begun to disperse. Only a single figure remained—he thought it must be Perry—waving a white handkerchief in a wide arc. The wake grew behind them like a furrow cut in the water. At the house on Salt Hay Road, his aunt and grandfather would sit down to dinner tonight in a kitchen emptied out. The ferry's wake stretched like a path that would lead him home, and he imagined diving off the stern rail into it and swimming back. The ferry swung out through Pine Gut. The houses of Drowned Meadow were a cluster of white and brown surrounded by the patchy green of the storm-damaged trees. Clayton felt his sister's hand on his arm. He kept his gaze on the churning wake. Out of the corner of his eye he thought he saw his brother-in-law take in his tear-stained cheeks. A part of Clayton longed to bury his face against Nancy's shoulder. But Robert's hand was around her waist with an easy possessiveness, and she was leaning against him. Clayton's eyes stung. The wake blurred before him. Long Island became a low dark shape on the horizon. He watched as it flattened and broke, into a line like a raft of scoters, into a smudge like smoke, until there was nothing left behind them but the water and the sky.

In the house on Salt Hay Road, Scudder sat in the living room by the cold woodstove. After a time, Mavis came in and sank into the chair beside the daybed. Scudder noticed for the first time that her face had lost much of its roundness. She had never looked old to him before. Closing her eyes, she let out a little whimper, almost inaudible.

Scudder felt as if he were watching her at a terrible remove, impotent and helpless. The feeling was eerily familiar. He tried to trace it back to its origin in his past, but his mind moved with arthritic slowness. He leafed through his many years like pages in a book that had gripped him at the time but that he could now only imperfectly recall. At last he realized what the feeling reminded him of: that awful night he'd spent on the beach in 1890 as the three-masted schooner he and Kelley never spoke about was gradually wrecked on the bar. He saw again the distant figures falling without sound into the wash of the indifferent water. He had buried his wife and two of his children, he thought. Here was Mavis, the last of them. He was overwhelmed with a tenderness he had no way to express.

"Can I teach you cribbage?" Scudder asked at last. It was a

question that took all the meager brightness he could muster. Mavis turned her wide, dark eyes to him, and he felt that he would do anything in his power to comfort her. He'd been too hard on her all this time. He had teased her about the one real consolation with which she tried to ease her many heartaches.

Scudder tried for a moment to give God the benefit of the doubt. For Mavis's sake, he tried to imagine Him. And what came to his mind, forgive an old sinner, was not a God who was omnipotent at all but an ancient God, all-seeing but deeply tired, a God who watched the people on the earth He had created the way Scudder had watched those doomed figures in the rigging of the wrecked ship. God heard their cries in the darkness; He loved them and He wished he could reach them. But He was very, very tired, and He was so far away. He could not save any of them, in the end.

Later

Clayton was not as miserable in Boston as he'd intended to be. In the spring of 1939, he discovered the Navy Yard. He was sorry Perry Gilpin couldn't see it lit up at night, the giant shapes of the grain and coal terminals on the skyline, the workers hurrying by as the shifts changed, the blue flame of the welding torches. There he was able to find odd jobs at the dry docks and the Ropewalk, and watch the construction of Gleaves-class destroyers, of destroyer escorts, and high-bridge and low-bridge Fletchers. He kept a list of the ships he'd seen built: *Mayrant, Trippe, O'Brien, Walke, Madison, Landsdale, Gwin*.

But at night, in the small room off the front hall of the apartment he never thought of as home, he dreamed repeatedly of searching for something along one of the faint, narrow paths made by the deer as they crisscrossed the marsh through the spartina. Or he would dream of houses collapsing in silence while he watched but could not move. Sometimes he imagined running away and returning to Fire Neck. Once, when he was fifteen, he saved enough money for a train ticket, and even went to South Station and waited on line. At the ticket window he faltered, imagining his aunt's expression when she opened the door and saw him. Nancy kept in touch with Mavis and Scudder, writing frequent letters and talking on the phone. But he'd been back only twice since the hurricane, preferring to exile himself in Boston when Nancy went to visit. He didn't mind staying with Robert, who sometimes listened to Fibber McGee with him on the radio and never questioned him about where he went after school: "Just no juvenile delinquency, or it'll be my head on a stake." Clayton couldn't imagine facing Mavis again, couldn't think of any way he'd ever make amends.

"Where to, then, son?" asked the white-haired man at the ticket window.

"Nowhere," he murmured, ducking away. "Sorry."

August Scudder lived just long enough to see the country join the war, dying of pneumonia in February 1942. Clayton traveled from Boston with Robert and Nancy, who was six months pregnant. They arrived at the house on Salt Hay Road after dark. Clayton felt his chest tighten as he got out of the car and saw the lights from the kitchen windows shining on the snow. Mavis met them at the door, and Clayton was taken aback by how small she seemed. As he stepped inside, the kitchen closed around him, as if in his absence it had diminished as well. The warm air smelled of streusel and the fresh loaf of bread steaming on the counter. He hung back as Mavis embraced the others, patting Nancy's belly and leaving a dusting of flour on the green fabric of her dress. When she turned toward him, Clayton found he couldn't meet her eye. He glanced down in the direction of her shoulder. "You're scraping my ceiling," she exclaimed, giving him a brisk hug. Feeling her arms pressed around his chest, he remembered how, after Captain Kelley died, she used to snatch him close and whisper a prayer above his ear. He'd hated it at the time. Now he caught the faint smell of yeasty dough and lilacs in her thinning hair, and wished she would hold him a moment longer.

At the funeral, Clayton stood in the cemetery with his sister and brother-in-law, hemmed in by drifts of dirty snow. Mavis swayed for a moment beside the grave, and Clayton wanted to put a hand under her elbow; she seemed frailer out of doors, exposed in the raw air. But he kept back, afraid of imposing.

The minister who gave the eulogy praised Scudder's heroism and spoke of how he'd risked his life to save the lives of strangers. He quoted from the Bible: *Although he had done no violence, and there was no deceit in his mouth* . . . Clayton shifted uncomfortably in his stiff, cold shoes and kept his mind on his grandfather, how he'd stood in the kitchen doorway on that summer night, alive through sheer will. *He poured out his soul to death* . . . Clay pictured him sitting on the porch wreathed in tobacco smoke, frowning over the cribbage board with a look of cunning on his weathered face.

The last time he'd spoken with Scudder on the telephone, at Nancy's insistence, Clayton had been on his way out the door to meet some friends. Impatient, he'd half listened to his grandfather's querulous voice talking about Pearl Harbor while wondering if the girl with the short red hair who liked Tommy Dorsey would dance with him if he got up the nerve to ask. "Armor-piercing bombs," Scudder cried at the other end of the line. "Think of the poor bastards in the hold . . ." What agitated the old man more than anything was the thought of the sailors trapped on the capsized *Oklahoma*.

Back in Boston after the funeral, Clayton took the day off from high school and enlisted in the Navy. He was nearly eighteen years old. He told himself he owed it to his grandfather, though in his heart he'd never planned to stay in Massachusetts. Walking back from the recruiting office, he wondered if he'd be assigned to one of the ships he'd watched being built at the Navy Yard. They'd finished the *Matagorda*, a Barnegat-class seaplane tender, in December.

It was dark when he got back to the apartment, and he paused for a moment before opening the door. His sister lay on the sofa, her belly cradled in her arm. She started guiltily at the sound of the door, then saw it was him. "I'm so tired today," she said, apologetic. "It'll have to be eggs for dinner again." She shifted on the sofa, making room for him.

He remained standing. "I joined the Navy," he told her baldly. "I'm waiting for my boot camp assignment."

He watched her mouth open, as if she'd been hit. Her face was puffy already from the weight she'd put on; he had the strange sense that he was catching a glimpse of her in some unhappy future. Of course, he'd expected her to make a scene, hardening himself to the thought of it as he walked back from the recruiting office, a swagger in his step.

Nancy didn't speak. Clayton watched her eyes fill with tears. He was a block of ice, a stone. He wanted her to suffer. Since she'd made him leave Fire Neck, he'd lived in their apartment like a lodger, out of it as much as he could be, returning to sleep in the little room off the front hall that they would soon need, he knew, though no one had yet said it, for the baby.

He waited for her to catch at his hand and beg him not to go. He wanted to tell her how he had to do his part, that he wasn't a boy anymore, that she couldn't stop him. What did school matter? The country was at war! A reckless certainty filled him that his ship would be torpedoed by German subs. He saw Nancy standing in the doorway with a telegram that announced his death in the line of duty somewhere off the coast of France.

Turning toward the wall, Nancy wiped her face with her sleeve. Clayton swallowed, waiting for her to say something. After a moment, she reached out and ran her fingers over the silver paint on the tall metal radiator against the wall. The paint, thickly applied, was flaking in places. Clayton watched as she pried at a daub with her fingernail, revealing a patch of dark brown beneath it.

"So I won't be here to see your baby," he found himself saying. And then, superstitious because he'd just imagined his own death, he added quickly, "I mean, I'll be at sea."

She looked up from the radiator's peeling paint. Her eyes were wet, her gaze pained but steady. "That was the biggest scare of my life," she said. "The hurricane. I didn't know if you were dead or alive, Clay. Now you want to scare me like that again."

He didn't know how to answer this. It wasn't his fault, he wanted to shout. Frozen in the hallway, his swagger gone, he tried to break free of her eyes. In his mind he could see the kitchen of the house on Salt Hay Road and his aunt's face in the lamplight as she looked up at him.

Nancy moved her hand from the radiator, and for a moment he thought she was reaching toward him. Instead, she rubbed her large belly, her hand moving with an unthinking, abstracted tenderness. "You used to climb into my bed at night and cry, you know." Her voice had softened. "After Mother died. You've probably forgotten that." Clayton looked away from her. She'd always lord it over him, he thought, that she remembered things about his childhood that he couldn't. He felt trapped in the narrow hallway, like a cave of the past, his sister immobile on the sofa. The smell of the soap from the laundry next door oppressed him. "You were so small then," Nancy said. "I remember the feel of your little ribs, like a rabbit's."

Two weeks later he left for boot camp in Newport, Rhode Island. It was raining, and Nancy refused to merely drop him off at the bus station but waited with him for the bus while the rain flattened her hair. When it was his turn to board, she held him too long, sniffling into his shoulder. He felt embarrassed by the lump in his own throat, and by her obvious, pregnant bulk. Suddenly he realized that the other recruits might mistake their relationship, and he disengaged himself more firmly than he meant to, just as she was telling him she loved him. She stepped back, hurt and confusion in her face. "I have to go," he mumbled. Grabbing up his bag, he hurried onto the bus. From his seat on the aisle he could feel her eyes on him. His face burned with something like anger, and he did not turn, although he saw her faintly from the corner of his eye, a pale blur like one of the ghostly apparitions supposedly captured by photography in the pamphlets his aunt and Captain Kelley used to read. Finally, the last recruit took a seat and the bus pulled away, rain streaking the windshield.

After her father's death, Mavis sat every night in the kitchen on Salt Hay Road alone. Across the field, the lights shone in Captain Kelley's old cottage, but she had never gotten over her dislike of Judith Purlowe. Since the hurricane, the house smelled more than ever of the marsh, as if the mud had seeped into the plaster. At night as she lay in bed the walls creaked around her as if threatening to come down.

One morning she walked over to the boatyard and asked Sam Burnett if he could recommend a builder, just to look it over for her. "It sounds silly," she confessed, "but I'm worried it's going to fall in on me."

Sam's gnarled fingers worked on an eel pot as he nodded, his pipe clenched in his teeth. "Nothing's sturdy like it used to be," he muttered. "The whole world's coming down around our ears."

The builder, when he came, walked through the house with a stern, critical eye. Silently, he sighted along the outside walls, heaved himself against the frames of doors, while Mavis followed behind, trying to guess what he was seeing in the mundane contours of each room. "Solid," he announced at the end of half an hour. He slapped the kitchen wall for emphasis. "No need to worry. This one's built to last."

Mavis paid him and the next day put a hand-lettered FOR SALE sign in the front. The house might be safe, but she didn't want to live there anymore.

With the money from the sale and from Mr. Washington's bequest, she bought a one-story cottage inland in Ronkonkoma, away from the Great South Bay and the ocean. Through a friend from church, she found work at a bakery. It was the first job she'd held since Mr. Washington died, and she enjoyed earning her own money again. She knew exactly what needed to be done, and she was good at it. Six mornings a week, she got up in the dark to make pastries and to punch and mold the bread dough into loaves before the owner came in to work the counter.

The bakery stood near the train station, and Mavis sometimes noticed a gaunt signalman pass on his way to work while she was setting the rolls and buns in the window before opening. One morning in February she could see his breath in the cold air, a tiny ghost cloud of vapor. He trudged into the light from the bakery window, and she glimpsed a black bow tie at his neck. Mavis found herself smiling, reminded of Captain Kelley and the kitchen on Salt Hay Road. Outside on the cold street, the signalman stopped, confused by her sudden stillness in the window and her expression. Their eyes met for a moment. The rolls steamed in the basket in Mavis's hand. On impulse she thrust a handful into a brown paper bag.

The signalman in his black jacket had continued on his way. He was walking toward the station, his back to her, his narrow shoulders hunched, when Mavis opened the door. The bitter cold made her breathless. "Wait," she managed to call, "wait!" He turned in surprise, and she held out the paper bag.

His name was Stanley Hoose, and he was a widower with three children. He courted Mavis all winter and all spring, and they were married on the first Sunday in June. Nancy and Robert came down from Boston for the wedding with little Helena, who was teething and wailed loudly at the start of the service, until one of the Hoose children slipped her a whip of black licorice. Mavis, stately in lavender crepe as she walked down the aisle, felt a momentary panic as she realized that this marriage, like her first, was starting during a war. Then the minister addressed them, *Dearly beloved*, and she looked into Stanley's calm blue eyes. When her turn came, she answered with a steady voice.

One night, a few weeks later, Mavis lay awake beside her sleeping husband. The full moon shone in through the bedroom window and made a great bright square on the opposite wall like a door into another world. Outside, a lone bird trilled, hesitated, trilled again. Mavis was afraid that if she got out of bed and went to the kitchen, she might wake her husband, who had to get up early for work. So she lay as still as she could and watched the square of moonlight inch slowly across the wall. Had there been a sign in the caskets she'd seen from the dress shop window before her first marriage? Did God hide messages in the shapes of clouds? The image of Ramsay's turnip-headed baby came back to her, without pain, like a photo in a newspaper story. In the next room her three stepchildren slept; that night at bedtime, the youngest had shyly kissed her. And then she remembered Clayton as a boy, watching reverently as she rolled out pie dough. She felt with a shock how far away he was at that moment, on a ship halfway around the world, and it made her afraid. Mavis murmured a prayer for his safe return.

She tried to keep her eyes open, but her lids were growing heavy. Maybe the signs she'd looked for didn't matter. Maybe no one ever knew for sure, and she could only pray and hope God heard her. She felt her husband stir in his sleep and pull her toward him. The door on the wall slanted into a diamond that wanted to tell her a secret in the language of diamonds. Mavis leaned forward, amazed, because she understood what it was saying, and found herself slipping into a dream. The bird warbled in the tree outside the window, fooled into song by the brilliance of the moon.

In Boston, Nancy woke to the rattle of an early-morning delivery truck passing on the street. Robert's side of the bed was empty, his pillow cold. A cat mewled in the backyard, where the laundry lines hung, but the apartment was quiet. Confused, she slipped out of bed. In the semidarkness of the kitchen, she could make out the counter clean of coffee grounds, the dishes neatly stacked; if Robert had left for work early, he hadn't eaten breakfast first. On her way to Helena's room, she glanced into the front parlor. And there was the still form of her husband, stretched on the gray sofa, with his feet tucked under a pillow and the baby asleep on his chest. Mesmerized, Nancy sank quietly into the armchair and watched them as they slept.

Slowly, the morning light brightened. It shone on Helena's rounded cheeks and her small pink mouth, which moved as she dreamed. Objects emerged from the dimness, and Nancy saw the dust she'd missed on the surface of the oak sideboard, the painted wooden rattle Mavis had sent, on the floor. The light fell on the fine lines around her husband's mouth and on the gray hairs mixed with brown on the patch of chest between his pajama buttons. He seemed, in that moment, heartbreakingly mortal. One of Helena's chubby legs kicked free of the flannel blanket, and Robert opened his eyes.

Nancy leaned forward and kissed him. "Why didn't you wake me?" she whispered.

He smiled sleepily at her. "I tried. You might as well have been hibernating." Stretching, he sat up, gingerly cradling Helena, and Nancy moved next to him on the sofa. She leaned against his sleep-warmed side and looked down at Helena's perfect half-open mouth, the curl of her dark lashes against her cheek. A frown passed across her face, momentarily creasing her blunt, dimpled chin.

"What woke her up?"

"Those Boston roosters," he answered, yawning. "She has her mother's ears."

Clayton's ship was preparing to leave Hawaii when he got Nancy's first letter. *I imagine this will be hard to learn, but Mavis has decided to sell the house.* Reading this on deck, the smell of tar and decay in the tropical air, Clayton felt the shock like a blow to his gut. *She says it's too big for her now,* Nancy's letter went on. *I think, perhaps, it holds too many memories.*

There was only one place on a ship with a crew of over a hundred men where Clayton knew he'd have some privacy. At the door that led to the engine room, he snapped on a pair of headphones and hurtled down the ladder into the stifling heat. The farther south they'd gone, the more unbearable it had become. Now the 6-cylinder Cooper Bessemers throbbed around him, drowning out all other sound. The sweat started on his face. He felt it soak his uniform with a feeling almost of relief. The noise, the staggering heat, the sense that the rivets might pop at any moment from the walls, all of this helped to ease the pain spinning through him like the sparks of a Catherine wheel.

Closing his eyes, he imagined himself back on Salt Hay Road. In his mind, he moved through his grandfather's house room by room, as though he could clutch it to him and hold it through his faithfulness alone. He stayed until the deckhand on watch, coming down to check the engine gauges, jumped, and nearly dropped his clipboard at the sight of him.

Clayton came to love the ship, the USS *Remorseless.* On deck, surrounded by the vast Pacific, he thought how big the Great South Bay had once seemed. It was like comparing Starke's Boatyard with the Boston Navy Yard. Some of his shipmates spoke longingly of home and complained about the endless stretch of ocean, the quarters, the food. Clayton welcomed it all. He felt older day by day, as if the ship were bearing him away from the vestiges of his childhood and his sister's apron strings.

Three Samoans worked as mess cooks on board, big, bronze-skinned men with dark hair. They were held in awe for their massive arms and their easy familiarity with both the officers and the landscape. They'd joined, Clayton learned later, as part of the Fita Fita Guard, and it was a mark of their status on board that no one ever teased them about the grass skirts of their dress uniform. One morning, as Clayton tied a stiff new pair of dungarees to a heaving line to soften in the ship's wake, one of the Samoans approached him, a sleek blue flying fish on his platelike palm. He reached out with meaty fingers and gently extended one delicate silver "wing" like a fan before handing the fish to Clayton almost formally, in silence. Clayton took it aft to his cabin like contraband and spent his free time sketching it until his bunkmate complained about the smell. It was the first thing he'd sketched since the whale on Fire Island on the day his uncle died.

Anchored in the lagoon of an atoll one afternoon, a couple of the men succeeded in catching a hammerhead shark, using heaving lines and homemade hooks. Clayton hurried to watch it being hauled out of the water on the boat davits. Huge and gray, its bizarre eyes staring from fleshy stalks, it thrashed a long time slung over the side while members of the crew took swipes at it with boat hooks. Finally, the second mate came down from the bridge and shot it once in the head. The huge body went still, and after a moment the crowd dispersed, considering the show now finished. Clayton stayed, saddened but fascinated. Now that it was safely dead, the fishermen winched it nearer, until it hung close enough to touch on the other side of the rail. It was well over ten feet long. Blood flowed from the gunshot in the blunt head and from its mouth, bristling with teeth. Probably a greater hammerhead, Clayton thought, though he didn't know for sure. Welch, the boldest of the shark fishermen, lashed his Bowie knife to a pole and hung over the bulwark. "All kinds of stuff inside a shark," he called over his shoulder, cutting roughly into the great belly, the way you'd gut a bluefish or a bass. "My buddy on the *Ontario* found a can of yellow paint!" An instant later they were astonished as half a dozen sleek gray forms with misshapen heads plummeted from the jagged opening in the shark's gut. They splashed into the water like a series of small bombs and swam away. Clayton stared after the flicking of their tails. "It's a cannibal!" shouted Welch, who'd nearly dropped his knife overboard in surprise and now tried to cover his confusion. Clayton didn't correct him. The dead one was a female, of course, and the smaller sharks her viviparous young.

Later the Samoans showed them how to cut out the jaw-bone of the shark and remove the perfect, jagged teeth. There were hundreds of them, and Welch let him keep a handful.

One evening, anchored at Ulithi, Clayton jostled with the rest of the crew on their way to the fantail to watch a movie. They'd joined a convoy of nearly a thousand ships, and the ocean, usually so empty, seemed as crowded as a city street. It struck him, as he stepped out of the hatchway and onto the deck, that around them in either direction every other ship's company would be congregating in the twilight for their movies too. To the west lay a small atoll, studded with palms like a desert island in a cartoon strip. An Essex-class carrier was anchored astern, the USS *Barnaby*. Out of the corner of his eye, Clayton caught a blur of movement. In the next instant the *Barnaby*'s flight deck exploded. A black cloud burst over it. General quarters sounded on the *Remorseless*, and Clayton began running forward toward his station in the engine room. Above him lunged a Japanese plane, so low he could see lines of rivets on its aluminum belly. He followed it with his eyes, powerless, the way he'd felt in his dreams of falling houses. The plane passed low above them, dove directly into the island, and exploded in a ball of fire.

Later, the general speculation was that the Japanese pilot had mistaken the atoll for another carrier. Darkness came fast on the Pacific. It would have been hard to see anything clearly at twilight and they would have been flying low for a long time to make it that far undetected, with so many ships at anchor. Clayton wondered. Part of him wanted to believe the pilot had passed over their ship deliberately. A weakness on his part, he knew, and thought of his grandfather and the nest of swallows on the mast.

He did not write to Nancy often. He felt a resentment toward her that he couldn't put into words and remembered the stilted weekly letters he'd been made to compose at the kitchen table under his aunt's stern eye after his sister first left Fire Neck for Boston. But when mail arrived onboard, he hoped for her letters in spite of himself. In one, Nancy told him the war had already changed things at the museum. Instead of expanding the collection, Robert was now assisting on a huge book called *A Check-list of Birds of the World*. In another, that Clayton was now uncle to a little girl named Helena, after their mother, the loveliest and most stubborn baby in the world. *She has her father wrapped around her tiny finger. When she cries, her chin wrinkles, and she reminds me of you.*

Mavis sent a short, dutiful note to tell him she was remarrying. Reading it, Clayton felt an echo of the pain the loss of the house had caused him. He would be missed at the small ceremony in Ronkonkoma, the letter said. Later, Nancy wrote to describe the wedding, and added that while they were on Long Island they'd stopped in at Fire Neck. The grounds at Washing-

ton Lodge were being used for Victory Gardens. Clayton imagined lines of staked tomatoes and peas where the manicured lawn
had been, and beyond them the copper beeches where the
cockatoos used to perch on sunny days. To please her, Nancy
continued, Robert had driven down Salt Hay Road. She
knocked at the old house, but no one had answered the door.
The greenhouses were all gone, of course, along with the old
wisteria trellis and the climbing roses. The house had been
painted yellow, and the windows were different, the panes larger
and without mullions. *It was like seeing a stranger's eyes looking out
at you from a familiar face.* Reading this, Clayton had a sudden,
vivid memory of his uncle on the ladder set against the house,
pulling a slab of dripping honeycomb from between the walls
like a magician. He stuffed the letter on the bottom of his seabag and did not read it again.

A few nights later, he dreamed he was on his way to the
mess room when he noticed a small hatchway he'd never seen
before. Behind it, a set of worn stairs led to the kitchen of his
grandfather's house, and when he sat down, no longer in his
uniform but in a pair of flannel pajamas, he heard his aunt's
soft, uneven singing: *Everybody has a sweetheart underneath the
rose, Everybody loves a body, so the old song goes . . .*

He woke on the fantail, the ship at anchor. Above him hung
the bright southern stars for which he'd invented his own con-
stellations: the Nine of Hearts, the Queen of Spades. A cool
breeze blew off the water. He could hear the soft splash of
something swimming nearby, the slap of waves against the hull.
His dream of the house came back to him, and he felt the
habitual paralysis of his guilt, and how it had followed him
doggedly, mile after oceanic mile. He had never spoken to
Mavis about Roy, or the night he'd returned home to Salt Hay
Road through the aftermath of the hurricane. And he never

blamed her for wanting to wash her hands of him. Standing in the kitchen that night, he'd felt their makeshift family pull apart like a house in a storm, like an island made of sand.

It was only after something broke into its individual parts that you saw how miraculous the whole had been, how fragile. He should have known this from all the sketches he'd made of dead things that had once been living.

On the train Clayton heaves his seabag onto the luggage rack above him. The war is over. Already he has traveled halfway across the Pacific. Now he's on the *Empire Builder* from Portland, through Spokane and Minneapolis, all the way to Chicago. And from there to Boston, on the far side of the continent.

Turning toward the sunny window, he takes out the much-crumpled paper and reads it again, holding it close, so that no one in the surrounding seats can see it. It's a citation from the Commander of Amphibious Forces, United States Pacific Fleet: "For excellent service in the line of his duty . . ." He knows it by heart but needs to see it written on the official letterhead to fully believe it. "Through outstanding effort and determination, displayed in the face of extremely hazardous conditions . . ." The destroyer ablaze, the smell of hot metal and melting rubber, the heat rippling as he ran toward it, tripping over the hoses. "By his utter disregard for personal safety, his coolness and promptness in action, he was an inspiration to all." Behind him, someone coughs. He folds the letter quickly and tucks it away.

Two days earlier, he'd been on deck as they neared the mouth of the Columbia River, an hour or so before dawn. The wind off the coast carried the smell of damp earth and greenery. Even in the dark, he felt the land pressing in on the ship from either side as they left the open water and moved upriver. Blurred and glittering, the lights of houses on the shoreline stirred his memory: a ferry, and his sister at the railing. After his years in the Pacific, surrounded by the ocean's tang and brine, the night air seemed thick with half-forgotten scents. As they passed Astoria, there was a rank oily smell from the salmon cannery. Later, the scent of sawdust and pine as they drew close to the dark shore to avoid a tug and log boom.

And then, astonishingly, he caught the brackish rot of marshland. He'd closed his eyes, breathing it in. Something moved in his chest then, like a fish flicking back into water.

Out the window of the train, a beaming man on a sunlit billboard lathers his pink face with Lifebuoy shaving cream. With sickening clarity, Clayton remembers the Japanese sailor with his chin sheared off, eyes widened in surprise, on the enemy freighter they'd cleared from Apra Harbor, how wading through the half-charred bodies floating in the rank, blood-warm water he'd felt compelled to roll them over, one by one, searching for a face he knew he wouldn't find. Across the wide Pacific, Clayton has pulled men from burning ships, from sinking ships and ships aground on coral reefs, and it was never his uncle he pulled out of the waves. If he lives for all eternity, he knows it will never be Roy.

He thinks of the USS *Barnaby* exploding before his eyes in a billowing black cloud, the screams of her sailors as they tried to swim through water slick with burning oil. He risked his life to save them, to salvage what he could. It is not his fault that he survived when so many didn't. It is not his fault. The shame he has carried halfway around the world weighs on him, a small but infinitely heavy burden he longs to set down.

He imagines the railroad track already behind him, cutting across the country like the wake of a ship, and fingers the letter again.

The landscape is in shadow now, and lights glow in the houses they fly past. Clayton thinks of the man in the red knit hat who used to skate the Lord's Prayer on the frozen surface of the Great South Bay. The skater must have liked the challenge of it, having competed, Roy told him, in Canada and Europe. Or perhaps, thinks Clayton, it was a private form of worship, etching the words with the stylus of the skate blades while the shadows lengthened and the cold air rose off the ice where the scooters had raced all afternoon. A wistful, ironic prayer, as if anyone watching from on high could read the looped cursive letters in the fading light.

The train pulls out of the darkness into a station. Beneath a lamppost, a woman stands alone, smoking a cigarette. Living on a ship, surrounded by other sailors, Clayton finds women as foreign as dry land, civilian clothes, peace itself. Around him, passengers bustle toward the doors, hauling luggage and parcels. Outside, the woman takes a last drag and flicks the glowing butt of her cigarette away. It arcs into the darkness like a shooting star. Clayton follows it with his eyes as it hits the platform floor and skitters away, throwing off its tiny sparks of light.

The train moves on, carrying him toward what is left of his

family: his sister, his niece, his aunt. He is a war hero, he reminds himself, with a handful of shark's teeth in his pocket. But he feels afraid. Coming ashore has shaken him, like a bottle in which some sediment has rested undisturbed at the bottom by means of a studied immobility.

A longing, a homesickness, grips him like a cramp, and he remembers waking in the spring in the house on Salt Hay Road to the call of the bobwhite quail. He feels, like the phantom pain of an amputated limb, the loss of the house. The train lurches, picking up speed. He is moving toward the Atlantic now, away from Leyte Gulf, from Mindanao, Tawara, Ulithi. He thinks of his little niece, safe in Boston in the room that had been his. Someday, when she's older, he can take her to Fire Neck. He is beginning to doze. He will show her the swallows along the Barto River in September. His eyes are closing, and now he sees the sky along the riverbank, thick with the migrating birds that have congregated every year in enormous flocks since before there was an America, a Germany, a Japan. The birds dart and weave over the darkening marsh. Swirling, they mass into something fluid and distinct, like a transparent bead of mercury, like smoke. The cloud rises and falls in twisting paisley shapes, the movement hypnotic, like the licking flames of a campfire on the beach. Then a rip appears in the belly of the cloud and the swallows begin to tumble through the hole, slowly at first, and then faster and faster, pouring like sand through a clear funnel. The cloud empties like a balloon losing air. The last birds vanish for the night to their roosts in the cattails and the high-tide bush, and the dark sky is a blackboard, wiped clean.

———

All this time, he thinks, he has held it against Nancy that she took him away from Fire Neck. It was easier to blame her for his misery than himself. He should have told her the day he left that he loved her. His eyes open on a dark window, where, for an instant, a boy in a sailor suit stares back at him. Something rattles in his chest. He is twenty-one years old, but he understands what it is. His heart, in its cage of bones.

He imagines knocking on the green door of the narrow apartment in Boston, his sister's eyes widening in relief and surprise. "I missed you," he'll say, lifting her off her feet. "I want to meet my niece."

The compartment has grown stuffy, overheated. Outside, he sees nothing but scattered lights. The rhythmic movement lulls him. Eyes heavy, he feels himself drifting like a small boat in a current. He's going to see his sister, he reminds himself, he will finally tell her he is sorry. For a moment he can't remember why. And then it comes back to him how he went out to the beach that morning when he should have been at school. He shouldn't have gone. But his sister loves him, he remembers now. She will forgive him. His hands are tightening on the smooth wooden handle of the crab net as it rises above the water, and drops scatter, painfully bright. A flock of gulls wheels in the air. He is on a ferry, leaving the dock behind, leaving a white blur that swings back and forth like a handkerchief waved in a wide arc. He is riding in a dark car down a potholed lane, a boy pressed half asleep against his sister's shoulder as they travel together down a bumpy road toward a room that smells of bread dough and potato peelings.

Acknowledgments

I am deeply grateful to the following for their help with this book: Sarah Burnes, Jennifer and Peter Clement, Gary Clevidence, the Fine Arts Work Center in Provincetown, Peg Hart, Courtney Hodell, John Kuegel, Jhumpa Lahiri, Celia Pastoriza, the late Dennis and Betty Puleston, the Rona Jaffe Foundation, Tom and Kathleen Scheibel, the late Bob Starke Senior, and Jill Shulman. Thank you also to John Starke for the ducks, and to Jay Watson for the wren.

Of the many books I consulted in my research, I am particularly indebted to *Bellport and Brookhaven: A Saga of the Sibling Hamlets at Old Purchase South*, compiled by Stephanie S. Bigelow for the Bellport-Brookhaven Historical Society; *A Wind to Shake the World: The Story of the 1938 Hurricane*, by Everett S. Allen; *Wrecks and Rescues on Long Island*, by Van R. Field; *Shipwrecks in New York Waters: A Chronology of Ship Disasters from Montauk Point to Barnegat Inlet, from the 1880's to the 1930's*, by Paul C. Morris and William P. Quinn; and *The Boston Cooking-School Cook Book*, by Fannie Merritt Farmer.